Through the Glass

A Novel

Amber Willems

Print ISBN: 978-1-954063-00-6
eBook Edition: 978-1-954063-01-3

All scripture quotes are taken from the New King James Version of the Bible.

This book is a work of fiction. All names, characters, and incidents are creations of the author's imagination. Any similarity to actual people or organizations is purely coincidental.

For more information about Amber Willems and her books please access the author's Facebook Page at:
Living Among the Amish/Amber Willems

Cover Design: Chuck Miller

Published by: Fortress Publishing

FORTRESS
PUBLISHING

Dedication and Acknowledgments

To Josh, the love of my life. Because of you, I have had the beautiful privilege of knowing what true love is.

To Mom and my sisters for always believing in me, supporting me, and cheering me on at every turn.

Special thanks to Chuck for his assistance and camaraderie as we walked through this great adventure of writing and authorship together. So grateful you are a part of our family!

And above all, to the Maker and Creator of all things good and beautiful. You are faithful to those that trust in You. May my life be a statement of gratitude. You have made every one of my deepest dreams come true.

"Delight yourself also in the Lord, and He shall give you the desires of your heart." **Psalms 37:4**

Prologue

A knock sounded on her office door.

"Come in," Dani called, but didn't bother to look up. She was ahead of schedule for the day's tasks, and as an editor for the Arizona Republic, she knew days like today were rare.

Someone came in and shut the door behind them. This got Dani's attention and she looked up to see Denise, a secretary from down the hall and Dani's closest and dearest friend, after her brother Jeff.

"Oh hi, Denise!" Dani smiled. "Come on in and sit down."

Dani swiveled in her chair to reach the cabinets behind her. "Let me show you the new chocolates I got at Gabriel's. You'll love them!"

"Dani." Denise touched her arm.

Dani saw the look in her friend's eyes and froze. She had never seen such a look of pain and fear on Denise's face.

"Denise? What is it? Is your grandmother in the hospital again?"

Denise started to cry. She tried to say something, but her voice broke. She shook her head.

"Oh, Denise!" Dani instinctively hugged her, but Denise pushed her back and held onto her arms with more strength than Dani thought Denise had in her slim little body.

She looked into Dani's eyes. "Dani, your brother's been in an accident."

Dani stiffened. "What?! Where? Where is he, Denise?!"

"It happened on Highway Thirty-one."

Dani grabbed her purse and stuffed her cell phone into it.

"Where is Jeff, Denise? Which hospital is he at? Did anyone notify Dr. Mathias?"

"Dani, he's not seeing any doctor."

Dani's shoulders relaxed and she breathed a sigh of relief. "Oh, good! So, he's not hurt? You really shouldn't scare me like that, Denise!"

Denise started crying again, but this time—thank goodness—she was able to speak. "Dani, Jeff was in a very bad accident. He was pronounced dead at the scene."

Everything around Dani and inside her darkened. Her purse hit the floor, contents spilling out, but she didn't notice.

She stared at Denise for a moment. She couldn't breathe. She couldn't think.

Suddenly, almost with a will of their own, her feet moved. She walked out of her office and headed down the hall. She had to get out. She had to go. Somewhere, anywhere.

Denise scrambled to scoop up Dani's things and catch up to her.

"Dani, where are you going?"

Dani heard the question, but she couldn't answer. She didn't want to think enough to answer.

She just kept walking.

"Dani!" Denise tried again.

Finally, Dani got into the elevator, and Denise realized she was heading to the underground parking lot.

Thankfully, there was no one else in the elevator.

"Dani, what are you doing?"

"I need to see him. I need to find him." Dani's voice and whole body trembled, but she stood stiffly. She felt like if she so much as leaned against the elevator wall, something

2

inside her would break, and she would lose what little bit of control and composure she was desperately hanging onto.

"Listen, Dani, let me drive you. I'll take you wherever you need to go."

"I can drive myself," Dani snapped.

The elevator dinged as it reached their desired floor, and Denise muttered something under her breath.

She scrambled to keep up with Dani.

Amazingly, considering the state of mind she was in, Dani found her car. She yanked on the driver's side door, but it was locked.

"It won't open!" She started to panic. "It's locked!"

She walked to the other side of the car and began frantically trying those doors, but Denise stopped her.

"Dani, calm down. Here," she said, holding up Dani's purse. "Here's your purse."

Denise slipped it onto Dani's shoulder.

"I need my keys." Dani began searching through her purse.

"Dani, listen to me." Denise held Dani's shoulders, forcing her to still. "Look at me," she said. "I am going to drive you. You can't drive, Dani. You can barely walk straight. I'll take you anywhere you need to go, okay?"

Dani knew she was right. She searched Denise's eyes, stricken and terrified. "Tell me it isn't true!" she demanded. "Tell me he isn't dead!"

Denise pulled Dani close, tears streaming down her face. She would have given anything in that moment to be able to tell her friend what she so desperately wanted to hear.

For some illogical reason, Dani's reaction was to stiffen under Denise's touch. It was as if accepting her compassion would somehow give validity to her terrible words. Denise knew she had to tell her more.

"We had just been told of a bad accident on Highway Thirty-one and had even sent out a nearby reporter to cover the story. As soon as he got there, he called in to let us know your brother was involved. The police confirmed that it was Jeff."

Dani's body went limp as the truth seeped in like a horrible, evil disease. She began shaking violently as sobs tore through her body. She had never known a person could cry that hard. She slid to the ground, oblivious of her designer slacks or the grimy garage floor, oblivious to everything and everyone around her.

The next few days were a blur. She went through the motions of planning Jeff's funeral and talking to people. So many people. The funeral felt like an out-of-body experience where she did and said what she knew she was supposed to without even thinking about it. Her mind was still in shock and her heart was lying in the casket eight feet away as broken as her brother's body.

If only she could fix it. If only she could wake up from this terrible nightmare. If only she could make Jeff come back.

But she couldn't and time and life insisted on moving on. Little by little, the fog had lifted and Dani was able to more fully grieve. Her pain, which had begun as excruciating and unbearable, eventually settled into a dull ache. She was learning to turn everyday reminders of Jeff into sweet memories instead of painful remembrances of all she had lost.

Still, the memories were inevitable and the reminders were everywhere since she was still living on the old ranch they had grown up on. When Daddy followed Mama to heaven eight years ago, Jeff and Dani had inherited the beautiful Arizona property and decided to continue sharing the large house.

Neither of them had married yet, which had been a constant source of good-hearted teasing between them. At the time of his death, Jeff had just started dating a lovely girl.

4

The fact that they hadn't had time for their relationship to grow more serious was one consolation to Dani in the midst of so much sorrow. At least there wasn't another girl having to go through the pain of Jeff's death like she was dealing with.

As she started to accept her life as it was now, Dani began thinking about going on a long vacation or even moving. As much as she loved the ranch and the Arizona mountains, she knew it would do her good to distance herself from all the memories for awhile. It was time. Her heart needed a break from the memories.

She dreamed of renting a beach house up in Maine and spending whole days just walking in the sand, listening to the ocean. Or maybe she would get a cabin in the Smoky Mountains and let the peace of the beautiful trees and blue mountains soothe her soul. Or maybe she would go some place more exotic like Italy of Japan and get lost in the wonders of another culture.

Maybe she would do something unusual. She was competitive by nature and had always enjoyed challenging herself. Maybe she would climb a mountain or train to run a marathon. Maybe she would write a book or learn a language or a musical instrument.

Dani let her mind wander over the endless possibilities. Whatever she chose, she suddenly realized that a shift in her healing had begun.

She had begun to dream again.

"For now we see through a glass, darkly; but then face to face: now I know in part; but then shall I know even as also I am known." 1 Corinthians 13:12

CHAPTER ONE

Dani smiled to herself as her little car rolled along with the light highway traffic. Two days ago, she never would have imagined her weekend plans would include an invite to an actual Amish home for supper. She wouldn't have thought that there were any Amish even living in Arizona.

She pulled off the highway and onto a smaller road. It took her away from Phoenix and into a clean, quiet residential area. Glancing at the directions in her hand, she turned onto a side road and began searching for the right house number. She smiled as she spied the small ranch. Beautiful hanging baskets hung along the porch, making a stark contrast with the dusty brown of the desert sand around them.

Dani walked up the sidewalk and onto the porch, but an elderly man opened the front door even before Dani could knock. She assumed from his Amish clothes and long, white beard that he was Leroy Hostetler, the man she had talked with the day before.

"Welcome," he said, smiling kindly.

"Thank you." Dani returned the smile. The two shook hands and an Amish woman hurried over from another room, quickly wiping her hands on an apron. Her hair was parted down the middle and neatly tucked under a crisp, white kapp.

"And this is my wife, Emma," Leroy introduced.

"Hello!" She shook Dani's hand warmly. "You must be Dani."

"Yes. Thank you so much for having me over."

"Oh, we're happy to have you."

"Well, come on in." Leroy motioned for her to enter. "I don't think I'll ever get used to this Arizona heat."

"I imagine it is quite different than Ohio," Dani commented.

"Yah, that it is."

"Supper will be ready soon, but make yourself at home in the living room," Emma said, excusing herself as she headed back to the kitchen.

Leroy led the way into the living room and Dani was surprised to see to see a young Amish man sitting at a desk in the corner, working on paperwork of some kind. He looked up when they entered and Dani blinked. She had never thought of Amish men as especially good-looking, but this man was strikingly handsome. He stood quickly and offered his hand with a friendly, but slightly shy smile.

Gorgeous and unassuming? Dani noted. It was a lethal combination.

"This here is our grandson, Willis," Leroy introduced.

"Hello," Dani said, suddenly feeling shy herself.

"Hello," Willis returned.

"Willis is actually from Ohio, but he works for a furniture company that has to haul items out west every so often," Leroy explained. "Usually they have someone ride along with the driver to help unload the furniture, but this time Willis asked if he could go since they would be driving right

7

close to us this time."

"How nice." Dani said simply. *What was wrong with her?* She was rarely at a loss for words or this self-conscious. For some reason, the young Amish man's presence made her feel oddly off-balance. How could a guy she had just met have such an effect on her?

Emma quietly entered the room. "Yes, we are so grateful to get to see him again," she said, catching the last bit of their conversation. She turned to Leroy. "Supper is ready, then."

"Well, let's eat." Leroy rubbed his hands together.

"Everything smells fabulous," Dani said.

She was amazed when she saw the table. Nearly every square inch of the table was filled with food. There was soft, homemade bread with strawberry freezer jam and steaming corn where a pat of butter still melted. A large dish held some kind of meat with mushroom gravy and another bowl was piled high with fluffy mashed potatoes.

"Wow!" she exclaimed. "You shouldn't have gone through so much trouble."

"Oh, no." Emma shook her head. "It wasn't any trouble."

They took their seats and Leroy asked Willis to say the blessing. Willis' prayer was simple and sincere.

There was a brief pause after the prayer was finished, and Leroy set his napkin on his lap.

"Willis, why don't you start the meat," Emma suggested.

Willis dished himself out a helping and Dani couldn't help noticing the way the muscles in his arm tensed and bulged as he lifted the heavy dish. He certainly was a man used to working hard. He handed the dish to Dani. As she took it, their fingers touched and a rush of warmth shot up her arm. Dani looked up and caught Willis' eyes. She averted her gaze, but felt her cheeks blush. What in the world had come over her? She tried to shake her ridiculous feelings.

8

Dani dished herself out a scoop and passed the dish to Emma. She avoided looking at Willis for a few moments as she let her blush fade and she steadied her emotions.

As they passed bowls, they all began conversing easily. Dani savored every bite of Emma's delicious cooking, but she couldn't help sneaking peeks at Willis every once in awhile. Since he looked to be about her age, she was interested in understanding the Amish from his point of view.

Or at least that's what she told herself.

Dani helped herself to another warm slice of homemade bread and smiled to herself. She still could hardly believe she was sitting here, having dinner with an Amish family. What a crazy turn of events had transpired in the last couple days.

It all started as she was going through her brother's things. She had been putting off that job, but now that it had been over three months since his death, she had decided it was time.

She was working on his computer files, organizing the articles he had written and sending the ones that could still be published to his editor. It was slightly unusual to use the articles of a deceased reporter, but Dani had offered them and since she was an editor and knew what they wanted, they had agreed. It only seemed right that anything her brother had worked on should be given the chance to be published.

Although reading her brother's words often brought tears to her eyes, Dani loved going through Jeff's writing. It was as if she was having one final conversation with him.

She had been working on Jeff's articles for several hours one day and was just about to click on another file, when a title further down the page caught her eye.

"The Life of the Amish" it read.

"What?" Dani almost laughed. In her entire life, she had seen an Amish person in their state only once. What was Jeff doing writing about Amish people? What did he think this

9

was—Pennsylvania?

Now her curiosity was piqued, so she opened the file and began reading.

The article told the story of how Jeff had actually come across an elderly Amish couple living outside the Phoenix area and how he had asked them to share about their lives.

Dani was mesmerized. She knew so little about the Amish. She was drawn by the unique way they lived and the couple's obvious love and faith.

According to the article, Leroy and Emma Hostetler had needed to move to Arizona because of Leroy's health. Even though there was a small Amish community outside of Phoenix, it was clear the couple dearly missed their home in Ohio. At one point in the interview, Emma had broken into tears as she described missing the daily interaction she had enjoyed with her children and grandchildren.

"Now," she said, "it's too expensive for their large families to come here. Maybe we can visit them once a year, but that is all we can do because of our medical bills and all. The little ones will change so by then."

Dani was surprised to learn that the Amish usually were not allowed to travel by airplane, so if any family member did want to visit, they would have to take a bus or rent a van and pay someone to drive them.

Dani was fascinated as the Amish couple described their life in Holmes County, Ohio, and she read the entire article.

When she finished reading, she stood up to look out the window.

For reasons she couldn't understand, a deep sense of loss and longing had suddenly come over her as she read about the Amish families. It was beautiful the way they all lived in such tight communities surrounded by each other.

With her brother's death, she had now lost every member of her immediate family.

Loneliness fell over her like a dense fog.

Besides her best friend, Denise, Dani realized her social life was nearly nonexistent. For the first several weeks after Jeff's death, a few people from her church had stopped in to see her, but as time went on and she didn't return to church, the visits and calls eventually stopped except for occasional calls from the pastor.

She had always been a faithful churchgoer, but after Jeff's death, she just couldn't bear to set foot again in the church that he had been such a part of. It was also the place where she had seen his face for the last time here on earth and had said her final goodbyes.

She knew her faith in God was real, but since Jeff's death she found herself somewhat distanced from Him. At a time when she should have leaned on His strength more than anything, she felt slightly betrayed by Him.

She wanted to get back the relationship with Him she once had, and she longed for the sweet peace that had filled her life. Maybe soon she could get away where she would be less distracted and could think through what was going on in her heart.

Her thoughts went back to the article she had just read. That was another thing enticing about the Amish—the peacefulness of their lives. Their world was so much less busy and cluttered as they simply worked and lived together without all the options most Americans had.

What an ideal setting to grow in your faith and walk with God.

Suddenly, Dani had a wild thought, and she laughed outright. *What if she were to go and live among the Amish herself?*

She laughed again. It was such a ridiculous idea.

But the more she thought about it, the more she thought of aspects about it that didn't seem so crazy. She was certainly drawn to the closeness of a community, something she desperately missed right now.

Besides, hadn't she been thinking just the other day that she should get away from the family ranch and all its memories for awhile? As she started to accept her life as it was now, Dani had begun to think about going on a long vacation or doing something unusual to distract her from her loss. As much as she loved the ranch, she knew it would do her good to distance herself from the memories for awhile. It was time. Her heart needed a break.

Maybe this Amish idea was it.

For one thing, she needed to know more about the Amish to know if this plan could even work. She turned from the window and back to the computer to start researching.

Dani guessed most of the Amish had never been online in their life, yet there was more than enough information about them out there. That was a good thing for her, she supposed.

She found that while there were Amish in over half of the states, the biggest communities were in Ohio, Indiana, and Pennsylvania.

It surprised her to learn that the Amish varied quite a bit from those that were not allowed to even ride in a vehicle except for medical purposes, to those that were allowed to own and drive tractors. There were whole church groups that were quite wealthy and others who barely scraped by. Some even had regulations on how much money they were allowed to make. From what she could tell, most had the same foundational doctrines, but each church group might have a different interpretation of how they were to be lived out.

Several hours had passed as she continued her research. She hadn't found a single thing to discourage her venture. In fact, what she read only intrigued her more.

Another thought hit her. What if she was to contact the Amish couple Jeff had interviewed? She certainly could get their advice on this wild idea of hers, but would they be willing to talk to her?

It wouldn't hurt to ask.

Dani began the search for the Amish couple's phone number or address in Jeff's filing cabinet. Although her brother had been fairly organized, with all the hundreds of contacts he had made over the years, it took her awhile to find Leroy and Emma Hostetler.

"Aha!" she exclaimed, pulling out a sheet of paper in triumph. There was an address and a phone number on it, but a glance at the clock told her it was probably too late to call this evening.

She had a hard time falling asleep that night as thoughts and questions raced through her mind. The idea just felt so right, but she would know a lot more if she could talk to Leroy and Emma.

In the morning, she could hardly wait until it was a decent hour to call the couple. When she finally did, she was a little disappointed to get their answering machine. She decided to leave a message.

"Hi, my name is Dani Chadwick. I came across your name from an article my brother Jeff did with you and I wondered if you would mind at all if I could talk with you—not for an article or anything—just for personal reasons."

Dani left her phone number and hung up the phone. She breathed out a sigh. She didn't know how the Amish couple would respond to such a strange message.

Two hours later, the phone rang and Dani dashed to answer it. "Hello?"

"Hello, is this Dani Chadwick?"

"Yes." Dani smiled. From the man's Dutch accent, she knew right away that it was Leroy.

"So, you're Jeff's sister?" Leroy asked.

"Yes."

Dani and Leroy talked for a few minutes about Jeff and then the conversation turned to Dani's reason for calling.

13

Dani didn't tell Leroy about her idea to live among the Amish, but Leroy must have been able to tell that she had a lot of honest questions about their faith and way of life. That, or he had sympathy for her because of the loss of her brother.

"Why don't you come over some time for supper?" he asked.

Dani was speechless. She had never expected an invite. "Really? I would hate to impose."

Leroy laughed a gentle, easy laugh. "My wife would be delighted to have company over. Besides, I'm sure she would be glad to meet you. That way, we could talk in person about whatever it is you want to know."

And so, two days later, she found herself sitting at a kitchen table, chatting with three Amish people, and enjoying one of the best meals she had ever tasted.

After the meal, they all lingered around the table and the conversation turned toward her. Dani took a deep breath and began explaining to them her big idea and why she was really there.

"Do you think that is something I could do- live among the Amish for a time?" Dani asked.

Leroy smoothed his beard thoughtfully and everyone around the table was quiet for a few moments while they thought through her question. Dani glanced at Willis and found he was already watching her, an intrigued look in his eyes. He seemed slightly embarrassed that she had caught him watching her, and he glanced over at Leroy.

"Well," Leroy took a deep breath. "I can't speak for the leaders, but my guess is that you could probably do that. I doubt very much that they would forbid you to be there, but I don't know for sure. What do you think, Willis?"

Willis thought a moment before responding. "The Amish people are naturally shy of outsiders," he said, "but you certainly seem to have good intentions and considering the circumstances, I can see why you'd be drawn to the Amish ways."

"It's a little out of the ordinary," Emma put in, "...but, if you're willing to live under their rules and all, I don't see why the leaders would say no."

They talked about different aspects of Amish life Dani would have to get used to.

Dani asked many questions and had so many more she wanted to ask, but she didn't want to take the couple's precious time with their grandson. After about an hour, she decided it was time to go home.

"Thank you so much for inviting me over," Dani said gratefully

"I'm just glad if we could help in any way," Emma said. "Jeff was such a nice young man. I was happy when Leroy told me we were going to meet his sister."

When it was her turn to shake Willis' hand, she turned to him. "It was nice to meet you," Dani said politely, determined to keep her emotions in check.

"You too." His eyes were gentle and kind. "Perhaps our paths will cross again sometime in Ohio." His mouth turned up into half-smile.

"Yeah, maybe they will," Dani said, refusing to think about how adorable that expression was on him.

"Feel free to stop in any time," Leroy said as Dani stepped out the door.

"Thank you. I appreciate your help so much."

Leroy waved and she returned the wave.

Dani had so much to mull over on her way home. The gentle and quiet attitude of each of her new Amish friends had been so calming. The whole atmosphere of their home was one of peace. If the Amish in Ohio were anything like them, it would be the perfect place to balm her wounded heart.

At home, Dani settled on her porch swing and pulled one of its pillows onto her lap. It creaked as she pushed off with her toe to get it swinging.

She sighed and looked out over the mountains. What a gorgeous backdrop to her childhood. The sun was just setting, and she realized how often she had taken for granted the beautiful sunsets here in Arizona. The entire eastern sky was pink, but as it neared the place where the sun had disappeared, the color intensified by degrees into a final shade of vibrant orange.

Shadows began to fall over the mountains, darkening the divots and valleys. How many times had she missed this display of color and splendor? There was so much beauty in this life she took for granted or simply failed to notice.

She knew now what a gift each moment of life was, and she treasured each special time she had shared with her dad and Jeff before their deaths. She wished that she had gotten the chance to have some memories of her mom before she died when Dani was only two.

While she had loved hearing about life from an Amish perspective, listening to them tell how intertwined their lives were with those around them in the community had stirred in her an acute sense of loss and aloneness.

Dani pushed her toe into the porch floor again to keep the swing rocking.

Why did everyone in her life have to die? She felt like her entire life was etched by loss, bookmarked with obituaries.

If she had been Amish, she would be surrounded by family of all ages. She would probably have aunts and uncles and cousins nearby instead of spread across various states like they were now. Even her friends would feel like family since they would have grown up together and likely stayed near each other all their lives.

Dani's thoughts took another turn. If they had been Amish, Jeff wouldn't have been driving a car and he wouldn't have died.

Dani stopped her train of thought. It was ridiculous and

unproductive to think about the "what-ifs" of life. She had done enough of that after Jeff's death. What if Jeff had taken a different route? What if he hadn't heard of the story he was heading out to cover? What if he had stopped for lunch first? What if that other driver hadn't looked down to change his stupid radio?

She supposed that every person goes through those types of questions when they lose a loved one. Life was so fragile. One wrong turn, one moment too late, one second for the driver to go left of center, and it was all over. Like a single puff of breath on a flickering candle flame, a life could be put out in a instant.

The sky gradually grew darker until all color had melted away and stars began to appear. Dani loved the peacefulness of the night. Only the occasional stomp or snort from a horse in the nearby stables broke the silence around her.

Expect for the loneliness, it didn't bother her to live in the big ranch house all alone. While some people might be uncomfortable having so much space to themselves, this old house felt more like a haven—a safe place—to her. Her daddy had built this house and she had lived here her entire life. It was like a dear, old friend that also remembered her childhood memories along with her—sliding down the large wooden stairs on pillows and couch cushions, chasing Jeff around until Daddy told them to stop running, or the way their tall Christmas trees barely fit in the living room. The house had fingerprints all over it from the people that had touched her life the most.

She had always been an independent person. Maybe that was why she hadn't formed more of a network of friends around her. With Jeff and Denise, she really hadn't felt the need for more friends. She did hope to find a best friend one day to marry, but she hadn't found anyone to fit that description yet. She wasn't in a hurry. She was content to let life happen.

Now she wondered if being so independent had been a mistake. Surely God intended humans to be connected to one another. Yet, it seemed like in this age of technology and unlimited access to each other, many seemed to keep their lives so busy and conversations so shallow that they were losing the art of real fellowship and friendship.

Dani smiled as she realized the Amish, even with their lack of phones, internet, and transportation, were far ahead of most Americans when it came to closeness among family and friends. They were the ones that really knew how to stay connected.

It sounded inviting to get rid of so much clutter and extra, useless things and to choose to live simply. To be in a community where nearly everyone not only did the same things every week, but also lived so close it wasn't anything out of the ordinary to pop in at someone's house or have them stop in at yours.

Dani had an intense longing to become a part of something like that, but she knew she needed to be sure it was the right thing for her before she made her decision. Over the next several days, she spent a lot of time thinking and praying about it.

It didn't take long for her to feel certain about what she should do.

She would make a trip to Ohio.

CHAPTER TWO

Dani decided to call Denise. Her best friend should be the first to know of her new plans.

The phone rang several times before Denise picked up.

"Hello, Shelby's residence."

Even at home, Denise had a perfect professional voice on the phone.

"Hey, Denise. It's Dani."

"Hey, Dani!" Denise brightened. "How's it going?"

"Good, actually. I have some news for you."

"Oh? Whatever it is, it must be good because you sound excited."

"I am, but I'm not sure you will be when I tell you."

"Okay...What is it?" Denise sounded skeptical.

"I decided what I'm going to do this year."

"Yeah?"

"I'm going Amish."

Dead silence filled the other end of the line. After a long pause, Dani laughed. She knew how preposterous it must sound.

"You're kidding, right?" Denise asked.

"No, I'm not. I'm going to become Amish."

Now it was Denise's turn to laugh. "Dani, are you serious?

I mean, I expected some kind of crazy, out-of-the-box idea coming from you, but going Amish?"

"Yeah, I know it's pretty wild, but I think this is what I should be doing."

"But..." Denise stammered. "How? I mean, why?"

"I've been reading a lot and their close community and simple lifestyle sounds just like what I need right now."

"So, you'd actually wear the bonnets and stuff?"

"Sure."

Denise's voice was serious now. "Dani, I hope you know what you're getting into. I mean, isn't that a little much? It's like you're joining a cult or something."

Dani chuckled. "It's not really a cult, Denise. Sure, they live out their beliefs a little different-"

"A lot different," Denise interrupted.

"Ok, a lot different, but they still base their religion on the Bible."

"I don't know about you, but I have never read in my Bible where it says you have to wear bonnets and black clothes and can't drive cars."

"I know it seems crazy, Denise, and I don't expect you to understand. I just feel like I need to do this. It's perfect for me. I've done a lot of research and even more thinking and praying. I don't know how to explain it, but I just feel like this will be a good thing for me."

"Kind-of like joining a monastery for a month."

"Yeah, exactly like that. I just need a place of simplicity where I can get away from things here and sort some things out, you know."

"What you really need is a man, girl," Denise said matter-of-factly.

Dani rolled her eyes. She knew her friend was good-hearted, but she was also a chronic match-maker.

"Chronic" in the same sense as a "chronic disease" or a "chronic headache." She wielded her cupid's arrow everywhere she went, her goal and mission: to find all supposedly miserable, depressed, single women the only solution to all their problems—a man.

They, on the other hand, did all they could to stay out of her crosshairs.

Dani sighed. She would like nothing more than to look out her window right now to see a man sent straight from God Himself on the front steps holding a bunch of roses behind his back and smiling charmingly at her. But wishing it hadn't produced a man for her anymore than Denise's hints and prodding had. She would find a good man when the time was right, if that was in God's plan for her.

"Oh, and I just met this guy at our church, Dani!" Denise continued.

Dani grimaced. *Here we go,* she thought.

"I was going to wait and invite you two over or something."

"Denise!" Dani scolded "Tell me you weren't going to set me up in some kind of blind date at your house without me knowing?!"

"Well," Denise took on a defensive tone, "I didn't think you'd agree if I told you."

Dani was speechless. *Why didn't she just leave me and my love life alone?*

Apparently, Denise was undaunted by her response.

"He is new to our church, but he seems so alive for God, Dani! He's got to be around your age, never married, and he's cute!" she finished in a sing-song tone like the one you would use to entice a three-year-old to eat his peas.

"Not interested," Dani said flatly.

Denise's tone turned to whining. "See, I knew you wouldn't come if I told you. You don't even give things a chance."

For maybe the first time since she met him, Dani pitied Denise's husband, Rob. The way Denise effortlessly switched from begging to pleading to guilt trips to condemnation had her head swimming.

Unfortunately, it worked.

Dani didn't know why she agreed to come over on Sunday. She suspected it was more just to prove to Denise that she could do it than anything else. It certainly wasn't because she really wanted to meet this guy.

Ok, so she might have been a little curious, but very little and only "curious," not "interested".

And there was a big difference between those two.

"I'm still going to go Amish," Dani warned her.

Denise laughed. "Ok, but at least I'll know I tried."

Whatever. If it made her feel better.

As soon as Dani hung up with her and put the phone down, she had words with herself and grumbled at the stubborn streak that had gotten her into trouble once again.

Well, the deed was done. At least she could anticipate a tasty dinner and some pleasant conversations. Hopefully, Denise would behave herself and there wouldn't be too many awkward moments. She had experienced too many of Denise's set-ups to have many positive expectations for the evening.

Dani rolled her eyes.

On Sunday afternoon, Dani dressed comfortably. She wasn't in the mood to dress up and certainly wasn't in the mood to try to impress this guy. She was just going to try to enjoy the evening as best as she could. She had enjoyed every other time she went to Denise's house. Rob and Denise had a charming home and Dani loved playing with their two little girls.

She was determined to have a nice time again.

She showed up early on purpose, hoping to beat "the guy," whatever his name was. Denise had forgotten to mention that little detail. The last thing Dani wanted was for Denise to have more time to get his hopes up and to show up with her squeals of, "Here she is!"

Thankfully, her plan had worked. He wasn't there yet.

Dani followed Denise into the kitchen where Rob was chopping up lettuce for a salad. The little girls, Allie and Heather, came running into the room when they heard her voice and she bent down to give them hugs.

Dani loved kids. When they love you, they're not afraid to show it. That was one of the biggest things that stunk about being single. Dani couldn't wait to have her own kids someday.

The girls were still in their church clothes, silky dresses and ribbons and tights and all, so after they finished telling Dani hello, Denise sent them up to their bedroom to change.

"Can I help with anything?" Dani asked, walking into the kitchen.

Rob looked up from the cutting board. "Actually, you could take over here for me if you want. I need to check on the grill."

"Sure." Dani took his place at the counter and began cutting tomatoes.

"So," Denise asked, "you nervous?"

"No." Dani looked her in the eye. "Denise, no match-maker stuff this evening, okay?"

Denise pursed her lips.

"I mean it. I'm not really even open to dating right now. I have things I need to figure out before I'm ready for the next stage." Dani pointed her paring knife at her. "Promise you'll behave tonight."

"Fine," Denise sighed. "But I'm not promising to not help you along. Girl, you need some serious flirting lessons."

Oh brother. If she wanted to flirt with a guy, Dani was sure she could figure it out on her own. Besides, she wanted a guy to like her for who she really was, not because she had charmed him into it.

"Oh, here he is!" Denise said excitedly, just as Dani had

pictured she would.

Glad I'm not you buddy, Dani thought. She did actually pity the guy. Here he was expecting to meet a lonely, single woman and who knows what else Denise told him, when she really wasn't even ready to date anyone right now.

Dani made sure to have things to keep her busy.

Denise brought him into the kitchen.

"Dani, this is Greg."

Dani came around the counter and shook his hand politely.

He wasn't bad. He was actually quite cute. And it hadn't been lost on her that his eyes lit up when he saw her.

"This is great to meet you and come here," Greg said enthusiastically to both of them. "Other than you, I don't get many invites, except from my single buddies—Christian, single buddies, of course. I try to not hang out much with unChristian guys. All they want to talk about is girls and sports—you know, worldly, carnal stuff. Just not a good influence."

Dani tried to nod understandingly. Had he really just said all that in the first conversation he ever had with her? Dani smiled. At least she wouldn't have to worry about drumming up interesting conversation tonight. This guy could talk a mile a minute.

"Denise!" Greg exclaimed, spreading his hands out wide as he looked into her newly painted and decorated living room. "This is awesome! It looks great!"

"You like it?" she asked, pleased with the compliment.

"Oh, yeah! This is great!"

Dani continued cutting up veggies for the salad while the two of them talked colors and furniture. She looked up at Greg, able to assess him from a distance now.

She had learned to judge guys like she was checking off some sort of list in her head.

He was cute. Not too short, not too tall. Not fat, but a little thin.

He was far too talkative for her taste. Although she would be grateful for it tonight, it would drive her up a wall to be around it all the time.

On top of that, Denise had made a big mistake. Dani guessed Greg was quite a bit younger than her, probably in his very early twenties while she was twenty-eight. So much for being the "same age." Dani appreciated the compliment in thinking she was younger, but felt bad about her setting Greg up for a dinner date that wouldn't go anywhere.

Rob came in through the sliding door.

"Hey Greg!"

"Hey man!"

The two hugged.

"Wow!" Greg dramatically sniffed the air. "I can nearly taste those burgers, they smell so good."

Rob smiled. "Well, I think they're done so we can go ahead and eat."

"Awesome!" Greg rubbed his hands together.

Denise went to call the girls and Dani carried the salad bowl out to the covered porch while Rob got together the other items from the kitchen.

Greg followed Dani out, carrying a menagerie of salad dressing bottles.

"So," he said the moment he reached her at the picnic table, "Denise tells me that you're going on a big trip this year."

Dani smiled. "That's the plan."

"I think that's so cool, like going on an adventure, a quest to find yourself."

Dani wasn't sure she would ever call looking for herself "cool," but she knew what he meant.

"Yeah," she said, "I'm hoping to broaden my horizons and have some time to heal more from my brother's death and get closer to God."

"That is awesome! I really admire your boldness to do something like that."

As obnoxious as this guy must get at times, his bright attitude with everyone was sweet.

Dani watched as he arranged the dressings next to the salad. "Thanks, but I don't feel like I'm being that brave-"

"How scary can the Amish be, right?" Greg laughed. "But, no, I mean I think that you're brave to go live in a totally foreign culture like that. That is just so cool! I have a friend in college that went and lived with a bunch of hobos for awhile just to understand what their lives are like."

Now hobos she would be scared of.

Greg was still talking, "He came back with long hair and had lost fifteen pounds, but he had such a great perspective of them and now he's a part of a ministry to reach out to homeless people."

"Wow, that's really great."

"Yeah, there's so much out there we don't know about, so many people groups—even in our own country, our own backyard that are so different from us."

Dani nodded.

The girls came running outside, Denise and Rob following behind, each loaded down with food.

Over their simple dinner, Greg and Denise did most of the talking with Rob and Dani filling in here and there.

Dani was pleased. She could relax and enjoy her time here. Although Greg gave her enough attention that she knew he was interested in her, he wasn't annoying and he talked just as much to the others.

Dani envied Greg's boundless energy. He was like a six-year-old boy in an adult body. Greg could singlehandedly keep them all and the dog entertained. Just watching him was enough to make anyone tired. It made Dani feel old.

There was such a contrast between him and the Amish guy she had met the other day. While Greg was energetic and sometimes said things before he thought, Willis had such a peaceful aura of confidence and maturity. Dani hadn't been able to help being attracted to his quiet strength.

The evening ended pleasantly when Denise told the girls it was time to get ready for bed and Dani decided it was time for her to head home. Greg followed suit and they all said their goodbyes and thanks for the enjoyable evening.

Dani headed out to her car and started to call out a farewell to Greg. She turned toward where his car was parked, but was startled to find he was right behind her.

"Oh!" she said, surprised.

"I thought I'd walk you to your car, if you don't mind."

"Okay." Dani was flustered and not sure what to say.

Greg opened the car door for her and smiled.

"Thanks," Dani said. Not knowing what else to do, she got in. "It's been good to meet you. I've had a nice evening."

She didn't remember feeling this awkward since she was in high school and she hated it.

Greg leaned against the car. Having him that close and having to look up at him didn't help her discomfort.

He smiled and pushed back away from the car.

"So," he said, "would you want to hang-out sometime? Just something casual like a movie or something?"

Man! She wasn't expecting to have to go into this.

"Um…" Her brain scrambled to find the right words. She always hated the "I'm not interested in you" speech. How do you reject someone kindly?

"I'll call you sometime," Greg promised. "Have a good night, Dani." He waved.

Before Dani could get a word out of her mouth, he was gone. She shook her head in amazement and shut her door.

"Goodnight to you too," she mumbled to herself as she turned the key in the ignition.

She thought about Greg all the way home. She hoped he called her soon. As much as she hated telling a guy that she didn't want to date him, she hated it even more if she felt like she was leading him on and getting his hopes up.

She just hoped Greg would forget about her.

CHAPTER THREE

Dani's phone rang at seven o'clock the next morning. She was usually an early riser, but she had let herself sleep in this morning. Groggily, she reached for the phone.

"Hello."

"Hi, Dani. This is Greg."

Dani blinked, trying to wake up. She squinted at the clock again. *Greg was calling her at this early hour?*

Greg was still talking. "Oh, I'm so sorry. It sounds like I woke you up. Do you want me to call back later?"

Yes! Dani thought, but she was already up. She might as well bite the bullet.

"No, it's okay, Greg," she said.

"I'm sorry, it's just that I just found out about this rodeo thing going on today. I know you guys have horses and all, and I thought that might be something you'd be interested in going with me to watch."

Dani yawned silently. "That's a nice thought, Greg, but I don't think it would be a good idea for us to hang out together."

"Why not?" Greg asked, disappointment etching his voice.

Dani cringed. Last night, she had decided that her plan of action would be to place her refusal on their age difference.

That should be less personal, and it was one—if very small—reason on her list.

"Greg you seem like a really sweet guy, and I enjoyed our evening last night, but I think our age difference—"

"Age difference?" Greg interrupted her with a laugh. "Aren't you twenty-eight?"

"Yes."

"I just turned twenty-seven. Do you only date guys that are your exact age?"

Wow. So much for her strategy. Greg was the same age as her?

Now she did feel old.

She stammered for words.

"Listen, Dani," Greg said, "this won't be the first time a girl told me no. If you don't want to go out with me, just say so."

Dani ran her hand through her disheveled hair.

"I think you're a nice guy, Greg, but I'm going to be leaving on my trip soon and I don't know when I'll be back."

She decided honesty was best and she continued, "I just don't think you and I would be a good match."

"Opposites attract," Greg reminded her, and she could hear a smile in his voice.

"I know," she said, "but I think it would be best if we just stay as friends."

"I'm wounded!" Greg surprised her with his switch to mock pain. "I'm not the man Dani's been waiting all her life for! She doesn't even like me." He boo-hooed in fake tears.

Dani smiled in spite of his goofiness. She knew he was trying to hide his disappointment and lighten the mood. He really was a great guy in a lot of ways, but definitely not the one for her.

Greg's tone turned serious. "I appreciate you telling me what you were thinking. I've had some girls that take a long time to tell me outright and that wastes a lot of my time and energy."

As if he didn't have enough energy to go around.

He went on, "I enjoyed my evening yesterday, too, and getting to meet you. You are a special girl, and I hope your trip goes well. Hey, maybe we'll see each other again at Denise's or something."

"Yeah." Dani could still tell he was little bummed, and she felt bad about that. "It was great to meet you too, Greg."

They hung up, and Dani sat in bed a minute before flopping back onto the pillows. She blew out a long breath.

There. That was over.

She snuggled back into her pillows. Even if she couldn't sleep now, the bed felt so good, and she wasn't ready to get out of it yet.

She must have fallen asleep again because the phone woke her up a second time. Not sure if she wanted to answer this time, she peered through her sleepy eyes at the clock. Twenty after eight. High time to get up anyway.

She sat up and swung her feet to the side of the bed. She reached once more for the ringing phone.

"Hello?"

"Dani?" It was Denise.

Dani winced. She wasn't awake enough yet for Denise to start grilling her about Greg. Why hadn't she checked to see who it was before answering the phone? She stretched.

"Good morning," she said sleepily.

"You're just now getting up?"

"Yep."

"Oh, sorry I woke you. I was sure you'd be up by now."

"Yeah, it's fine." Dani stifled a yawn. "Time to get up anyway."

"Soooo?"

Here she goes.

"What did you think of Greg?" Denise asked.

"I thought he seemed nice. Sweet... and high energy."

31

"I could tell you two hit it off. Greg's just great, isn't he?"

"Denise, I'm not going out with him."

"Why? Why not?" Denise sounded just as disappointed as Greg had sounded earlier, if not more.

"He's just not my type. He's too busy. It would drive me crazy."

"But you just said he was sweet."

"He is. The energizer bunny seems sweet, too, but I wouldn't want to live with it."

"That's too bad. We just love Greg, and I was hoping I finally found you someone you would like."

"I do like him, Denise, but only as a friend and a guy, not as husband material."

"Oh well. I'll just have to keep trying."

"I wish you wouldn't"

Denise ignored Dani's comment. They had been down that road enough times to know it was a dead-end street. Denise refused to lay down her cupid 's bow and arrows, and Dani continued to wish she would.

"So," Denise asked around a bite of something. "Do you know yet when you're leaving for your trip?"

"I'm not sure yet. I just finished all of Jeff's files so I'll probably leave sometime next week."

"Make sure you keep in touch with me while you're on your Amish expedition."

Dani laughed. "You make it sound like I'm going out into the jungle and might not make it back. I'm not even leaving the States."

"When *are* you coming back?" Denise wondered.

Dani thought a moment. "I don't really know."

After Jeff's death, she had decided to leave her position as an editor for the *Arizona Republic*. Her boss had tried to get her to stay, but she couldn't handle the stress like she had before, and her heart wasn't in it anymore.

She had enjoyed working again on her family's ranch.

There was something therapeutic in the feel of dirt and sweat and the smell of horses and sweet hay, but since it had been run for many years by capable managers, Dani could truly come and go as she pleased.

"I'll probably just play it by ear," she told Denise.

"Well, if you must go," Denise said, resigning herself to the idea. Then she laughed, still incredulous at the idea. "I still can't believe you're doing this. You'll have to send me pictures of you in your Amish get-up."

"I'll see what I can do. They don't allow cameras, you know."

"What? Why not?"

"I'm not totally sure, but it has something to do with the passage about not making any graven image. They feel like a picture is an image so they don't permit pictures of people."

"Seriously? But you don't believe that?"

"Yeah, I know, but I'm going to be as peaceable as I can and follow all their rules if I'm going to live with them. If I'm going to do this, I'm going to do it right."

"Well, find a way to sneak me a pic. anyway. This is one thing I've got to see!"

"Okay, I'll see what I can do."

Denise sighed. "I'm going to miss you."

"Yeah, you go bother someone else with your matchmaking," Dani teased.

"Hey!" Denise retorted defensively. "I'll have you know that there's a couple in our church that just got engaged and I was the one who introduced them to each other."

Dani chuckled. "Good for them. I'm going to miss you, too, Denise. I'll call you if I don't see you before I leave."

"Okay. Be sure and do that."

They said their goodbyes, and Dani got ready for another day.

She took a bowl of cereal into the den. Now that she was done with Jeff's articles, she should go ahead and schedule her trip to Ohio. She probably should have done that sooner, but she wasn't sure how long the articles would take and if his manager would want more editorial help on them. Now that that was over, Dani felt ready to move on.

She had done quite a bit of research here and there and had discovered that there were many Amish communities in Ohio. The number of possible towns for her to stay in would have been overwhelming if she hadn't already decided to try to stay in Fredericksburg, the town Leroy and Emma were from.

A Google search on Fredericksburg wasn't able to give her much information about the city, but she was able to learn that it was tiny country town, smack-dab in the middle of an Amish community. It had a library, a bank, a school, a pizza shop, and one small corner grocery along with a few other tiny shops.

Perfect, Dani thought, *off of the main, busy tourist areas, but still an Amish community.*

After booking her flight online for next Tuesday, Dani grabbed a pad of paper and started making a list of all the items she should bring along on her "Amish expedition".

She smiled at the phrase Denise had coined. Maybe it was the perfect word to sum up what she was doing. Here she was, setting out to take in all the sights of a foreign culture. She was going to be there to live as a "native" and learn from the people. Like any great explorer, she was also on a quest —albeit more of a spiritual one, but just as precious to her as a buried treasure.

She was starting to get excited as she thought about the adventures that could be waiting just around the corner for her.

Little did she know what lay in store for her in Ohio. She would never have dreamed of what was to come.

CHAPTER FOUR

Dani landed in Cleveland, Ohio. Her first two impressions of the state were that the weather was chilly for late April, and that the trees and greenery were so beautiful. She had been used to seeing the brown sand and rocks and very little color of the hot Arizona desert. The bright green of the springtime landscape around her seemed so fresh and alive.

She picked up her rental car and headed out of the city toward Amish country. She had reservations for a hotel in Wooster, a town on her way and, from what she could tell from her GPS, the closest city to Fredericksburg. As she drove along, she marveled at the beautiful farmlands and the massive acreage of some of the farms. The fields of acres upon acres of tilled ground reminded her of the rolling expanse of the desert, only here the brown earth was broken up by old farmhouses and barns, and a faint dusting of green covered it in places where new crops were sprouting. Dani decided she liked the rustic and peaceful setting.

She reached Wooster within an hour. It was already six o'clock and Dani was too tired from her drive and long flight to head into Amish country today. She grabbed something to eat and checked into her hotel. In her room, she set her suitcase down and kicked off her shoes.

Man, did it feel good to get those things off. Dani wiggled her toes. Even though she had picked casual, comfortable clothes for traveling, her choice of her favorite boots had not been a smart one.

She flopped on the bed, belly first and reached for the pillows. Resting her head on them, she closed her eyes. It felt so good to finally be here. She had forgotten how tiring it could be to do nothing but travel all day.

After resting a moment, she opened her eyes and looked out the window across the room. It faced the busiest part of town. Most people wouldn't have liked that, but Dani thought it was perfect. She was ready to experience Ohio.

The city of Wooster looked much like any of the newer, mid-sized towns back home. The stores looked new and well-kept, giving the town a clean feel.

Although she was tired, Dani definitely wasn't sleepy. Six o'clock in Ohio meant three o'clock Arizona-time, and her body wasn't ready to go to bed for the night.

Dani decided she'd go out and see the town, so she showered and changed into fresh clothes. That refreshed her, and she grabbed her purse and hotel key.

Since it was more the people than the places that she cared to see right now, Dani decided to go to the one place that always attracted more people than any other store, a place that likely every adult American had visited at least once in their life, a place local humanity in every city thronged to.

She decided to go to Wal-Mart.

Dani pulled into the huge parking lot. Suddenly, she spotted a large, black object. Its box-shaped frame made it stand out among the sleek vehicles in the parking lot.

Her first buggy! Dani turned into the row. Sure enough, there was a horse tied to a long, horizontal pole. Someone must have put that up just for the Amish.

Dani smiled. A buggy station at Wal-mart!

There was a car behind her, so she had to keep moving. At the end of the row, she turned left into the main aisle in front of the store and looked for a parking spot.

Just as she was thinking how she might get to see some Amish today after all and hoping she could find whomever came out of that buggy, a large van stopped in front of her to unload its passengers at the curb. Suddenly, an Amish lady jumped down. Then one, two, three... four, five, six more Amish women and a baby disembarked.

Dani giggled like a little girl.

The ladies smoothed their skirts from their hop down from the van and pulled purses up onto their shoulders.

The van began moving and Dani followed it past the group of ladies.

Dani was mesmerized. She drove so slowly, a car behind her beeped. The whole group of ladies looked over their shoulders toward her, wondering what the commotion was about. Dani wasn't sure what else to do but smile and wave, so that's what she did. A couple of them raised a hand in a wave, but looked confused.

Dani chuckled and pulled into another row. Suddenly, an idea hit her and she drove back to the buggy station. To her delight, she found that the parking space directly next to the buggy area was empty, and she pulled her car into the spot.

She couldn't see anyone, and she wasn't about to go around peeking into the buggy, although it was tempting, so she headed inside the store.

Dani felt like such a tourist, but she tried to look casual. She knew that was silly because she looked like everyone else, but while the others were simply shopping, she was here on an adventure to see all she could. Things that were normal for them were fascinating to her. She guessed that there were very few of the other shoppers that felt truly delighted to be there like she was at that moment.

When she walked through the double doors into the store,

37

she saw an elderly Amish lady sitting on a bench. She had bags on her lap and piled next to her, obviously waiting for her ride. A little boy was sitting next to her, and he stared at Dani. She smiled, but he just continued to stare back blank-faced.

In the store, Dani meandered through the various departments, discreetly on the look-out for Amish. If she spotted one, she moseyed down that aisle pretending to look at the items, sometimes picking out something she would use later and setting it in the shopping basket she had grabbed.

She felt like she had as a kid at Disneyland, looking for the various characters who walked through the amusement park. Cinderella had been the one she was watching for. Fortunately, they had found her within the first hour they were there because Dani could barely enjoy the rides for fear of missing "Rella". She had been so proud of the picture of her in Cinderella's gentle hug that she taped it to her bedroom wall where it hung for years.

And now look at her.

Dani smiled to herself. Although the people she was looking for weren't in costume, they would have stood out in California more than Minnie herself walking around in the supermarket. This wasn't a day job for these people to pretend to be someone else. This is who they were and what they believed in.

It felt a little silly to be looking for people, but Dani didn't care. This was the most fun she had had in a long time.

In one aisle, there was a young couple with a baby girl sitting in the front of the cart. She was absolutely adorable with her tiny Amish clothes and tiny white bonnet. She caught sight of Dani and watched her curiously.

"Hi," Dani cooed when she was close to her.

The little girl's eyes grew big, and she froze and stared at Dani. The baby's parents, who had been discussing an item a few feet away, looked back, a surprised expression on their faces.

"She's so cute!" Dani said, this time to them.

The couple smiled nervously and looked back at the baby, but didn't say anything. Dani was afraid she had worried or offended them somehow so she kept moving.

In the shoe department, she hit the jackpot.

While she had no intentions of buying any shoes when she walked into the store twenty minutes ago, once she spotted the two Amish women in the shoe section, Dani remembered that she could use a more comfortable pair of shoes for walking around in Amish country tomorrow.

Dani tried not to look conspicuous as she made her way down the aisle, inching her way closer to the women. One of them was sitting on the little bench, trying on shoes, while the other was helping her by bringing different sizes or styles.

Dani got close enough to be able to hear them, but she soon discovered that was pointless because they were speaking in Dutch. She was able, however, to notice the types of shoes they were considering—simple and completely black. Dani realized it would be smarter to buy a pair that she could wear when she lived with the Amish. No sense buying a pair now and another one later.

A thought struck her and she decided to be bold. She walked closer to the women.

"Excuse me?"

They both looked up.

"I was wondering if I could ask you a question?"

"Yah, sure," the older lady on the bench responded.

Dani wasn't quite sure how to phrase it, but now that she had started, she pushed ahead.

"This is going to sound pretty strange to you, but I'm hoping to become part of an Amish community for a while. I was wondering if you could tell me what shoes would be appropriate to buy?"

The women looked as flabbergasted as if Dani had just told them she had a spaceship waiting outside to take them home. They gave Dani a once-over and she knew how she must look to them. Even though her outfit of jeans and short-sleeve sweater were conservative to her, she knew she looked like a total "Englisher" to them with her highlighted hair and long, beaded necklace.

The women finally remembered that they had been asked a question.

"That so?" the lady on the bench said, pretending to take it all in stride.

"Well, that is my hope."

"What church are you going to be a part of?" the other woman now asked curiously.

"I'm actually not sure yet, but I'm hoping something not too old-order." Dani felt odd, speaking and thinking in their in their lingo about being "English" and not going "old-order."

"It'll make a difference where you go," the older woman pondered. "Do you know where you'll live?"

"I'm hoping to find a place to rent in Fredericksburg."

The woman nodded thoughtfully. "There's several churches in that area, but probably biggest groups are Tobe or Dan May."

Tobe? Dan May? Dani had no idea what those words meant, but she stayed quiet. She was a stranger enough without showing these ladies how ignorant she really was.

The older woman on the bench motioned to the shoe on her foot.

"In most churches, these or those in that box should be fine."

Dani caught herself just in time to force herself not to grimace. The black pair on the woman's feet was what she had always considered "old-lady shoes." No doubt they were comfortable, but with the gathered stitching around the top of the shoe, it was just too much for Dani.

The others in the box were tennis shoes, completely black with no logos or writing on them. They were so plain they could just have easily been boy shoes. Inside, she cringed, but at least they were a little better than the old lady shoes.

"Okay, thank you," Dani said.

"We'll be here a bit longer if you want to look around and see if there's something else that suits," the younger lady added, probably noticing Dani's lack of enthusiasm.

Dani was grateful. "Oh, thanks! I'll be quick."

Dani swiftly scanned the ladies' shoe aisles and came back with three boxes of shoes.

She held out the first pair for inspection. They were also tennis, but more modern, athletic looking ones with a stripe of lime green around the bottom and matching green laces.

The two ladies thought a moment.

"Usually, we don't like color in our shoes, but I think the Tobe church might be fine with it."

"Maybe if she switched out the laces," the other woman suggested.

"Yah, might be."

"That's okay," Dani said. "I don't want to buy anything that might be offensive to some." She set that box down and opened another one. "Here, what about these?"

"Yah, those are nice." The older woman nodded.

"My daughter has a pair like that," the other woman commented. "I don't think you'll have any trouble with those."

Dani was relieved. The approved shoes, while still being completely black even down to the laces, were actually cute with even a slight heel and were definitely feminine. She could walk around in these without completely destroying her fashion sense.

"Thank you so much!" she said. "I really appreciate your

help."

"Sure thing." The women smiled and waved.

As she turned away, Dani heard the women quietly talking to each other in Dutch again, obviously talking about her and marveling about the unusual experience.

Yeah, I bet you don't see that every day. Dani smiled wryly, thinking how she was going to be the talk of their circle of women. She could just picture a group of Amish women gathered around a quilt, amazed and laughing about this English woman who thinks she's going to be Amish.

As she continued to make her way through the store, Dani saw several Mennonites. She had learned in her newly-acquired knowledge of all things Amish and Mennonites, that the easiest way to tell the difference between the two was by their bonnets or head coverings. The Mennonites wore a white kapp made of mesh of some kind that sat further back on their heads, while the Amish covering was made of a more solid white fabric that you couldn't see through.

Dani came to the hair and cosmetics department and she spied a group of Amish girls. At least Dani thought they were Amish. She was puzzled to see few of them wearing store-bought and modern sweaters or tee-shirts over their plain clothes. It looked odd and Dani tried to be discrete as she tried to figure them out. She was shocked when she realized that they were looking at a section of mascara, of all things, and one girl held a packet of stylish barrettes, ones that were definitely too fancy for Amish standards. Another girl had a package of foam curlers in the basket hanging off her arm.

Hmm...

Dani decided against talking to them, but she listened to their giggling and discussion for a minute while she pretended to look at something.

For some reason, she felt sad and slightly disappointed. She certainly had nothing against make-up or fancy hair accessories, but she knew these girls' parents and church did. Seeing a group of Amish girls sneaking off and going against their authority somehow rubbed off a bit of the glow of purity she had formed around the Amish people. It was the same feeling she would have had if she had seen Cinderella after her shift at Disneyland in her jeans and tee-shirt and would have realized she had just been acting all along.

At this point in their lives, these girls were doing some acting of their own.

Dani finished her shopping and checked-out without encountering any other Amish.

She made her way back to her car and loaded up her bags. Just as she shut the trunk, an Amish man walked past her, pushing a cart. He pulled up to the parked buggy and began organizing his groceries into the small cargo area.

Dani spied a woman waiting in the front seat and, bolstered by her success with the shoe women, Dani decided to be bold again.

"Excuse me?" she asked the man.

"Yah?" He looked at her curiously as he set a box of something in the back.

The man had a long, scraggly beard that easily reached to the middle of his chest. His clothes were very plain and he wore a black vest over his white shirt. A wide-brimmed straw hat sat snuggly over his head instead of the black felt ones she had seen on the Amish men in Wal-Mart.

Dani said hello to the woman in the front, who had poked her head out to see what was going on.

"I'm new here," Dani continued, speaking to both of them now, "and I'm looking for an Amish place to stay in the Fredericksburg area. Would you happen to know of any?"

The man pursed his lips in thought. "I caun't think of

any," he said in a strong Dutch accent. "My wife haus some family that way, but we don't get over there often with it bein' so far, so I caun't say as I know the area all that much."

"Oh, where do you live?" Dani knew she was being far too nosey, but the Amish man didn't even seem to notice.

"Isht about three miles east of here." He gestured with his hand.

Dani thanked him for their help anyway, and the man smiled. She was surprised to see his teeth were dark, obviously tobacco-stained. His grin could have easily rivaled that of the roughest mountain redneck's. Dani hadn't even realized Amish were allowed to chew.

She waved goodbye to the woman in the buggy and got in her car, puzzling over what the man had said. He was three miles closer to Fredericksburg, yet to him it was "so far." Fredericksburg was only another twenty miles or so away.

Then it dawned on her that this couple was probably Swartzentruber Amish, one of the oldest order of Amish still around. They weren't allowed to pay a driver to take them anywhere except for medical needs. To drive a buggy the twenty miles to Fredericksburg would take awhile. That would also explain the difference in their clothing from the others she had seen in Wal-Mart.

Dani returned to the hotel, pleased with her outing. She hadn't expected to see any Amish, let alone talk to some. She could hardly wait to see what tomorrow would hold.

44

CHAPTER FIVE

Dani's day started off with a lovely morning. She woke up rested and ready for a new day. As she enjoyed the hotel's complimentary breakfast, she perused through a local paper looking for homes for rent or anything that might clue her in to what the area was like.

She didn't find much in the way of lodging. Rent seemed to be a little cheaper here than it was in most Arizona cities, but nothing seemed to fit her needs.

Back in her room, she gathered up her things. She had decided to dress even more conservatively today in a comfortable skirt and modest top.

She laced up her new shoes and walked over to the long mirror hanging in the bathroom for a better view. Tilting her foot sideways, she smiled satisfactorily. Not bad. They were actually quite cute. Dani knew she would soon be wearing anything the Amish told her to, cute or not, but somehow it soothed her feminine soul to at least have a pair of attractive shoes.

The drive to Amish country was beautiful. Dani had decided to go directly to Fredericksburg to look for a place to stay first before doing any more sight-seeing.

She turned off the highway onto a smaller, two-lane road.

The countryside was so peaceful and different from what she was used to. Dani couldn't get over all the greenery everywhere and she loved seeing the cows and horses grazing in the pastures.

Suddenly, she saw a buggy up ahead. She applied the brakes, but still came upon it faster than she had expected. She hit the brakes harder and slowed the car to a crawl. She hadn't realized just how slowly buggies moved. No wonder it took the Amish couple she had met in the Walmart parking lot a long time to get to Fredericksburg.

She waited until it was very safe to pass. As she slowly drove around the buggy, Dani saw that the driver was a woman. She was resting her foot on the outside trim of the buggy and the edge of her dress flapped in the breeze.

Dani was nervous that her car might spook the horse. She could imagine how frightened their horses back on the ranch would be if a car passed this close to them.

This buggy horse didn't even seem to notice her and simply kept plodding on. Its body was wet from the sweat of the exercise, but Dani could tell the buggy with its light frame and load was easy for the horse to pull.

She gave the horse a wide berth before sliding back into her lane.

Just outside of Fredericksburg, there was another buggy on the road. The road had turned curvy now, and this time there were two cars ahead of Dani also waiting on the buggy.

Dani watched in amazement as each of the cars gunned their engines and sped around the buggy, one of them barely giving the horse enough space. Yet, the horse trotted on, undisturbed.

Dani was duly impressed. Maybe she would learn a thing or two about horse training while she was here.

Before she could pass, a blinker on the back of the buggy suddenly lit up.

"Oh! Okay!" she said, surprised.

Barely slowing down, the buggy glided into a driveway.

In Fredericksburg, Dani parked at the little grocery store on the corner and went in. She wasn't hungry or needing anything, but she walked through the few aisles. The store was quite small, but carried most of the regular mom and pop grocery items—soda pop, chips, and a variety of basic produce items. Unlike others, though, this store also had a row of bulk food items. Dani smiled as she read some of the labels. She had never seen "donut mix" or "root beer extract" before.

After she looked around, which didn't take long, she headed up to the counter. The cashier was a middle-aged, pleasant-looking English woman.

"Can I help you?" she asked.

"I'm actually looking for a place to stay here in Fredericksburg," Dani said. "Maybe a bed and breakfast. Would you happen to know of anything like that in the area?"

The woman thought for a minute.

"Sorry, I just can't think of any, but there's got to be something around here. Maybe check down at the shoe store across the way. It's run by Amish and they might be able to point you in the right direction."

Dani thanked her and headed out. She had to wait on a dual-cab truck at the one intersection in Fredericksburg to cross the road. Although the driver looked like a teenage English boy, Dani could see that the truck was packed with Amish men. Several of them stared curiously as they passed.

Dani crossed the street and went into the shoe store. Bells jingled against the door and the rich odor of leather hit her.

An Amish woman stood at the counter, pricing shoe boxes with an old-style sticker gun. She glanced up and smiled a greeting without missing a beat in her work.

Dani looked around. The first impression that struck her was that there was so much black. Huge black barn boots

47

all the way down to tiny black baby shoes. Nearly everything was in black—black scarves, black bonnets, black felt hats for the men, black socks, black suspenders, and black shawls.

On a whim, Dani decided to buy the tiniest pair of Amish baby shoes she could find. The ones she picked out looked just like the old-lady shoes the Amish woman in Wal-mart had worn, but unlike those, these tiny ones were absolutely adorable.

She took them up to the counter.

"Hello," the Amish woman said quietly and rang up the shoes.

After Dani handed her the amount, she asked the woman if she knew of a bed and breakfast or some other place she could stay in Fredericksburg.

"It'll be for an extended period of time," she added. "I'm hoping a few months or so."

"There isn't a bed and breakfast, as you might say," the woman said. "There are some that have a basement or a room they might rent out if you're going to be here awhile. Let me think..." The woman rubbed her forehead absentmindedly as she thought.

"I know Davids' just moved into Jonas' place," she said, thinking out loud. "Rueben Weaver might have something though..."

She looked up. "Would it work for me to check around and then maybe get back with you?"

"Oh, that would be great," Dani said.

She pulled out one of her old business cards. Just as the card slipped from her fingers, Dani realized she had made a huge mistake. It was too late. She watched the woman's face, hoping she didn't read the card and would just set it next to the register, but she held it up to look at it.

As Dani feared, the woman's face clouded. She must have noticed the section on the card saying Dani was an editor for the newspaper in Arizona.

Inwardly, Dani kicked herself. *Nice going, Dani.*

The Amish had naturally become leery and uneasy with most reporters. Understandable, they preferred to be left alone and undisturbed by the outside world.

Dani could tell the woman was trying to decide what she should do now, so she jumped in.

"Oh, I'm not here working for a newspaper," Dani said, feeling awkward and clumsy. "It will probably sound strange, but I'm actually hoping to join an Amish community."

One eyebrow raised.

"You're not here for reporting?" the woman asked skeptically.

"Oh, no!" Dani shook her head. "Not at all. It's completely for personal reasons. I'm not even working for that paper anymore."

The woman searched her face, and Dani could tell she wasn't buying her story. Seeing no other choice and seriously needing this woman's help, she decided to tell her story.

When she got to the part about Leroy and Emma, the woman interrupted her.

"You know Leroy and Emma Hostetler?" she asked.

"Yeah, I got to meet them and their grandson, Willis."

"That so? Yeah, Willis lives just down the road from here, and we know Leroy and Emma real well."

Dani continued with her story and by the end of it, she had made her first Fredericksburg friend.

The woman was smiling again now and chatting away about a few rental possibilities.

Inwardly, Dani breathed a sigh of relief. *Thank You, God.*

"I'll have to give them a call here and get back with you," the woman said.

"Okay." Dani paused. "Do you mind if I ask you a question?"

"No."

"I thought the Amish weren't allowed to have phones."

"Oh, and you're wondering how it is that I can call them up?"

"Well, yes, if you don't mind."

"Most of us around here are allowed to have phone shanties."

"Phone shanties?"

"Yah, it's a small shed up by the road. We usually check the phone in there a couple times a day to see if someone left us a message or whatnot."

"Oh," Dani said, pondering this new information. "So you're new-order Amish?"

"Well, by the books we'd still be old-order, but we're pretty high in the old-order church."

Dani nodded as if she understood every word the woman just said.

A look of concern crossed the Amish woman's face. "I do have to warn you, though, I'm not sure how the church will take to an outsider coming in. We've had a few come through here, but they rarely stay. Just don't be surprised if they're a bit stand-offish."

"Okay." Dani nodded.

"Oh," the woman smiled, "and I probably wouldn't throw around that part about your job with the newspaper."

Dani grimaced. "Yeah."

"My name is Mary Weaver, by the way." She smiled. She glanced up at the clock behind her. "Well, most check their phones around noon, so I best do my calling."

"Oh, yes. Thank you so much!" Dani said, gratefully. "It's so kind of you to go out of your way like this for me."

"Oh, sure thing. Not a problem."

Dani waved as she went out, the jingling bells hitting gently against the door behind her.

She walked back across the road, but instead of going

to her car, she crossed yet another street on the other side of the grocery store to the little pizza and ice cream shop on the opposite corner. She figured she might as well have her lunch now.

She paid for a sub and Pepsi and sat down near a window where she could watch the town.

Across the road was a bank, which was surprising because this town didn't seem large enough to have their own bank. On the other corner was the smallest library she had ever seen.

Most of the traffic seemed to be work vehicles—mostly trucks and big vans—with an occasional buggy. Dani watched in amazement as an eighteen-passenger van passed by, pulling a huge trailer with a Bobcat skid loader on it.

Now that's something you don't see everywhere.

A work truck parked near her window, and Dani watched as the English driver and three young Amish guys jumped out and headed into the shop. She quietly ate her sandwich and listened to the group. She smiled as she heard them order their lunch in Dutch. The very English girl behind the counter seemed to easily understand every word.

They all took their food into an adjacent room. Dani heard a television turn on and after a few minutes, she could tell they must have turned on a sports station. A few of the Amish kids talked animatedly, but she had no idea what they were saying.

She finished her sub and balled up the wrapper. As she threw away her trash, she could see into the room where the others were. The guys all faced the television, occasionally throwing out a comment or pointing to something on the screen.

Dani headed outside, smiling to herself. Even the Amish men liked their sports.

She got back in her car and checked the battery on her phone to make sure she had plenty of power left so she wouldn't miss Mary's call. She turned the ringtone volume up as high as it would go.

Looking at her map, she tried to decide what she should do next. She really had nothing else to do in Fredericksburg until she knew what was going on with her boarding situation. She decided she might as well head into Berlin, the biggest tourist area in Ohio, to see some of the sights.

It took about thirty minutes to get to Berlin. The mood of the scenery shifted once she got into the midst of the town. People were everywhere, obviously tourists and shoppers. The stores lining both sides of the street, though quaint, were definitely not Amish. Dani didn't see any stores she wanted to shop in today so she kept driving. Someday she'd like to browse more, but from the looks of it, it would be an all-day thing.

Denise would love it. Maybe someday Dani could bring her up here for a girls' get-away.

Dani had seen a sign for an old Amish house that had been turned into a museum of sorts. That sounded like it could be interesting, so she headed there.

She took the tour and walked along with the rest of group, charmed by the rustic and simple life portrayed by the old hand pump in the kitchen and the worn quilts in the bedrooms.

The tour guide mentioned that there was a buggy ride available outside, and Dani joined a few others talking to an elderly Amish man outside who was obviously the buggy driver.

He smiled at Dani. "Would you be wanting a ride?"

"If there's room."

"Oh, yah, sure. We've got plenty of room."

He motioned for everyone to get in, and Dani climbed up beside an older couple and settled back for the ride.

She looked around at the inside of the buggy. She was surprised at how little there really was to keep the Amish safe inside the buggy. Of course, they didn't go fast enough for it to be dangerous, but if a horse got spooked or a car hit them...Dani shuddered.

The Amish man drove them on a paved path that wound around a large pasture on the museum property. It was a relaxing ride. The others chatted and laughed at one point when the horse relieved itself. Dani contemplated again what a big difference it would make if everyone had to move this slowly. You would be forced to slow down and take time to talk with whomever was with you. You wouldn't be running in every direction all the time, that's for sure.

There would be a lot more time spent staying close to home, a lot more doing without and making do. Dani wondered how much time it actually might free up by forcing someone to cut out many things they had come to think of as necessities that really weren't.

She smiled at the paradox. Here were the Amish without cars and with transportation that went five miles an hour, yet they got more done, kept up their homes and gardens beautifully, and had more time for their relationships.

We really haven't done ourselves favors by making everything move faster, Dani thought as she looked out over the peaceful pasture.

After the buggy ride, Dani checked her phone. She still hadn't heard from Mary, so she decided to go to a cheese factory not far from where she was.

She took her time there, wandering through the store and trying the many samples. Cheese was definitely one of her weaknesses, and she had never seen a place with so many samples. She loved the odd flavors like "smoked pizza" or "moon cheese," and she picked out several to take with her.

After seeing everything, she stood at one of the windows to watch the Amish men making cheese. They had hairnets over their long hair and beards and stirred the watery cheese mixture with long wooden paddles. There were Amish and

Mennonite girls in another section, deftly slicing, cutting, and wrapping chunks of cheese to sell.

Dani's phone vibrated in her purse and rang at the same time, making her jump. She quickly headed to a quieter spot as she answered it.

"Hello?"

"Hello. Is this Dani?"

It was Mary.

"Yes, this is Dani."

"Okay, well, this is Mary Weaver from the shoe store in Fredericksburg."

"Yes. Hi, Mary. Were you able to find a place for me?"

"Yes, I was. There's an older couple that has a basement room they're not using now, and they would be willing to let you stay there if you'd like."

Mary went on to explain the details and named the rental price, which was much less than Dani had expected.

"All their children are grown with their own families now, so John and Martha don't like having so much space to themselves. You'll enjoy staying with them." Dani could hear a smile in Mary's voice. "They're a spunky older couple."

Okay...spunky Amish?

"What church do they belong to?" Dani wondered.

"Oh, yah, they go to the Tobe church."

"Is that new-order?"

"Well, Tobe is still considered old-order, but they aren't very low. They still have things like phone shanties, English drivers and such. Oh, and you might be interested to know that Martha's sister is married to one of Emma's sons, so in a way they're somewhat related to Emma and Leroy."

"Really?" Dani was pleased. Somehow, just knowing John and Martha were close to her friends in Arizona made her feel more comfortable about living in their home.

"Thank you so much for your help, Mary," Dani said

gratefully. "I'm not sure what I would have done without you."

"Oh, yah, glad to help. I'll just let them know to expect you sometime today, if that's what you want."

"That would be great. Thank you so much."

Mary gave Dani directions to John and Martha's home, and Dani thanked her again. After they hung up, Dani decided to pick out a few more cheeses and a couple squares of fudge to give to Mary as a thank-you gift.

The afternoon was beginning to wane, and Dani was anxious to get to Fredericksburg, so she headed there after grabbing a bite to eat at the only drive-through she saw in Berlin.

Twenty-five minutes later, and after dropping off the cheese for Mary at the shoe store, Dani pulled into a long gravel driveway. Narrow ruts ran down both sides of the drive from buggy wheels. Two other lanes branched off and led up to huge Amish homes, but she knew from Mary's directions that neither one was John and Martha's home.

Probably relatives to them, she thought, observing the carefully landscaped yards. One had laundry hanging on a line that connected to a pulley attached to the second story of the house. What must have been an ordinary picture to the Amish was nearly post-card perfect to Dani, other than a few unmentionables discretely hung between larger items.

Dani smiled and looked back to the drive in front of her. A beautiful, two-story home stood at the end of the drive, its stonework contrasting with the clean white siding. A matching out-building sat perpendicular to the house, framing in the parking area. Dani slowly turned the corner and parked there.

She breathed a sigh of relief. *Well, Lord, I'm here.*

She stepped out of the car and headed up the walk. Tidy flower beds skirted the house and encircled a pair of flowering trees in the yard, lending color and beauty to the serene landscape.

Dani knocked on the door and jumped when someone inside squawked very loudly.

"Come in!" the raspy voice shrieked. Dani couldn't tell whether it belonged to a man or a woman. She hesitated, feeling uncomfortable to simply open their door. This certainly wasn't what she had expected.

"Come in!" she was sternly commanded again.

Okay. She reached for the doorknob.

At that very instant, the door opened. Embarrassed, Dani quickly dropped her hand, but the white-haired Amish man in the doorway looked down at it.

"Oh, I'm so sorry! I thought someone told me to come in," she explained awkwardly.

"Yah, someone did." The man chuckled. He held the door open. "Come on in."

"Maybe I should say some*thing* did," he added, pointing to the living room, a mischievous grin on his face.

It was then that she spied a large bird cage in the corner.

"Come in! Hello!" squawked the boisterous occupant, bobbing its head.

A parrot.

Dani smiled, and the Amish man laughed as if he had just witnessed the funniest thing he had seen all week.

"Hello!" the parrot called again, swinging upside down.

"I'm John," the man said, turning to her and holding out his hand.

"And I'm Dani." Dani shook the man's big hand.

"Welcome. I hope Methuselah didn't scare you too much."

An Amish woman bustled into the room, wiping her hands in her apron.

"Well, hello!" she said cheerfully. "You must be Dani."

"Yes."

"Well, here let me show you to your rooms." She

motioned with her hand for Dani to follow.

"There's a door in the basement you can use to go outside if you want," Martha said as she led the way down the stairs. "It's a bit unhandy to get to since it opens to the backyard, so feel free to use the front door if you wish."

"Is there one you would prefer me to use?"

"No, just use whatever suits; it doesn't matter to us. We're pretty used to people comin' and goin'."

They reached the landing, and Dani looked around. Directly in front of them was a cozy area with couches, a rocking chair, and a recliner placed around a huge braided rug. A kitchen complete with attractive cabinets and a matching dinette filled one corner.

"Feel free to use the kitchen, too." Martha pointed. "There are pans and dishes in the cabinets. Just use whatever you want."

"Thank you. This is amazing!"

Martha opened the door to what must have been the bedroom and waited for Dani to walk into the room first. A bed took up half of the room and it was covered with one of the most beautiful quilts Dani had ever seen. She touched a seam almost reverently, knowing all the work that must have gone into making the piece of art.

"This is so lovely," she commented.

"Oh my! I made that over five years ago."

"Wow," Dani said, smoothing a wrinkle. The various shades of rich purples and blues harmonized perfectly in an intricate pattern of diamonds and strips.

"This must have taken a month just to cut out," she marveled.

"Yah, it did take awhile," Martha admitted, "but I had help. My granddaughter helped quite a bit with the piecing, and my aunt came over several days to help with the quilting part."

"I only know the simplest sewing basics. I sure would

love to know how to make something this beautiful with my own hands."

"It is a gift that can be learned." Martha smiled at Dani. She opened a closet door.

"Now, if you need more space or hangers, just let me know," she said.

"Oh no, that's plenty, thank you."

"There's a bathroom on the left, too. Just put whatever you want in there. We hardly even use it anymore."

Dani followed her out of the room, and Martha showed her where there were towels, washcloths, and extra toilet paper. This was turning more into a hotel than a rental.

"This is so nice," Dani told her.

"Well, I hope you like it." Martha shut the towel cabinet door. "My granddaughter and her husband were the last ones to stay here while they built their house and that was nearly four months ago, so we're just glad to put the place to good use."

She started back up the stairs, and Dani joined her. For her age, Martha sure kept moving.

"We'll have supper ready in a bit," she said. "You'll join us?"

"Oh, thank you, but I already ate."

"Oh." A hint of disappointment etched Martha's voice. "Well, do you want to settle in a bit and come up for some pie?"

"I'd like that," Dani said, her taste buds watering already.

She slipped her shoes back on at the door. John was in the living room with a newspaper. He quickly folded it and started to get up.

"Here, let me help you with your things," he offered.

"Oh, please don't bother. I just have a couple bags and I can get it all in one trip," Dani said.

She had purposely packed lighter than she liked to force herself to not bring too much of home with her. Just like the shoes now on her feet, she wanted to establish her new Ohio, Amish self by buying things here.

John sat down reluctantly as Dani insisted again.

Dani pulled her bag and suitcase out of the trunk and set them on the driveway. She spied the plastic bag of cheeses she had purchased for herself. She didn't remember seeing a fridge in the little kitchen, but surely the Amish had a way of keeping things chilled.

I hope John and Martha like cheese, she thought, hanging the bag on her arm.

She shut all the car doors and picked up the handle to her luggage.

Inside, John wasn't in the living room anymore, and Dani could hear silverware clinking in the dining room where they apparently were eating their dinner.

Dani was surprised to realize what a soothing sound that was to her. Just knowing there were others in the same house was unexpectedly reassuring to her. She hadn't lived in the same house with another person, or pet for that matter, since Jeff's death. She hadn't realized how much she had missed the presence of another person.

She quietly took her things downstairs and started making the space her own. She was completely unpacked within a half hour. Hoping she had timed it right, she headed upstairs.

Dani followed the sounds of dishes and found the kitchen. Martha was clearing the table.

She smiled when she spied Dani. "Did you get all settled in?"

"Yes, thank you."

"John is outside doing a few chores, but he'll be back in a bit."

"Can I help with anything?"

"Oh, my, no. Why don't you sit down and relax." She motioned to the kitchen table.

Dani noticed a refrigerator in Martha's kitchen. She

wondered how it worked since the Amish weren't allowed to have electricity. She had so much to learn about these people.

"Oh," Dani held up the bag of cheese, "I picked up some cheese earlier in Berlin. Do you all like cheese?"

"Well, yes, we do, but you could put it in the small ice box downstairs if you want. John turned it on again after we talked to Mary, so it should be getting cold soon."

So there was a fridge downstairs.

"Oh, no," Dani said. "Please take it. You don't know how much I appreciate you opening your home to me."

Martha looked at her sympathetically, and Dani knew Mary had probably told her the whole story.

"Well, okay," Martha said, taking the bag. "I'll slice it up sometime for all of us to have with crackers for an evening snack. This is really good cheese," she said as she took the cheeses out and read the labels.

"I thought so, but then I like most cheese," Dani said.

"So do I." Martha smiled.

John came in and settled into one of the chairs. Dani caught a faint whiff of hay and the smell of horses. She was overwhelmed with a feeling of comfort as she was reminded of her own home and the smells that had surrounded her entire life. It was a curious thing how a simple smell can instantly take you somewhere and wrap you in warmth.

John smiled kindly at Dani. "You like apple pie?"

"It's my favorite."

"Goot, cause that's what we're havin'. And my Martha here makes the very best in the whole county."

Martha threw him a look. "Now, Dat, you know that's the same recipe half of the church women make and every single one of them is a fine cook."

"Well, I like yours best," he said matter-of-factly.

"Why don't you go and bring in the ice cream," Martha

suggested.

John chuckled as he left to get ice cream.

Dani was curious where they kept the ice cream if it wasn't in the refrigerator, but she didn't say anything.

"Now." Martha set a beautiful pie on the table.

"It looks too pretty to eat," Dani said.

"Don't you start too," Martha said. Dani watched as she deftly cut the pie into eight even pieces. She set a slice on each plate. Tiny apple cubes and thick syrup oozed slowly onto the plates.

John came back in with a bucket of ice cream, and he scooped a dollop onto the plates before returning the ice cream outside to wherever he had gotten it.

He soon was back and they started to dig in.

"Wow," Dani said after her first taste. "This is really good."

"Thank you," Martha said humbly.

"What'd I tell you, Ma. Isn't this the best you ever had?" John asked Dani, pride showing on his face.

Dani smiled, more at him than anything else. "Definitely," she agreed.

"Okay, now," Martha said. "Dani," she said, changing the subject, "Mary told us that you want to join the Amish for a while."

"I would really like to."

"We'll have to talk to the leaders soon," John told her.

"You came at a good time," Martha said. "We have our church service this Sunday, so you will be able to meet more of the people and more of the leaders will be able to meet you."

"More of the leaders?" Dani wondered.

"Yah, well, Dat here is one of the deacons." Martha pointed her fork at John.

"Really?"

Could her luck have gotten any better? Maybe she had

been right about God's blessing on this trip.

"Yah, well," John set his fork on his empty plate and relaxed back in his chair, "from what we heard from Mary, sounds like a goot thing you're doin', to us at least. We'll have to see what the rest say and how it goes."

Bless you, Mary.

"I certainly don't want to cause any trouble," Dani said.

"Are you willing to wear a kapp and plain clothes?" Martha wondered.

"Oh, yes," Dani assured her. "I was hoping you might be willing to take me under your wing and make me into a fine Amish woman."

Martha's eyes sparkled. Dani couldn't tell if it was out of humor or the anticipation of a challenge, but she could see her already making a list in her mind of all the things she had to fix about this English woman sitting across from her at the dining room table.

A knock sounded on the front door, setting off the parrot again, and John went to answer it. Martha started clearing the table, and Dani got up to help.

She was wiping off the table with a wet washcloth when John came back in with the visitor. Dani looked up to see the newcomer and she started.

It was Willis, the young man she had met in Arizona at Emma and Leroy's house. Their eyes met, and a broad smile spread across Willis' face.

"Hello," he said simply.

"Hi."

"Dani, this is Willis," Martha said. "He's our nephew. He lives with his family in the second house off our lane."

Neighbors, huh?

Martha turned to Willis. "And this is Dani Chadwick. She's planning on staying with us for awhile."

"Welcome," Willis said, his eyes twinkling. "So you made it after all?"

Dani smiled. "Yes, I did."

"You two have met before?" John asked, surprised.

"Yah," Willis answered. "I met Dani when I was at Daudy and Mommy's in Arizona."

"That so?" John asked.

"Well, what do you know?" Martha said incredulously.

Dani smiled and continued wiping the table.

"I just brought over the eggs," Willis said, turning to Martha. "John wasn't sure where you were wanting them."

"Oh, here, I'll just take them," Martha said.

Willis carefully set the cartons into Martha's arms.

"Well, I best be going." He wiped his hands on the front of his homemade trousers. "Mom has us all working like dogs to get ready for church."

Willis must have noticed the puzzled expression on Dani's face because he turned to her.

"We're having church in our shop this Sunday," he explained.

"Oh." Dani smiled at her ignorance. *Of course.*

"Ack," Martha sympathized. "So much has to be done. Tell Ina to please let me know if there's something I can do."

"Okay. We have a lot of help, and Mary's been over most days to help us, but I'll let her know," Willis said, heading to the doorway. "We'll see ya," he said to them all before leaving.

Dani wondered at the turn of events. The thought had crossed her mind that she might meet up with Willis at some point, but to be neighbors? She was pleased to feel like she already had a friend of sorts in this Amish community.

And Mary? She couldn't help but catch that and wondered if she was Willis' girlfriend or whatever they called it in Amish. He definitely seemed to be marriage age for the Amish, and Dani was sure she wasn't the only girl to notice his good looks. Maybe she would get a chance to observe a dating Amish couple while she lived here.

She certainly hoped so.

John settled in with his paper again in the living room.

Martha looked at Dani. "So, will you be wanting to do some shopping for Amish things tomorrow or do you have other plans?"

"No, that sounds wonderful, if you'll point me in the right direction."

Martha paused for just a moment. "Would you mind if I went with you?" she asked.

"Oh, no, not at all. Actually, I'd prefer it. I really know very little about which church allows what."

Martha chuckled. "Yah, it can get confusing even for us."

"What time would be a good time to leave tomorrow?" Dani wondered.

"Oh…" Martha thought for a minute. "Maybe around ten, but it doesn't really matter, so whenever you want to leave is fine."

"Sounds good."

They said goodnight, and Dani thanked Martha again for the delicious pie and headed downstairs.

It was a bit early to go to bed, but she decided to get ready and just let her mind and body relax in bed. Once she got comfortable under the heavy quilt, she realized just how tired she was and she set her alarm on her phone for the next morning.

Lying back against the pillows, Dani sighed. *"Thank You, God,"* she began to pray, closing her eyes and marveling how easily everything was coming together so far. She let her mind and prayer wander.

"Teach me whatever it is I have come here to learn."

CHAPTER SIX

Dani woke up to the smells and sounds of bacon cooking upstairs. The aroma made her stomach gurgle, and she wondered how she had been able to sleep through all the popping and sizzling, not to mention the scraping of dishes and pans.

She lay there awhile, just listening and soaking it in. It took her back to all those mornings when she was awakened by Dad's clattering around in the kitchen and the pleasant conversation with whomever of the employees had stopped in. Dad was a firm believer in starting your day off with a hearty meal, and he was good at it. It wasn't long before his cooking drew in any hungry soul on the ranch.

Dani remembered moseying her way downstairs and finding her spot at the table, still in her pajamas.

"Good morning, Sugar Blossom." Dad would smile at her and make her up a plate of whatever combination of eggs, potatoes, ham, pancakes, sausage, bacon, or biscuits he had decided on for that morning.

Dani breathed in the smells coming down from the kitchen now and smiled contentedly.

After she got ready for the day, she wasn't sure what to do. They hadn't talked about meals or food being included in the rental arrangement, but Martha had acted like she had expected her to eat with them last night. On the other hand, she had mentioned Dani could use the kitchen. Dani decided that, as enticing as the breakfast upstairs smelled, she wasn't going to impose, so she rummaged through her stuff to find whatever food items she had stashed in her purse and suitcase.

She would have to get more food today. Thankfully, she wasn't a big eater, and the two granola bars she found would be enough to tide her over until lunch.

Dani found a small saucepan and filled it halfway with water. She set it on the gas stove to heat up for her coffee. She would have to get used to not having a microwave.

She opened cabinets and drawers until she found a spoon and a mug. She was so grateful that she had thought to bring some instant coffee. Dani dug a couple of sugar packets out of her purse.

She took her coffee and granola bar breakfast over to the living area. The couches and chairs were arranged by the sliding glass door, so she had a lovely view of the morning outside and even the remainder of a sunrise.

Not an Arizona sunrise, she decided, but still beautiful.

Dani tucked her feet under her and sipped the coffee as she let herself wake up and enjoy the peacefulness of the morning.

She could see Martha's huge garden in the backyard. She could only imagine how much time and work it took to keep it so neat and weed-free. Dew still hung on the spider webs nestled in the grass.

Beyond the yard and garden, there was a woods. It looked deep and Dani knew she would be exploring it one of these days. She had always been enthralled by trees and forests, probably because she didn't get to see them much in

Arizona, except for her family's annual camping trip to Flagstaff when she was growing up.

She was delighted to spot a squirrel bounce casually across the yard, its fluffy tail flowing along to the movement of its body.

"Hello!" a sharp voice startled her before she realized her feathered friend upstairs was yelling again.

"Vas is dat? Vas is dat?" the bird called.

Dani nearly spit out her coffee. She quickly swallowed it down and held her stomach as she shook with silent laughter. Even the parrot spoke Dutch! It was the most hilarious thing she had ever heard.

The parrot rasped out another string of Dutch, and Dani fought hard to keep her laughter quiet. She sighed as her fit of laughs died down.

What an awesome way to start a morning!

When she was ready for the day and it was nearly ten o'clock, she made her way upstairs. The incredible smell of warm bread greeted her as she opened the door. She was amazed to see twenty or so loaves of bread on the table, some in bags already and placed in neat rows on the end of the table and some still cooling on racks.

"Good morning," Martha greeted her. She started bagging the cooled loaves.

"I see you have been busy," Dani commented, impressed.

"Yah, I'll be done soon and we can go. Sorry you have to wait."

"Oh, no. I'm in no hurry at all," Dani assured her. "I would have helped you if I had known, though."

"My sister Ina—Willis' mom—stopped in last night and wondered if I might make a few loaves for church," Martha explained. "They're planning on bread soup and we usually use day-old bread from the bakery for that, but someone else already claimed it."

"Bread soup?" Dani couldn't help asking.

67

Martha grinned. "Ain't you ever had bread soup?"

"No." Dani shook her head.

"Well, it probably is more of a plain folks' thing. It is a little different, but it's cheap and that can be important when you feeding over three hundred people."

"I'll look forward to trying it."

Martha twisted a twist tie on the last loaf of bread and started carefully stacking the loaves into a large cardboard box.

"Alright if we stop by Ina's to drop these off?" she asked.

"Oh, sure," Dani said. "And if you'd like to stop anywhere else while we're out, please let me know."

"Okay." Martha folded the flaps on the box down.

"Here, let me take that," Dani said.

She was glad when Martha let her. For all the spunk this woman had, Dani was sure her age had to catch up with her eventually.

Dani realized she hadn't thought about whether Martha was even allowed to drive in the car with her. She had just assumed she could.

"Would you like to take the car or buggy?" Dani asked casually.

"Well, do you mind if we take the car?"

"No, not at all."

Dani set the box of bread carefully in the backseat.

Martha directed her to which lane led to her sister's house, and Dani offered to carry the bread in. Martha agreed, but she said she'd go along.

Dani carried the box up the steps.

"Ina?" Martha called through the screen door.

A cheerful voice inside called something in Dutch which must have meant "come in" because Martha promptly pushed open the screen door.

They found Ina and several other older Amish girls in the kitchen busy working on something that smelled heavenly. A

68

few smaller children watched them curiously.

"I brought your bread over for you," Martha said.

"Ah, thank ya, Martha. You can just set the box on the table there," Ina told Dani.

"You must be Dani," Ina smiled kindly at her.

"Yes."

"Welcome to Ohio."

"Thank you," Dani smiled back.

Martha went over to look at whatever the women were doing. She fell back to talking in Dutch.

Dani winked at one of the little girls staring at her. The little girl smiled shyly and looked down at her bare toes. Dani looked around the house, noticing how clean and orderly everything was even in the midst of their busy day.

The screen door opened, and Dani turned to see Willis coming in. A surprised look crossed his face, but he quickly recovered.

"Hello." He nodded and smiled.

"Hi."

Willis looked at the box next to her. "I see Martha's been baking this morning."

"Yes. She is amazing."

Willis just smiled knowingly. He turned to tell his sisters something in Dutch before heading back outside.

Martha was still talking in Dutch, and several of them looked Dani's way so she knew they must be talking about her. Ina looked Dani up and down and said something to Martha.

"Oh, yah?" Martha said, looking at Dani. She switched to English. "Sorry," she said to Dani, "we get so used to talking Dutch, we forget not everyone understands it."

"That's okay," Dani said. She had been taking in the surroundings and really hadn't minded until now.

"Ina here was just saying you might be able to fit into one of Rebecca's dresses," she motioned to a young woman

69

chopping onions on the other side of the counter. Rebecca glanced up and smiled at Dani. She did look close to her size.

"I really have more than I need, if you want to try on a few," Rebecca offered kindly, wiping her hands on her apron.

"Really? Are you sure you don't mind?"

"Yah, come and I'll show you."

Dani followed her up the stairs and into a huge bedroom that must have been hers. From the three beds in the room, including one full-size bed, Dani guessed Rebecca must share this room with her sisters.

Rebecca rummaged through a closet and laid a dress on the bed.

"Do you want to try one on now to see if it fits?" she asked.

"Sure," Dani agreed.

"We often wear aprons over top our dresses, but you can just try on the dress for now," Rebecca said, setting aside the apron piece.

Rebecca showed her how to pin the dress, since there were no buttons or zippers. Dani hadn't counted on that. She watched carefully as Rebecca showed her how to weave the straight pins through the fabric.

"Just come down when you've tried it on," she suggested and shut the door behind her.

Okay. Here goes.

Dani slipped into a dress and cautiously pinned six pins through all the layers of fabric to close the bodice. It seemed risky to rely on straight pins to keep your clothes together, but with all their emphasis on modesty, Dani was sure the Amish ladies knew what they were doing.

After several tries, Dani finally got the pin and the fabric to lay right, at least as good as she was going to get this morning. She had thought pinning corsages on was tricky.

That was nothing compared to folding in the fabric on the front of a dress just right and securing it with a pin running vertical. Her neck was tired from looking down so long.

Spying a tall mirror, Dani walked over to it.

She had to smile. She definitely wasn't an Amish woman yet, with her short hair brushing the shoulders of the plain dress. She pulled her hair back to try to visualize her Amish self better.

Dani turned to inspect the dress.

Not bad, she thought. Much to her surprise, she actually looked pretty good in it. It felt a lot different than her jeans and sweaters, more feminine. It had been so long since she had worn such a long, flowing dress. She felt like a little girl playing dress-up.

Dani decided her pinning job would hold for now, and she headed downstairs for the real test before the pros.

Everyone looked up from their work when she came down.

Martha smiled at her. "Ah, looks like it fits real nice."

Dani nodded and looked to Rebecca. She was smiling, her eyes twinkling. Dani knew she must be quite the sight—an English woman in an Amish get-up.

"I don't think we'll even need to take out the hem," Ina commented.

"Nay," Martha agreed. "What do you think?" she asked Dani.

"I like it."

"Here, let me get some others for you," Rebecca offered.

"Are you sure? I feel so bad taking your clothes."

"Oh, no." Rebecca waved her off. "I'm glad to do it."

"Rebecca here is our seamstress," Ina told Dani. "Trust me, she'll be happy to get out of other jobs to make a few more dresses for herself."

Rebecca returned and set a neat stack of dresses on the table.

71

"Please, at least let me pay for them," Dani insisted. After some resistance, she finally got them to let her pay for the dresses. Dani was sure to give a generous amount for each dress.

The door opened again and Willis stepped into the kitchen, carrying what looked like jugs of oil. He tried to hide a grin when he saw Dani, but she caught the twinkle in his eyes. He moved into the kitchen and set the jugs on the floor next to the counter.

"I think I'll be leaving soon to go pick up Mary," he told Ina. "Is there anything you need me to pick up while I'm out?"

Ina responded in Dutch, and Willis left the room with a goodbye nod to Martha and Dani.

Dani smiled to herself. Maybe living here she'd even get a chance to watch an Amish courtship. It sure would be fun to observe.

Dani turned to Martha. "If you don't mind, I think I'll change back into my clothes. I really feel strange in an Amish dress with my hair how it is."

Martha nodded understandingly.

When Dani came back down, she laid the dress on a pile of neatly folded dresses Rebecca had set on the table for her. Dani noticed that she had been thoughtful enough to give her several different colors of dresses—from sage green to a rich burgundy. Although she would have worn anything, Dani was grateful Rebecca had good taste in colors. When a whole dress is one color and one color only, it'd better be a pleasing one.

After changing back into her English clothes, Dani thanked Ina and Rebecca again and followed Martha back out to the car. They made several stops for Martha, and Dani was able to pick up some much-needed grocery items.

Martha noticed what she was doing. Back in the car, she turned to Dani. "You know you're more than welcome to eat your meals with us."

"Oh, thank you, but I really would feel like I was imposing."

Dani again saw a faint look of disappointment cross Martha's face.

"It wouldn't be imposing," she said. "The house gets quiet with just me and Dauddy. Why don't you at least join us for suppers?"

Dani smiled. "I would love to."

Around lunchtime, they stopped at the pizza shop in Fredericksburg, the same one Dani had eaten at the day before and the only eatery around, from what she could tell. They both ordered subs, and Dani insisted on paying for them.

After lunch, they made their way to Rachel Hershberger's home, the village kapp-maker, Dani deducted. Martha told her that Rachel was expecting them, so at some point Martha must have slipped to the phone shanty to call her and set up the appointment.

Rachel's home was distinctly more modern than Martha's, but when she greeted them at the door, Dani found she was still very much Amish. She welcomed them in and got right down to business. She led them into her large sewing room, and Dani was struck with the lovely oak cabinets—Amish-built, no doubt—and a countertop lining an entire wall to make a spacious work area. A variety of white and black kapps lined another wall. Dani hadn't realized that there were so many shapes and sizes. There must have been twenty or more out on display.

"I sew for several church districts here," Rachel explained as she saw Dani glance at the wall of caps. "What you'll want are these."

She pulled several different sizes from a row of caps. She left some smaller ones in the same style that graduated all the way down to what must have been a baby size.

"Here, have a seat." Rachel pulled out a chair and placed it near a large mirror on the wall. "You'll need to put your hair up to try these on for size. Did you bring anything to put it up with?"

"No." Dani grimaced. *How had she been that stupid?*

"No matter," Rachel said. "Here, you can just keep these." She laid a netting of some kind and some hair pins on the counter.

"Oh, thank you," Dani said gratefully.

She paused a moment to decide how to use Rachel's set of tools of the trade. She really wasn't sure what to do with them, and Rachel noticed her hesitation.

"Would you like me to help?" she asked kindly.

"If you don't mind, so I can see how you're supposed to do it."

"Sure," Rachel said, gently parting Dani's hair down the middle. "There's not really a set way of doing up your hair. As long as it's under the covering, it doesn't really matter."

In the mirror, Dani watched as Rachel clipped her hair on each side of the part, then formed her hair into a ponytail. Rachel twisted the hair into a bun, but the layered ends stuck out in several places. Rachel folded the hair net over itself to make it smaller. She tried to capture all the ends in the net and secured it with pins.

Not the most attractive, but it would do for now.

"There," Rachel said and picked up one of the coverings. She placed it carefully on Dani's head and looked it over critically. After trying two other sizes, she looked over to Martha.

"This one looks like the best, not?"

"Yah, I think so," Martha agreed.

"Most women pin on their covering to be sure it stays on," Rachel told Dani, reaching for a pin cushion. "If you look in the mirror, I'll show you how I do it."

Dani bent her head down toward the mirror and watched

as Rachel carefully put the tip of the pin in about an inch then twisted it around to go the opposite direction and poked it back out of the covering.

If there was one thing she was learning today, it was that she was going to be getting a lot better acquainted with pins. These Amish women used pins for everything. For a girl that didn't even know if she owned a single safety pin, Dani had her work cut out for her.

After Rachel put two more pins in, she stepped back.

"Well, what do you think?"

"It looks goot." Martha smiled.

Dani took her first real look in the mirror at herself. Before her sat an Amish woman. Well, an Amish woman in jeans. Wearing a covering certainly wasn't the most flattering hairstyle she had ever done, and she would probably do it a little differently than Rachel, but it would work for today. For the first time in her life, she thanked God for her nice hairline.

She turned to face Martha. "I look Amish," she said, pleased.

Martha smiled and glanced at the rest of Dani's get-up.

"Oh, right." Dani grinned. "Besides the pants and all."

Martha laughed. "You're turning into an Amish maidly little by little. Now we just need to put the dress and covering together."

Rachel had several coverings already made up in her size, so Dani bought two and also a larger black one the ladies informed her that she would need. Dani took their word for it, and soon she and Martha were back in the car and heading home.

After some small talk, Dani asked Martha, "Do you mind if I ask you a question?"

Martha smiled. "No, I don't mind."

"Please tell me if I ask too many questions or ask something that makes you uncomfortable."

Martha chuckled. "You'll find soon enough that we Amish people are a curious bunch and we like to ask a lot of questions. We really don't think anything of it, and you certainly won't bother John and me with them."

It crossed Dani's mind that if the Amish were such curious folks, why hadn't Martha asked her much yet about her own life. Surely there were a lot of things they must wonder about this English woman in their house. Then it dawned on her that Martha was probably just giving her time to settle in and get to know them better. Martha's questions were likely more personal than Dani's were, and she was patiently waiting until she felt Dani was ready.

Dani smiled at the kind woman next to her.

"So," Martha settled in her seat, "what do you want to know?"

Dani had so many questions, but she decided on two for the time being.

"I read that the black covering is worn when you are out in public, but there were several women I saw in Wooster that only wore their white one. When do you know whether or not you need to wear the black covering over your regular white one?"

"Oh, we usually wear the black ones when we go to special meetings, to church, weddings and such. It provides extra modesty."

Dani nodded. She was still a bit unsure, but she figured she could just ask Martha whenever she needed to know how to dress for the day.

"We usually take them off there, though," Martha continued. "They're not very comfortable to wear all day."

Okay.

Dani decided to move onto her second question. "How can you tell the difference between the different churches and their coverings?"

Martha smiled. "Yah, I can see how that would be

confusing to you. Some kapps are different shapes, even ever so slightly, and sometimes they vary in how many pleats on the kapp."

"Pleats?"

"Yah, the flattened folds of material."

Martha pulled out one of Dani's new kapps and showed her. Dani hadn't even really paid attention to the fact that there were folds, let alone count to see how many there were. At a glance now, there must have been a dozen or so neatly pressed and perfectly spaced pleats.

Martha went on, "There is often a set number of pleats on the coverings."

Dani was amazed. "And the different church groups have a rule about how many pleats you should have in your covering?"

Martha smiled. "They often do. You will learn how important unity is to the Amish people. The leaders have set clear boundaries, so we don't unintentionally cross the line."

It seemed to Dani that there were likely more rebellious ways to cross the Amish line than by putting an extra pleat in your kapp, but what did she know?

"With tomorrow being Sunday, is it okay that I go with you?" Dani wondered.

"Oh, certainly, but you might wish you hadn't. It's a very long service, and it's completely in Dutch and German."

"That's okay. If I'm going to do this, I'm going to do it all the way. Is it fine for me to wear my Amish things now or should I wait?"

Martha shook her head. "No, I talked to John about it and we think you should go ahead and look Amish. It would be quite distracting if you were in your English clothes. I don't think you'll want to stand out that much."

Definitely not.

They pulled into the lane leading to the house. It was only

a little after four.

Dani parked and turned to Martha. "Thank you so much for helping me, Martha. I really don't know what I would have done without you. I think God really is working His hand in all of this."

Martha smiled tenderly and laid her worn hand on Dani's cheek. "I'm blessed to be able to get to know such a special child of His," she said gently.

Dani was struck with her kindness after she had only been with Dani one full day. She sat for a moment as Martha got out of her side of the car. It had been a long time since Dani had been touched in such a motherly way, and it had been wholly unexpected from this Amish woman.

Dani finally smiled and got out. She carried her groceries and newly acquired Amish wardrobe into the house after Martha.

"Supper will be at five-thirty," Martha called to her as Dani made her way to the basement door."

"Okay. Is there anything I can help with?"

"Oh, no," Martha said. "Just settle your things in down there. We're just having roast so the meal is simple tonight."

Dani smiled as she closed the stair door behind her. *Just roast.* She hadn't had such a nice home-cooked meal since her invite to Leroy and Emma's. Although she didn't mind cooking, it seemed like such a waste of time when she was only cooking for herself.

She placed her groceries in one of the empty cabinets and spied the small refrigerator for the cold items. She headed to the bedroom to put away her clothes.

She was still wearing the Amish kapp since they had come right home from Rachel's, and Dani decided since she had the time she should go ahead and redo the covering and dress now. She certainly wanted a little more practice before she had to get ready early tomorrow morning.

She laid out the four dresses from Rebecca. The burgundy

one was definitely going to be one of the dressy ones. The sage green one was pretty, and the light turquoise was an unusual color. Dani picked her least favorite, a county blue, to be her "home dress".

Pinning the front of the dress went easier than she had thought. She was grateful to notice Rebecca had pinned several pins into one of the dresses so she had some to use. The kindness of these women touched her heart. They thought of everything. It was a strange and wonderful feeling, knowing others were taking care of her, watching out for what she needed.

Dani looked at herself in a long mirror. She looked Amish alright. Her hair could use some help. It seemed weird to try to figure out a style for the couple of inches of hair that showed, and there wasn't a whole lot she could do anyway since all the Amish women she had seen so far parted their hair down the middle.

Dani loosened her hair and pushed it forward just a bit to keep it from looking so severe and slicked back. She then tried her best to twist her hair back into a bun and set the kapp on.

It took her several tries to get the pins in straight with twisting them around the way Rachel had showed her, but eventually she got the hang of it. It was surprising how much stronger the pins held that way instead of just poking them in like she normally would. The last thing she wanted at her first Amish gathering was a wardrobe malfunction.

After she finished, she took a deep breath and looked at herself again. Her hair was much better. Dani grinned. She actually made quite a cute Amish girl.

She looked at her English clothes draped on the bedpost. She knew once she began to be Amish she couldn't go back to her English clothes until she left Ohio. She studied her reflection in the mirror and looked herself in the eye for a long time.

Was she really ready to do this?

"*It's time,*" she whispered.

She pulled out her suitcase and pulled out the items she would still need. Then she folded up her jeans and sweater and placed them in the empty suitcase along with the rest of her English outfits. As she zipped up the suitcase, she felt like she was shutting the lid on her old life. In her new Amish clothes, she felt like she was now truly beginning her Amish adventure.

CHAPTER SEVEN

Dani could hear Martha setting dishes on the table and the Dutch conversation between her and John. She was just about ready to head upstairs when she remembered Denise's request for a picture of her in an Amish get-up.

She tried a couple times before she finally got a good photo on her phone's camera. She sent it off to Denise and waited a moment, knowing Denise would respond back. Soon, her phone vibrated, and she smiled as she flipped in open and read her message.

"Wow!!! You're really doing it! You look so cute! And hilarious. LOL"

Dani quickly texted back ":) Going very well. God has His hand in this. Don't know how long I'll have a phone, so don't be worried if you can't reach me. I'll try to call soon."

Her phone buzzed with Denise's response. "OK. Sounds good. Keep in touch. Love ya, girl!"

"Love you too."

Dani shut her phone and laid it on the dresser before heading upstairs.

81

Martha smiled as soon as she saw her, and John looked up from the counter where he was writing down something. His face brightened when he spied her in the plain attire, but he didn't say anything.

"You look right nice," Martha said kindly.

"Thank you. Is there anything I can help you with?" Dani asked.

"Oh, no. I've nearly got it."

"Now, if I'm going to be an Amish 'maidly', as you say, you're going to have to start letting me help with things."

Dani noticed the bread hadn't yet been sliced. "How about I cut the bread?" she offered.

Martha looked at her for a moment, then smiled as she handed her the bread knife.

"Alright, Maidly." She winked.

Dani smiled and began cutting the bread. It was so soft that it was a bit tricky to slice. It smelled wonderful.

John carried the heavy pan of roast to the table for Martha as she set out the few remaining items.

Dani took the seat she had had the night before, and John and Martha sat down. They quietly bowed their heads. Dani followed their lead and waited for John to pray. When a moment went by and he didn't, she looked up. Their heads were still bowed. Dani realized maybe they expected her, as their guest, to offer the thanks. She had no way of knowing whether this was true or not, but she figured it didn't hurt anything if she was wrong, so she began praying. Dani said a short prayer of thanks to God for His care over her and for leading her to such kind people.

At the "amen", John and Martha straightened. Dani noticed that they shared a look between them before John reached to serve the roast. Martha tried to hide a smile and busied herself with passing the bread to Dani.

Dani wasn't sure what to make of their behavior. She must have done something, but she knew she hadn't said anything strange in her prayer. She decided to forget about it.

The meal was fabulous. The meat was done perfectly and so flavorful.

"This roast is so good!" Dani said, savoring another bite. "It's even better than my dad's, and let me tell you, his cooking was famous on our ranch."

"You grew up on a ranch, not?" John asked.

"That's what we always called it. I still live in the old house I grew up in, but I don't actually manage the ranch anymore."

"Interesting." John scooped out generous helping from a bowl heaped with steaming home-grown corn.

"So, do you raise cattle then?" Martha wondered.

Dani finished her bite. "Well, it started off with cattle a few generations ago, but by the time my grandpa died, we had switched completely over to boarding horses. Now, that's all we do, but we just haven't given up calling it a ranch. We have improved our stables so we now have the ability to house over fifty horses."

"That so?" John asked, impressed. "And you have that many customers with horses?"

Dani nodded. "There are a lot of people that want to own horses in Arizona, but don't have the set-up for it. Usually we're completely booked up."

"Do you have a trainer or whatnot?" Martha wondered.

"Yes, he actually lives on the premises with his wife."

John leaned back. "We built a barn for a guy who does that. Maybe you'd like to see it sometime."

"Sure. I'd enjoy seeing how other people do it."

The conversation lulled for a moment, and Dani savored the delicious meal with each bite. She could have eaten the entire bowl of buttery sweet corn by herself.

She was going to have to watch her weight living here.

After dessert, Dani helped Martha and John gather up the dishes from the table. As they were finishing, the parrot began to make its voice known again.

"Care to join us in the living room?" Martha invited.

"Sure."

Martha led the way into the other room and fed Methuselah before finding a seat on the couch. She gathered up some kind of stitching to work on. John joined them and popped out the footrest on the recliner. He sighed as he settled back into the chair. Dani picked a comfortable spot on one of the couches and tucked her socked feet up under her.

"So," John started, "I was talking to the preacher today, and he was thinking about having a meeting tomorrow afternoon after the meal that way we could discuss some things with you."

"Certainly," Dani nodded. "Who all would be there?"

"Most likely it'll be the preacher and us deacons, but he may open it up to the other men in the congregation. This hasn't really happened before in our church—an outsider coming in for just awhile—so that will be up to the preacher."

"Sure." Dani understood, although she couldn't help feeling a little intimidated by the thought.

"I'll just let you know when we're ready to talk."

Dani nodded.

"Church starts at eight-thirty," Martha put in, "but we usually start walking over around eight."

She hadn't been kidding when she said it was early.

Martha went on, "If you need any help with your clothing or covering, please let me know."

"Yah," John added, "Martha has to use twenty-seven pins for a Sunday."

"Twenty-seven pins?" Dani asked in amazement.

"Yah," Martha smiled, "between my dress, apron and kapp. Did Rebecca give you that many pins?"

Dani shook her head. "I don't think so."

"Well, let me go get you some more." Martha got up and

headed into another room.

Dani was a little dismayed at the number of pins she would have to use. She had used maybe ten pins at the most this afternoon and that had taken her long enough. She already had apprehension as it was about her first Amish church meeting. She really didn't want to mess this up or start her first Amish Lord's Day stressed about her clothes.

Martha returned and handed Dani a small pin cushion with a section of pins stuck in it.

"Here," she said, "you can just keep this."

"Thanks, Martha," Dani said, taking the cushion.

"Why don't you get dressed in the morning and come up, and I'll help you with your apron since you've never done that before," Martha offered.

"That would be a big help." Inwardly, Dani breathed a sigh of relief.

John began dozing off and Martha looked tired, so Dani decided to excuse herself.

"Well, I think I'll head for bed. I'll come up before eight so you can pin on the apron and make sure I did everything else right."

"Sure thing." Martha smiled. She started winding up her thread.

John snorted awake and looked disoriented for a moment.

Dani tried to hide her grin. She thanked them again for the meal and said goodnight.

"Goodnight, Maidly," Martha said gently, her eyes twinkling.

Dani looked back at her and smiled.

The alarm woke her up in the morning at six. She had wanted plenty of time to get ready. She was hoping to have a few minutes to pray and quiet her mind before heading to church.

She showered quickly and slipped into her sage green dress. Painstakingly, she poked each pin into the dress. She sure hoped this got easier. Each pin took her about five tries before she was satisfied with how it laid. At one point, she pricked her finger. It hurt, but thankfully didn't draw blood.

Just getting the dress on took her about twenty minutes. Now for her hair.

She laid the hair things out on the counter and set the kapp nearby. Folding the hair net in half the way she had seen Rachel do, she hung it over a door knob to hold it for the time being. There was no way she would be able to fold it with one hand while holding the bun with the other like Rachel had done.

Carefully, she made the part and combed back the hair. Dani picked up several clips and slid them into her hair to hold it in place like she had seen Rachel do. This had to be one of the sturdiest hair-styles she had ever done. Even her pony-tails and French braids she had worn as a kid eventually got loose and fly-a-ways would take over, but there was little chance of that happening with this Amish style, where only an inch or two of hair that even saw the light of day.

Once she was satisfied her hair was twisted properly into a bun, Dani carefully set her kapp on and pinned it the way Rachel had taught her.

She studied her reflection in the mirror.

Not too bad.

She flipped the strings of her covering over her shoulders. It wasn't the most attractive she had ever looked, but she could live with it. She felt neat and tidy.

It felt strange to skip the next step in her normal routine, putting on her make-up. She had forgotten how much smaller her eyelashes seemed when she wasn't wearing mascara. Oh well, it was such a small price to pay. Her skin was probably thanking her for a break anyway.

Dani left the bathroom and gathered up the remaining items she needed for church: her Bible, notebook, apron and black covering.

Glancing at the clock, she was happy to see she still had thirty minutes left. She decided to heat up some water for coffee and picked up a blueberry muffin she had bought the day before.

It looked like a beautiful day outside. Dani carried her coffee and blueberry muffin to the porch swing she had spied attached to the underneath of the porch upstairs. She breathed in the fresh morning air. There was just something about nature that made you feel closer to the Creator.

Dani let her heart calm as she talked to God. She started with apologizing for her distance from Him in the last few months.

I still don't understand why you took Jeff or Dad from me, she thought bluntly. *I'm still angry at You for that. But I know I also can't live away from You, apart from Your presence. Help me, God! Help me sort through so many emotions.*

Her thoughts and prayers traveled to the way the doors had seemed to open so easily for her to be here in Amish country. It was one of those times when she just knew Someone else was orchestrating things. Dani could feel the workings of Providence. She felt grateful, while at the same time curious as to what lay in store for her. If God wanted her here, there must be a reason. There must be something here He wanted to teach her.

Guessing that it was nearly time to head upstairs, Dani went back inside. She rinsed out her coffee cup and brushed her teeth.

Upstairs, Martha was finishing wiping up the table. She smiled at Dani when she spied her.

"Good morning," she said.

Dani returned her smile. "Good morning."

Martha noticed her Bible and stopped cleaning. "Oh my, I didn't think of that. I'm afraid you shouldn't bring your

Bible," she said apologetically.

"Oh?" Dani said, confused.

"Yah, we only use German Bibles in church."

"Okay, I'll just put it back with my things."

Dani headed back downstairs. It felt so utterly wrong to be told she couldn't take her Bible to a church service, but she decided there was no commandment that said you had to take your Bible to church. It would be wiser to simply go along with it for today.

Back upstairs, Martha had disappeared somewhere so Dani waited for her in the kitchen. Martha soon returned, carrying four black books.

"Here," she said, handing Dani one, "this is the German hymnbook that we sing from. I want you to have this."

"But won't you need one?" Dani asked.

Martha chuckled. "When you're as old as I am and have sung the same songs all your life, you don't really need a hymnal anymore."

Dani gently took it. "Thank you," she said gratefully. She wouldn't be able to understand the German words, but maybe she could at least follow along.

Martha set the other books on the table and picked up Dani's apron. "Now, let's see about putting this on."

Martha held the apron up to her and picked several pins out of the cushion. She held them in her mouth as she slowly began pinning the waistband to the waist of Dani's dress. It made Dani so nervous whenever Martha talked around her mouthful of pins to explain what to do. She supposed by this time Martha must have mastered the art of holding pins between her lips without swallowing them. Dani tried not to think about it and listened carefully so that she wouldn't have to repeat herself.

After the waistband was secure, Martha pinned the shoulders. There were no ties on this apron like there were on a normal apron, so everything had to be pinned.

By the time she was done, Dani felt like a walking pin cushion. It wasn't uncomfortable, but she knew how many pins were holding her clothes together and it was an odd feeling.

John came in from outside. He was fully-decked in his black suit and hat. He looked as neat and tidy as Martha did.

He acknowledged Dani with a gentle smile before heading into another room. Martha placed her black bonnet over her white one and stood waiting for him. Dani followed suit, carefully putting on her own go-to-meeting bonnet. It was quite a bit bigger than the white one and there was little chance it would fall off unless they were hit with hurricane-strength gusts of wind. Thinking that was unlikely on a beautiful Sunday morning, Dani laid that worry to rest, grateful she didn't have to stick one more pin into her clothing.

John soon reappeared. "Bist du ready?"

Martha responded with a soft "yah" and they were off.

It was a glorious way to go to church. Instead of the bustle of traffic that was a constant part of Phoenix living, there were the trills of the birds' morning song and an occasional moo from the few cows in a nearby field. John and Martha walked slowly, almost reverently. Dani breathed in deeply and enjoyed the quiet, refreshing walk. She could get addicted to this.

When they reached Ina and her husband's home, they could see Amish families milling about. All were dressed similarly—the men in their crisp white shirts with black pants and jackets and the women in varying colors of the same style dress, topped by a white apron. Everyone was quiet and peaceful, even in their "hellos" as they waited their turn to go inside.

Dani entered what must have been a shop or huge garage during the week. The white steel that covered the outside of the building also lined the inside, giving a bright and clean feeling to the place. The concrete floor was swept carefully, and rows and rows of pews filled the entire building expect for a walkway along one side and a space in the middle.

The women sat in the rows by the doors while the men began filling up the rows on the far side of building.

There were tables on both sides of the door where many hats and black kapps were already carefully stacked. Martha took off her black bonnet and laid it with the others. Dani followed her lead.

Dani spotted Rebecca making her way toward her.

"Good morning," Rebecca said quietly. "We unmarried girls sit up front together. You're welcome to join us if you like."

Dani glanced up at the front. That was really the last place she wanted to sit. She was grateful, however, that this Amish young lady was reaching out to her and befriending her, so she agreed. She had noticed that she had been getting quite a bit of attention from everyone already, so sitting further back probably wouldn't make much difference anyway.

Dani followed Rebecca to their seats and sat down on the hard benches. The wood was polished smooth so as not to tear your clothes, but not having a back rest was going to kill her back. Dani tried to sit straight and help her back out as much as possible.

She was a little uncomfortable with all the men facing them and knowing she was probably being curiously scrutinized by the stiff and religious men across from her. She tried to forget about it and focus her attention on the Lord.

When it seemed like everyone was seated and things quieted down a bit, one man began singing a long note slurring up to another. Everyone joined in with him, singing long, very drawn-out words.

Dani was enchanted. She had never heard anything like it in her life. It sounded like something from medieval times and reminded her of the way monks might sing in the solemn, chanting sort-of way. The music had little medley and almost no tempo at all. Every once in awhile—perhaps at a new verse, Dani thought—the people would quiet down, and the one lone male voice sang alone a few notes again before everyone joined in.

Dani listened to the music, letting the flow and tide of the singing wash over her, calming her and making her feel a part of something very old and sacred.

She couldn't really tell when they switched to a new song since the differences were barely perceptible in the melody, if you could call it that. After awhile, the singing stopped, and a man in the front row across from Dani stood up.

He opened his Bible and began talking. There was no way Dani was going to understand a word he said. She couldn't even tell if he was talking in German or Dutch. This was going to be an interesting morning.

And long.

Dani kept her eyes on the preacher, but let her mind wander. She was going to have to do something through the next three hours of sitting there. Her backside was already numb from sitting on the hard benches. She decided to spend the morning productively by using the time to meditate and pray and think. She didn't think she had ever prayed or sat in one spot for three hours in one shot before. She decided to look at it as a wonderful opportunity since she was usually tempted during her prayer times to get up and go somewhere or do something.

Her mind wandered through the last several months. *Why was it that she had strayed from God?* She knew that she was still His child and could still talk to Him, but somehow their relationship hadn't been the same. There was something in her almost pushing Him away, keeping Him at arm's length. She was still going through the motions, but something had come between them. She knew that she was

91

the one keeping Him away, but she wasn't exactly sure why she was.

Was it because her faith in Him had been broken? That she somehow now doubted His goodness?

Or was it because she had this hidden motive to punish Him somehow for letting her brother die? She certainly knew she felt angry toward Him at times.

Was it because she wondered if He really was as powerful as she had always believed? Could He really have stopped Mama from dying of cancer or Daddy's heart attack or Jeff's accident? And if so, why hadn't He? Did He really care that little about her? If He did, how could she go on pretending He was her best friend?

So many people at the funeral and afterwards would tell her that all things worked together for good somehow and that God must have a plan in all of this. Dani fluctuated between wanting to roll her eyes and outright slapping the person. Of course, she just nodded politely instead as if she agreed with them.

Did they even realize what they saying? "Cheer up, God has a wonderful plan in the death of your mother, father, and brother. He'll work the deaths of all of your family into good."

It sounded so weak and cliché.

Dani knew that there had to be a God. The earth and universe were far too intricate and complex to have possibly happened on their own without a Creator. The many prophesies were fulfilled too exactly hundreds of years later to discount their merit. The crucial point on which all of Christendom hung—the resurrection of Jesus Christ— was far too documented and also proven by the disciples' suffering and death to ignore. No, God was there. Jesus was real.

There were times, though, when she wondered where He was.

Maybe she would find Him here, among the plain people of Ohio. Maybe she could glimpse Him again through the fog of her questions now that she was away from the place she had lost her loved ones and in a new world full of everyday simplicity, surrounded by a whole community of loving, gentle people.

Maybe here, in the peaceful setting of Amish Country, she could finally quiet herself enough to understand what was going on inside her heart and sort through all the raging emotions and questions.

Dani let her thoughts wander on. They were so intense that she nearly forgot the time and even the place.

Babies cried occasionally, and mammas took them out. Every once in awhile little kids had to be taken outside to the porta-johns. Little girls and boys sometimes switched between sitting on one side with their dad to sitting with their mom. Dani was amazed how well the children sat. She could not imagine English kids sitting this well for one-third of this time. Three hours was a long time to ask any kid to sit. But they did it, each of them. It was their life, and they would likely be doing this every other week for the rest of their lives.

Dani was startled out of her reverie when suddenly everyone turned around and knelt at their benches. She quickly joined them. It was such a relief to take a break from sitting on the bench. A man prayed, and since Dani didn't know what he was saying, she kept an attentive ear out for the end and rustle of people getting up.

They sat back down, and Dani's legs and backend screamed at her for putting them back on the hard bench. She tried to ignore them.

A different man got up and said a few things—maybe announcements?—and the service must have concluded as people relaxed out their reverent stillness and began gathering things together and talking among themselves.

Rebecca looked at Dani. "Well, was that longer than you expected?"

Dani smiled wryly. "It wasn't too bad except that my behind is complaining."

Rebecca giggled. "You get used to it."

Maybe.

"Once I started thinking, it made the time go faster," Dani said.

"Yah, that usually what I do too. It's kind-of goot, you know, to just have time to sit and think."

"Well, there's not much else you can do when you can't understand what is being said."

"I know." Rebecca nodded.

Dani was puzzled. "What do you mean? Don't you speak Dutch?"

Rebecca laughed a sweet, tinkling laugh. "Oh yah, I speak Dutch, much better than I speak English, but I can't always tell what all the preacher is saying if he's reading out of the German Bible."

"Really?" Dani was amazed.

"We had to learn the German language in school so we can read and write it, but most of us don't really know the meanings of all the words."

"So, your Bibles, you can't even understand what the verses are saying?"

Rebecca shook her head. "Not very well. Or the hymns in our song book either."

"Wow. I had no idea."

"Yah. Some of us have English Bibles in our homes. We know a lot of the Bible, like what it says, but most of us can't really tell you where a certain verse is or how it goes exactly."

"So, you know the concepts and principles in the Bible, but not necessarily the specific verse that teaches them."

"Yah, that's right."

This was a detail about the Amish Dani had never expected. Who would have known that some of the most strict, religious people in our country couldn't necessarily understand their own Bibles?

Rebecca glanced toward the door. "Oh my! I should be helping Mom. Sorry to leave you!" she said apologetically, hurrying to gather up her things.

"Oh, no, that's okay." Dani waved her on.

As Rebecca left, Dani turned to look behind her to find Martha. Several ladies still sitting on the benches stared back at her curiously. Dani spied Martha standing near the doorway talking with another woman, and she walked over to join her. A few of the Amish ladies she passed in the aisle smiled at her, but no one said a word.

Dani stood near Martha, but stayed a comfortable distance away so as not to crowd her or interrupt her conversation.

Everyone was slowly migrating outside by little groups. Dani watched as two little girls whispered to each other. They giggled, and one grabbed the other's hand to lead her outside. Dani wondered if the girls were sisters or cousins.

A young mother walked by, too desperately shy to even look at Dani. In her arms she carried a tiny baby, and Dani just barely caught the sight of his sweet little face peeking above the blankets as she passed.

A group of men walked out, talking as they went. Willis was in the group and he caught Dani's eye and nodded a friendly greeting.

Two women, one very elderly, made their way to the door very slowly. The old woman's hair was badly balding in the front. Dani realized that she had probably been parting her hair that exact way since she was a toddler. The thought of wearing your hair the same way your entire life was both odd and refreshingly simplistic.

Martha must have finished up her conversation because she turned to Dani. "You ready to eat?"

95

"Sure, whenever you are."

Martha led the way outside.

The scene outside was quite a bit different than it had been that morning. Instead of the solemnity and quiet, groups of people chatted. A group of men nearby laughed together at some joke, and three boys chased each other around the house.

A tent was set up nearby with tables and what looked like a buffet line. Martha and Dani got in line. Martha shared a friendly greeting in Dutch with a woman ahead of them.

The woman looked past Martha to Dani. "Hello," she said, smiling kindly.

"Hi." Dani returned the smile.

The line moved forward, and Dani watched as the girls behind the buffet tables served the food. She noticed one of them had Downs' Syndrome, and she marveled at the grace the girl tried so hard to achieve as she ladled soup into bowls. The girl smiled at someone's comment to her, and her huge grin made her already little eyes nearly disappear as her entire face lit up with joy. It was a beautiful sight.

They were served and sat down with their lunch of bread soup, salad, homemade pickles, applesauce and cookies.

Dani couldn't wait to try the bread soup. She tentatively took a bite.

"So, what do you think of bread soup?" Martha asked.

"Hmm..." Dani tasted another bite. "Not bad. It tastes like it has chicken broth for the base."

Martha nodded. "Yah, you're right. It also has onions and other spices in it."

The pieces of now very soggy bread were a bit unusual. Not something Dani would ever request, but not bad either, just very different.

There was one little girl sitting across from Dani, watching her over her own plate of food. Dani smiled at her, and she smiled back shyly, almost embarrassed.

"Are you one of Ina's girls?" Dani asked, thinking she had seen her the day before.

She nodded. "I'm Carrie."

"That's a nice name." Dani smiled. "How old are you?"

"Nine." Carrie fidgeted uncomfortably.

"Did you help make all this food?"

"Not much. Mostly Mama and the big girls did, but I cut up the bread."

"You cut up all the bread?"

She smiled and nodded.

"Wow. It must be a big help to have you around."

Carrie didn't seem to know what to say.

After a minute, Carrie asked, "What is your name?"

Dani smiled, pleased the girl was warming up to her. "I'm Dani."

Carrie looked confused. "Dani?" she asked.

"Yep." Dani took a bite out of her cookie.

Carrie still looked befuddled and Dani realized that the name "Dani" was a more modern name Carrie might not be familiar with.

"You've probably never heard that name before, huh?" she asked.

"I've heard it before, but not for a girl." Carrie hesitated. "That's my uncle's name."

Dani couldn't help chuckling at the solemn expression the girl wore, like she was afraid of offending her.

"Oh, dear," Dani said, still smiling. "I didn't realize I had an Amish man's name."

Carrie smiled and let a little giggle escape.

Dani took a sip from her cup of iced mint tea.

"This is really good," she said, motioning to her cup.

"Did you never have mint tea before?" Carrie asked, surprised.

Dani shook her head. "Nope. I like it though."

Carrie nodded. "Me, too."

Carrie had finished her food, and she looked around to see where her friends were. She scooted off the bench and picked up her tray.

"Bye," she said shyly and hurried off.

Dani smiled as she watched Carrie throw her plate away and join a group of girls about her age. They talked among themselves and skipped off to play, their kapp strings waving behind them.

Dani realized Martha had left, and she sipped the rest of her tea, content to relax and take it all in.

John came up beside her.

"We're ready to talk when you are," he said quietly.

"Oh, sure."

She swallowed the last of her tea and got up. After dumping her trash in the can, she followed John up to the house, a little anxious as to what she would find there.

CHAPTER EIGHT

John held the screen door open for Dani, and she entered to find the huge living room area was full of Amish men. All eyes were on her as John shut the door behind them and motioned for her to take a seat.

Dani was more than a little intimidated at the room full of sober, bearded men. She had heard of the seriousness and strictness of the Amish men in leadership. She hadn't found John to be that way, but maybe he had been the exception to the rule.

The man who had preached that morning stood up to shake her hand.

"I'm Mose Weaver," he said. Although he didn't out-right smile, the look in his eyes was kind and friendly.

"Hello. I'm Dani." She shook his hand. "Nice to meet you."

Dani found a seat, and Mose began.

"John, here, tells me that you would like to join our Amish group for a while."

"Yes." She nodded.

"As you probably know, we Amish are very careful with what we allow in our community. We strive hard to keep the outside world, outside."

Dani suddenly had a sinking feeling as she wondered where he was going with such an introduction. Maybe she had been wrong to expect to able to stay here.

"It's nothing against you as a person," Mose added. "It's just how we have to do things. The biggest concern we have is that by being here, you might somehow pull some of us—especially the young people—away from our faith."

Dani didn't know what to say. The thought had never even crossed her mind. *Had she really been so self-centered that she hadn't realized how her being here might affect the Amish too?*

"I understand your concerns," she told the men honestly. "You are afraid that just by me being here, I might negatively affect the young people by making the outside world seem more attractive."

Mose nodded.

Dani glanced over at John. He was looking down as if thinking, a sober expression on his face.

She pushed ahead. "My hope in coming here is to learn from you. I think the Amish have many things right that more modern Americans have forgotten. I can truly say that I believe God has led me to you. I have no desire whatsoever to encourage any of you away from your Amish faith. I would hope, rather, to learn from you and to be submissive to all the rules of the church for as long as I am here."

She thought she could sense Mose relax ever so slightly.

"We can't forbid you to come," the preacher said, stroking his beard thoughtfully, "and I doubt we would want

100

to if we could."

"I certainly don't want to be a trouble for you. I'll leave on my own if that's what you prefer," Dani told him. She knew it would be the right thing to do even though she would be deeply disappointed if she had to leave this place and these people she was already learning to love.

Mose held her gaze for a moment, and Dani waited for his decision. He turned to the other men and started talking in Dutch. Dani watched as the men asked questions and made comments. What she wouldn't have given to be able to understand Dutch right about then.

Finally after some discussion, Mose turned to Dani again.

"No," he said, "you can stay. It's not right that we guard ourselves so much that we cannot give to those that really have come to learn. I think you are one of those. You are welcome to stay so long as you continue under our leadership and no problems arise because of you."

"Thank you," Dani said simply, more relieved than she cared to show.

"Now there are some other details we should discuss, like your car. We think it would be best if you not drive your car while you are here."

Dani nodded. It would feel rather strange to lose that independence, but she would learn to get by without it.

"Also, do you have a cell phone?"

"Yes, I do."

"We would prefer if you not use it while here either."

"Sure," Dani agreed. She had figured that one was coming.

"Other than that," Mose leaned back into her chair, "you look like you're in good hands," he said, glancing over at John.

"You don't know how much I appreciate you letting me into your lives. I know it isn't something you do often or lightly, and I realize the gift you as a community are giving me." Dani looked around at all of the men. "Thank you."

Several of the men nodded, and John smiled gently at her. *He had wanted her to stay*, Dani realized. John had been really hoping she could stay. A warmth flooded her heart. Surely his opinion had largely influenced Mose's decision

The men started to disperse, a couple shaking her hand and offering their name and a few words of introduction, but most simply started chatting amongst themselves.

Last to talk to her were Mose and John.

Mose shook her hand again. "I hope we can be a blessing to you."

"You already have," Dani said. "I certainly hope I can do the same for you."

They headed back outside, little knowing the problems her being there might indeed cause for this quiet Amish community.

Dani spied Rebecca wiping off tables in the now deserted tent.

"Can I help you?" Dani asked.

Rebecca straightened. "Oh, you don't have to."

"I don't mind." Spying an extra washcloth, Dani picked it up. "Can I use this?"

"Sure." Rebecca smiled, giving in.

The two wiped tables in silence for awhile. Dani returned to Rebecca to rinse her rag in her bucket of soapy water.

"So," Rebecca asked, "are they going to let you stay?"

Dani smiled. "Yes."

Rebecca grinned. "Goot. I was hoping they would."

"Really?" Dani asked, surprised and pleased.

"Yah."

Rebecca hesitated and then added, "Frankly, I could use a friend right about now."

She began wiping off some chairs.

Dani thought about what she had said. She realized

Amber Willems

that she hadn't seen Rebecca with any group of girls even though, with all the young people, there must have been some that were her age. She would have assumed that Rebecca was just staying busy helping with church and all, but maybe there was something deeper going on.

Dani eyed her thoughtfully.

"Do you think you would be willing to do a huge favor for for me?" she asked.

"What's that?" Rebecca asked, a bit cautiously.

"Well, the leaders decided that it would be best if I didn't drive my car while living here aaaand..."she drew out the word, "I would really love if you would teach me to drive a buggy."

Rebecca's face broke into a grin. "You would?"

"Yeah. Is that something you wouldn't mind doing?"

Rebecca was still smiling. "No, that would be fun. I wouldn't mind at all."

They held each other's gaze for a moment, and something told Dani that they were well on their way to a sweet friendship.

"Are you staying for the hymn-sing?" Rebecca asked.

"Hymn-sing?"

"Yah, all the young people come and sing for a bit, then visit and have snacks."

"Rebecca, I don't know if you've noticed, but I don't know a word of Dutch. There's no way I can sing your songs."

"Oh, no one will care. We know you're new. Besides, sometimes we sing some English hymns. We are going to have to work on your Dutch though."

Dani made a face of mock hopelessness. "I know!"

"You should come, though." Rebecca nudged again.

"Oh, I don't know."

"You can sit by me; it'll be fine."

Dani looked doubtful.

Rebecca continued. "My gros-mommy says 'when you decide to go swimming, you've gotta give up the idea of being dry.' "

Dani wasn't quite sure what she was trying to say by the riddle.

"In other words," Rebecca explained, "if you're going to do something, you have to go all in. It isn't that fun to go swimming if you're going to try to keep something dry at the same time."

"Just jump in, huh?"

"Yah. If you want to be an Amish maidly, then you're going to have to do it all the way."

Dani looked at her, weighing her options.

"Okay, I'll come," she finally said, squeezing her cloth out for the last time and hanging it on the side of the bucket.

"Goot," Rebecca said, picking up the bucket.

"You're a pretty good negotiator for an Amish woman," Dani teased.

Rebecca grinned and carried the bucket to the edge of the yard. She held onto the rags and tossed the dirty water into the brush. Some men and boys began cleaning up the tables and chairs. Dani looked around to see that many of the Amish families had already gone home.

She saw John say something to Martha, and they looked around, obviously trying to find her.

"Oh, there you are." Martha smiled. "John and I are going to head home. You want to come now, too?"

"Sure," Dani said. "Rebecca talked me into going to the singing tonight."

"Did she?" Martha seemed pleased. "Well, now, that doesn't start until seven, so you'll have plenty of time to eat yet and walk back."

"Okay, sounds good."

They had a quiet afternoon and more simple supper. Dani could tell Martha was nearly done in by the day's end.

"Please don't wait up for me," Dani said. "I'll just come in through the basement."

"Okay." Martha nodded.

"Rebecca said that we sing for awhile and have some snacks before heading home. Is there anything else I should know about tonight?" she wondered.

"Dani," Martha said gently, "you're not going to mess-up."

Dani was a little taken-aback.

Martha went on. "You are so worried you are going to do something wrong. Even if you did, everyone knows that you're new and will give you grace. That's our way."

Dani nodded, still surprised at her insight.

"On another note," John's eyes twinkled mischievously as he glanced at Martha, "we should tell you that it's a custom for the young men to take the girls home after the singing is over."

"What?" Dani asked. "No, you're joking."

John laughed. "Not this time."

"Oh, John," Martha scolded.

"Rebecca didn't tell me about this," Dani said, a little alarmed.

"Don't worry," Martha said. "You're new and can just walk since it's so close. I really doubt anyone will offer to take you home. Besides, it's just as common for sisters to go home with their own brothers or sisters. The custom just makes a way for a couple to be together for a bit if they're interested in each other."

Dani hoped Martha was right. She never would have agreed to go tonight if she had known this. It wasn't that she was opposed to making male friends among the Amish, it was just that she wanted the friendships to stay just that and the hint of romance in this hymn-sing tradition worried her.

The last thing she wanted was to have to ward off more suitors, especially Amish ones! And falling for an English girl was the last thing they needed as well.

But she had told Rebecca that she would come, and their relationship was too fragile and new for her to back out now. Despite her trepidation, Dani enjoyed the walk back to Ina and William's house that evening. Walking was something she hadn't done much of before, seeing as she just drove everywhere and didn't take time to walk. Dani decided that she had been missing out on a lovely pastime, and she determined to do more of it in the future.

Rebecca was waiting for Dani outside, and she smiled when she spied her.

"Hello," she greeted her.

Dani returned the smile. "Hello."

Rebecca quietly led her inside the building. All the benches had been put away, and there were just the snack tables and several dozen folding chairs organized into two groups on either side of the room. Dani quickly noted that one side was for the boys and one for the girls.

Rebecca and she took a nearby seat. Some of the young people chatted and laughed softly amongst themselves until Willis announced: "Let's get started."

Books rustled and Rebecca handed her a different hymnal than the German one Dani had brought along. A number was chosen, and the young people began to sing. Dani tried to follow along even though she didn't know the words, thinking maybe she could at least follow the sounds so she knew where they were in each song. She soon found that that was nearly impossible. With the long, slurred notes, she couldn't even tell what they were pronouncing. With one song, they abruptly stopped when she thought they had two more verses, and with another, she came to what she thought was the end only to have them continue on with another verse.

Dani noticed the Down's syndrome girl several chairs away. The girl alternated between singing and staring at someone, which usually ended up being Dani most of the

106

time. Dani smiled at her once, but the girl just continued to stare as if trying to figure out who she was.

After about an hour of singing, the song service ended and the books were set aside.

The scene turned into a casual one with chatting and laughter.

"I'm going to get the snacks out," Rebecca told Dani, excusing herself.

"Oh, here, I'll help," Dani said, getting up with her. They began working on taking lids off containers of cookies leftover from lunch and opening bags of chips.

When it was all set out, Rebecca said, "We might as well get our plates while we're up here."

Dani really wasn't hungry. It seemed like all she had done all day was sit and eat. She wondered how these Amish girls ate so much and still stayed so thin.

She did take a cookie because she remembered how good they had been earlier.

They sat back down and began munching on the goodies.

Dani turned to her friend, "You didn't tell me about the buggy rides home."

Rebecca smiled. "I wanted you to come," she said simply.

Dani shook her head, marveling at her intuition. "Seriously, though, do you think one of the boys really might ask to take me home?"

Rebecca glanced over at the boys' side of the room. "I doubt it," she said. "It can usually take awhile to warm up to strangers, especially for us Amish. The boys don't usually ask to take someone home unless they're interested in the girl, you know, romantically."

"I hope you're right," Dani said, taking the last bite of her cookie.

Rebecca grinned.

After a while, some of the other girls sat across from Rebecca and asked her something in Dutch, so Dani simply sat and watched the group of young people. By now, a few of the boys and girls were talking together, although for the most part, the two groups were still separate. Even under their cloak of modest Amish ways, Dani could still pick out a couple of the girls that were the flirty type and a few of the boys that seemed more bold and rebellious.

Human nature seemed to be the same no matter where you went. Amish parents here had to deal with some of the same heart issues that a typical American family might, except maybe on a less blatant scale.

Dani watched as some of the couples began pairing up and leaving.

A girl got up and joined one of the guys with a shy smile. Dani noticed Rebecca was watching them. Dani caught the hint of sadness in Rebecca's eyes, and Dani knew she had just stumbled upon an insight into her new friend. Rebecca dropped her gaze and looked back at the girl talking to her.

Dani decided that it was soon time to head home as well, but she had noticed earlier that Rebecca had put out a water cooler of their delicious mint tea, so she got up to get a some.

She threw her plate in the trash and picked up a cup. As she was holding down the button to fill up her cup, someone came up and waited for her.

She looked up to see Willis.

"Hello," he said.

"Oh, hi!" Dani smiled.

She finished with her cup and moved out of the way for him to fill up his.

"You having a nice time?" he asked instead of getting more tea.

"Oh, yes. You're sister is such a gem."

Willis smiled and looked over to where Rebecca was sitting. He turned back to Dani.

"You heading home?" he asked, nodding at the hymnal in her hand.

"Yeah, I think I will soon, but I couldn't pass up another taste of this delicious mint tea again."

After a pause, Willis asked, "Do you want someone to walk you home?"

Startled, Dani quickly said, "Oh, no, really, you don't have to do that. I don't mind the walking."

"It's not far." He shrugged his shoulders. "And I don't mind either."

"Okay," Dani said, not sure what else to say. If she was honest, she really wouldn't mind the company. "Let me say goodbye to Rebecca."

Rebecca looked up as Dani reached her.

"I think I'm going to head home," Dani said. "Thank you for the nice evening."

"Oh, yah, sure." Rebecca noticed Willis waiting for Dani. "Is Willis walking you home?"

"Yeah," Dani said, a little embarrassed, though she wasn't sure why.

Rebecca's eyes twinkled with amusement as she glanced back at her brother. "Okay, well, we'll see ya. Oh," she stopped, "you want to see if tomorrow evening suits for you to come over for buggy lessons?

"Sure." Dani grinned. "Just plan on it unless you hear otherwise."

"You want to come over after supper some time?"

"Sounds good."

The two said goodbye, and Dani set her now empty cup in the trash before joining Willis. He smiled and led the way outside.

The night was now slightly chilly, but very fresh. Dani marveled at the stillness and quiet as they walked in comfortable silence. She had always enjoyed the deep peacefulness of the night.

"So, you've never had mint tea before?" Willis asked.

"Not iced like that. It's really good."

109

"I guess it's probably an Amish thing." He looked at her. "You must be learning a lot of new things you've never heard of before."

Dani nodded. "Yeah, but so far I like what I'm learning."

"Yeah?" he asked.

"You all have such a different way of doing things— of living, really. It's fascinating to me to see things from a completely different viewpoint than I am used to."

Willis smiled. "We might not be as different as you think."

Dani pondered that. From the limited exposure she had had with the Amish, Willis did seem different than the others. He seemed less Amish somehow, even more so than his own sister, Rebecca. Dani wondered what was the cause of that.

Loud chirping noises were coming from a nearby pond. It sounded like a flock of giant crickets were having a party.

"Is that noise coming from some sort of insect?" Dani asked.

"What noise?"

"That chirping noise."

"Oh, you mean the spring peepers."

"Spring peepers?"

"Yah, they're little frogs."

"Seriously?"

Willis chuckled. "Let me guess—you've never heard of those either."

Dani shook her head. "Nope. Wow, that's so different. I never knew frogs could make such a racket."

"Yeah, they'll go on like that for a few more weeks or so."

Dani listened to the constant peeping of the little frogs as the gravel crunched under their feet.

There was something she had been curious about ever since Willis offered to walk her home. She decided to just come out and ask it, even though she knew she probably shouldn't.

"Forgive me for being so nosey," she forged ahead, "but doesn't Mary mind you walking me home?"

"Mary?" Willis seemed puzzled.

"Won't she be waiting for you to take her home?"

Willis looked at her with a funny, almost mischievous, expression on his face. "Yeah," he said, "I'll be taking her home."

Dani had known this question wasn't a good idea, and now she felt the awkwardness of it. She couldn't quite read Willis' expression, but she had the vague sense he was enjoying her confusion.

He was kind enough to let the awkwardness only last a few seconds longer.

"Yeah, I'm sure she won't mind," he said simply.

Dani could see he was still hiding a grin, but she wasn't about to ask anything else on the subject. It was just another interesting tidbit into Amish life. Maybe the women here were so used to chivalry that it didn't make them the least bit nervous or suspicious if their man walked another girl home. Or maybe Willis and Mary's relationship was so strong that she implicitly trusted Willis. What a lovely kind of relationship.

"So, I hear you're going to be taking driving lessons?" Willis asked, breaking the silence.

Dani smiled. "I'm hoping to."

"Have you worked with horses much? John says you grew up on a ranch."

"Yeah, I did quite a bit with the horses as a teenager, but more horseback riding. I've never driven them pulling something."

"That must be beautiful, riding horseback in the Arizona mountains."

Dani looked over at him. "Yes, it is, especially in the

morning when it's cooler and the sun is just coming up over the mountains."

"Sounds like a picture."

"How far west have you been?" Dani asked.

"The furthest I've gone was to Arizona on that trip where I met you, and that was a first for me. I would enjoy seeing the Colorado mountains sometime. Some of my cousins took a trip there this year to go hunting."

"Yeah?"

"That's usually what we go West for."

"What do you hunt out there?" Dani wondered.

"Oh, it depends where you go. Some hunt for elk and some hunt for mule deer."

Dani had never heard of a mule deer, but she didn't say anything.

They reached John and Martha's house.

"Thanks for walking me home," Dani said, turning to Willis. "I enjoyed the company."

"It was my pleasure." Willis smiled. He touched the brim of his hat. "Good night," he said, walking backwards to face her.

"Goodnight."

Dani listened again to the night song of the spring peepers as she followed the sidewalk around the side of the house. Even after she shut the door inside, she could still faintly hear them as they called out into the night air.

CHAPTER NINE

It was still dark when Dani awoke to a different sound. She could hear the gentle crunching of tires on the gravel drive and the low rumbling of a diesel engine. The front door upstairs shut. A car door slammed. What was going on? *John must be leaving for work*, Dani realized.

She certainly wasn't ready to get up yet, so she snuggled back under her quilt.

An hour or so later, sunlight beamed its way into her tiny basement window. Dani stretched and sat in bed for a few minutes, letting her body wake up.

While she was eating breakfast, Dani noticed Martha out in the garden. She was dressed and her hair done neatly like always. It looked like she was pulling weeds.

Dani drank the last of her coffee and decided to join her. Even though she tried to work quickly, it still took her a half

113

hour to get dressed in her Amish attire and hair-do. When she finally finished, she spied Martha further into the garden but still weeding.

Dani stepped outside and shut the sliding door behind her. As she headed to the garden, Martha spotted her and smiled.

"Goot morning, Dani," she said cheerily.

"Good morning. What are you working on?"

"Oh, chust some weeding." Martha surveyed the garden. "A job that never seems done."

Dani knelt down next to the row and began pulling out weeds next to the tiny corn plants. "Well, maybe this year you'll have an easier time keeping up since you'll have an extra pair of hands."

"Oh, no, you don't have to do that," Martha protested.

Dani stopped and looked at her. "Now, Martha, you would expect an Amish maidly to help you, right?"

"Yah, I suppose so." One side of Martha's mouth turned up in a crooked grin.

"Okay, then." Dani returned to her weeding.

After she pulled the weeds next to the plants, Dani picked up a hoe that was lying in the dirt and began hoeing in between the rows like she had seen Martha do. She set to work chopping up the rich soil and destroying all the little weeds. It didn't take long for blisters to form on her hands, but she kept on, alternating between pulling weeds and hoeing.

The work was harder than one might think. The hoeing part alone was almost as good an exercise as her cardio workout at home. Pulling weeds wasn't physically hard, but it did get tedious to pull up each tiny, unwanted plant.

She enjoyed it at the same time, though, except for the blisters. It was actually quite relaxing to work outside. It was so different here with the sounds of the birds in the nearby woods and the gentle breeze that brushed away the heat from the warm morning sun. It was quiet and peaceful, quite a stark contrast to the noisy, busy work atmosphere that she had been used to in the newspaper office where there was a constant bustle of people coming and going and phones ringing.

As the morning drifted slowly by, Martha continued to work, so Dani did too. She had no idea what time it was, but it had to be getting close to lunch because she was starving.

Sure enough, after finishing the row she was working on, Martha straightened up. "Well, I guess that about does it for this morning."

"I'll finish my row here," Dani said.

"Okay, how about joining me for lunch when you're done?"

"Sure." Dani smiled. "Where do you want me to put the hoe when I'm done?"

"You can just put it inside the shop."

"Will do." Dani began chopping again and Martha went to the house.

It took Dani several minutes to finish hoeing her row. At the end, she rested her hands on top of the handle and looked over their morning progress.

It did look better. They had gotten nearly a third of the garden done. Dani hadn't realized how beautiful vegetables could be. A well-kept garden was nearly as lovely as a flowerbed.

She knew one thing. Whenever she saw gardens from now on, she was going to have more appreciation for the gardener now that she knew how much work was involved. Her muscles ached, and her hands and fingers were sore from the blisters and where hundreds of weeds had rubbed them raw. Dani had always thought of herself as a tough, country girl, so it surprised her to find out how soft she really was.

In the shop, she found where the hoes went, and she carefully hung hers next to the other tools on the rack.

When she turned to leave, she spied a buggy parked on the other side of the building. She grinned.

Walking over to it, Dani ran her hand along the smooth black metal and peeked inside. Even though it was dark, there was enough light coming in from the windows in the garage doors for her to see that there was only one bench in this buggy. Dani glanced out the windows and, not seeing anyone, she cautiously stepped up into the buggy. It leaned slightly, and the metal springs squeaked as she pulled herself up. She sat down in the first seat and let out a breath she hadn't realized she was holding.

She was in her first real buggy. It wasn't the huge tourist one in Berlin, but a real one an Amish couple actually used for their own personal needs. Dani smiled again and relaxed, looking out the glassless dash in front of her. She noticed the now limp reins and picked them up. She looked at them in her hands. Soon, she would be driving a buggy just like any other Amish girl.

Looking at her hands reminded her of her blisters and the fact that Martha was probably waiting for her by now. She set the reins back down and gingerly stepped out of the buggy.

Inside the house, Dani found a lunch that would more than satisfy her hunger. Martha had made delicious-looking meat and cheese sandwiches along with homemade pickles, applesauce, and cookies. Dani was delighted to find that her glass was also filled with mint tea.

"Martha, you didn't have to go through all this trouble," Dani said.

"Oh, my. It wasn't any trouble. I was making some for myself, so I might as well make one for you as well."

Dani shook her head. "Do you Amish ever stop working?"

Martha grinned. "No, not really."

She said it teasingly, but Dani suspected it actually might

be the truth.

The two had a lovely, peaceful lunch.

"I'm going to need to return my car to the rental agency," Dani told Martha as they were cleaning up from lunch. "What's the best way to get a ride back from Wooster?"

"Hmm..." Martha thought for awhile. "Well, we could just hire a driver, but my sister Ina's husband, William, and his work crew drive through Wooster quite often. We could check with him about a ride."

Okay

"Wouldn't that be an inconvenience for him though?" Dani wondered, hesitantly.

"He's often going right through there anyway and all you need is to be picked up," Martha said. "Trust me, the Amish men and their drivers are used to being asked to make extra stops along their normal daily route. It's what you do when you don't have cars."

"You do rely on each other a lot more, don't you?" Dani pondered.

Martha nodded. "And you learn to help each other and not worry about those little inconveniences. Tomorrow will be their turn to help you."

What a lovely community spirit. It reminded Dani of the old movie shows like *Andy Griffith* or *Gunsmoke* where neighbors helped each other and thought nothing of it. That sure was something American towns as a whole had lost.

"Okay, if you're sure," Dani said, still a bit hesitant. "I really don't mind just paying a driver." She always hated to make someone go out of their way for her.

"Yah, I'm sure. William's cell phone number is on the bulletin board in the phone shanty. He'll still be at work, so it would be a good time to call when he's still with his driver. Maybe they can even pick you up this afternoon."

"Okay," Dani said, starting to leave. Then she realized what Martha had just said. "Wait, did you say William has a cell phone?"

Martha smiled at her confusion. "It's his work phone. The Tobe Amish are allowed to have cell phones for work."

"Oh, okay." Dani tucked away that tidbit and headed outside.

The phone shanty was at the end of the lane just past William and Ina's house, so it was a decent stroll, but Dani didn't mind. She waved at Carrie and what must have been her younger brother as she passed their house. Carrie waved back happily.

As she got closer to the phone shanty, Dani saw that there was someone already in the shanty, so she waited outside, trying to leave plenty of room so the person had privacy.

Dani suddenly caught the face of the person inside and realized that it was Rebecca. Her friend looked downright nervous as she kept fingering her kapp strings. She wrote something down and placed the phone back on the wall. She tore off the piece of paper she had written on, carefully folding it into a small square, and tucked it into the side pocket of her dress. She stepped out and nearly jumped when she saw Dani waiting.

"Oh, I'm sorry. I hope you weren't waiting very long," Rebecca said apologetically.

"Don't worry a bit. I just got here," Dani assured her.

Rebecca still looked troubled.

"Rebecca, are you alright?" Dani asked, concerned.

"Oh, yah," Rebecca said dismissively, but Dani wasn't buying it.

She looked up at her. "I'm okay. I just have a lot of things on my mind right now. Maybe we can talk about it later if you're still up to learning how to drive buggy."

"If you're still willing to teach." Dani smiled.

"Okay, then, I'll see you later." Rebecca waved as she turned to walk back down the drive.

Dani watched her go for a moment. *What was troubling*

her dear Amish friend?

She turned back to the shanty and stepped inside, closing the door behind her. Everything you needed to make phone calls was right there in the tiny space. Paper, several phonebooks, a mug full of pencils and pens, and even an office chair were organized around a small counter.

Dani glanced up at the bulletin board. It was nearly full of of over-lapping notes and scraps of paper. After a bit of hunting through numbers for the horse courier, the leather shop, the vet, and at least a dozen other numbers, she finally found one for William's cell.

She still felt strange asking a favor from a man she barely knew, but Martha had been so sure that it was alright. Dani dialed the number.

"Hello," a man with a strong Dutch accent answered.

"Hello, is this William?" Dani could hear hammers banging and someone call out something in the background.

"Yah."

"Hi. This is Dani Chadwick, the woman who recently moved into John and Martha's home."

"Yah?" he said again, not helping her much.

Dani plowed ahead. "I'm hoping to possibly return my car to the rental place in Wooster one day this week, and Martha suggested that I ask you if your driver would be able to pick me up sometime on your way home from work."

"Ah," William thought for a moment. "Yah, that shouldn't be a problem. We'll be actually going through there today. What time were you thinking of?"

"I don't have a set time. I can be there anytime that works well for you."

"All right. Well, we usually go through Wooster around four or so, so if you want to be there around then, that should work."

"Okay, I'll do that," Dani said. "I really appreciate it."

Dani gave him the rental name and the street it was

located on and thanked him again before hanging up.

A glance at the clock on the wall told her that she had about an hour and a half before she needed to go. She decided to go ahead and get ready to leave so she could pick up some item she needed. Hopefully, she could find a store close to the rental place so she didn't have to drive around too much.

She showered and changed into a clean dress. She asked Martha if there was anything she needed at the store before she said goodbye and headed out.

Since today was a day of breaking from her English ways, Dani decided to also put an end to her cell phone, and she called Denise on the drive to Wooster.

Denise answered on the second ring with a happy squeal. "Dani!"

Dani smiled. *Gotta love caller ID.*

"Hey, Denise!"

"How are you doing, girl? I've been waiting so long to hear from you! I'm just bursting to know how it's going and everything."

It was good to hear her old friend's voice again.

"I'm good. I love it here, Denise!"

"Do you?"

"Yeah, it's so peaceful and simple—it's a whole other world here."

"Wow, I'm so glad for you, Dani," Denise said, a hint of wistfulness in her voice. "So, are you wearing the whole Amish get-up and everything?"

"As we speak." Dani grinned.

Denise laughed. "That is so crazy!"

"I know, but it's weird, Denise. It's been so easy for me to adapt to."

"Really?"

"Yeah, but I guess the real test will be after today though."

"What's today?" Denise wondered.

"You're not going to believe this, but I'm actually on my way to take back my rental car."

"Seriously?" Denise's expression held a note of awe in it. "So, you won't be able to drive?"

"That's right. And I'll have to turn my phone off as well."

"Wow! That would be hard!"

"I have a feeling it will be harder than the wardrobe changes."

"You're amazing, Girl," Denise said. "But, how will I be able to get a hold of you once your phone is off?"

Dani told her how she could still call out and gave her the number for the phone shanty.

"You'll just have to leave a message," Dani told her. "They'll let me know if you called."

The two friends chatted about how Rob and the girls were doing. Dani found herself thinking how busy their family was with soccer games and piano and ballet lessons and church services twice a week, not to mention all the projects Denise was into. Not that any of those things were wrong, and she certainly had never thought of it before, but now it struck her just how busy and cluttered their lives seemed.

Denise asked the question Dani knew she would eventually get to.

"Sooo," she asked, and the way she drew it out the word clued Dani into what was coming.

Dani rolled her eyes.

"Any cute Amish guys up there in Ohio?"

"Denise…" Dani said, warningly.

"Well, are there any?" She remained ever undeterred by Dani's grumblings as usual.

"I've only met one, but he's already taken so don't get any ideas," Dani said to appease her.

"Oh, I'm sure there's more than one handsome guy in a whole Amish community."

To tell the truth, Dani had hardly even noticed the other Amish guys. She didn't bother to explain that to Denise or enlighten her on the fact that most Amish youth would be married by the time they reached her age. Plus, any smart Amish guy would know how detrimental it would be to him as well as his family and entire community to have interest in an English girl.

And that was the last thing she had come here for.

Mercifully, Denise moved on to another subject.

They were still chatting when Dani turned into Wooster and spotted a dollar store. She pulled into the parking lot and finished her conversation with Denise, asking her to give a few people her new number. She sent hugs to the girls and promises to keep in touch.

Dani dialed the number of the couple that managed the ranch and left a message letting them know how to reach her if they needed to. Dani knew the ranch would go on the same as always in Mike and Becky's capable hands.

After she hung up, Dani looked at the phone in her hand before turning it off. She knew she had just ended her last phone call from her phone this side of Amish life. She had been used to using her phone all throughout the day, and it was going to be quite an adjustment to be without it. She felt like she was in the scene from *Apollo 13* where the astronauts signed off on their last communication with the Houston command center before entering the dark side of the moon where they could no longer receive or send a signal.

Dani held down the button to turn off her phone and watched it power down. The screen went dark.

See you on the other side Houston. This is Dani, the maidly, Dani slid the phone into her purse, *signing off.*

Dani picked up a few items at the store and drove down the street to the rental agency. Everything there went without a hitch, and she was soon waiting for her ride.

Dani sat where she had a good view of the road through

the large front windows. It was such an odd feeling. She had been a teenager the last time she had needed to wait for someone to pick her up in their vehicle. She felt a distinct loss of control as she stood there alone, waiting.

I suppose that is what dependence on others feels like, Dani mused.

She had been waiting twenty minutes when she spotted a van coming down the road and turn into the entrance. This must be her ride. The van was a large, fifteen-passenger van like the one she had seen the women at Walmart get out of, only this one had a ladder rack attached to the roof.

Dani spied William in the passenger seat, and she stepped outside. When the van pulled up to her, someone inside opened the side door for her.

Here goes. This was definitely a little out of her comfort zone, getting a ride from a vanload of Amish construction workers, most of whom she had never met, but she was determined to "get all wet", as Rebecca put it.

Dani said "hello" to the two men that scooted over to make room for her on their bench seat. Once she stepped up into the van, she could see the driver, a young guy. Mennonite, she guessed by his conservative appearance. Dani said "hi" to him as she sat in her designated seat and pulled the door shut.

The van pulled back out of the parking lot, and Dani reached to buckle her seat belt. After a minute of looking, she realized that there were no seat belts and that the men next to her weren't wearing any either. She felt utterly stupid and quickly sat up straight.

The van ride was almost uncomfortably quiet. Even though Dani could see four guys, and she could tell by a few subdued conversations behind her that there were several guys behind her, still for the most part everyone was content to be silent. The silence felt a bit awkward, and she pictured how different a van full of English guys would be.

There was some sort of music playing on the stereo, a style Dani had never heard before. It was just voices singing without musical instruments, but they sang in a somewhat whiney and very slurred way- almost like old country music.

The van meandered down back roads and into Amish driveways, dropping off the men at their homes. Each worker had a lunch box and usually left with a "see ya".

Dani recognized the scenery when they reached the area around John and Martha's home. Sure enough, the van slowed and pulled into the lane. It passed William's house and pulled up to John and Martha's home.

Dani gathered up her bags and offered to pay for the ride. The driver shook his head.

"It wasn't a problem," he said kindly.

Dani thanked him and William again for picking her up. As Martha had predicted, they both seemed to think nothing of it.

Dani jumped down and shut the door.

From now on, she was at the mercy of these people.

CHAPTER TEN

After a pleasant dinner with John and Martha, Dani insisted on helping the dishes. With only three of them, there weren't many dishes, and it was the least she could do for Martha.

"Do you think I could start helping you with making the meals?" Dani asked as she set a clean dish into the dish drainer. "Unless you'd rather I didn't."

"Oh, no, I don't mind," Martha said. A look of humor crossed her face. "Have you cooked much?"

"Only a little. My dad used to do most of the cooking, and after he died, my brother and I usually just did frozen meals or take out. I probably cooked once a month or so, but I only know the very basics."

Martha smiled as she picked up a bowl to dry it. "That's all right. If you want to learn, I'll be glad to show you. It's been so long since I taught my own daughters how to cook." A far-away look filled Martha's eyes as she looked out the kitchen window, obviously whisked back in time to old memories. Watching her, a wave of sadness came over Dani. She wished she had been able to have some memories like that with her own mom.

After the dishes, Dani walked leisurely up to Rebecca's home.

As she got closer, she could hear laughter and several voices talking. She smiled and knocked.

"Come in," William called out.

Dani entered into a wonderful Amish family scene. From his spot in the living room recliner, William smiled at her over the top of a magazine. Several of the children were playing a game on the floor in front of him, laughing and exclaiming in Dutch. In the kitchen, Ina and the older girls bustled about, picking up dishes from the table and putting away food.

"Come on in," Rebecca invited, motioning her into the kitchen. "We're just finishing up."

"Oh, please don't rush for my sake," Dani said.

Ina smiled at her. "How are you, Dani?"

"Good." She returned the smile.

Carrie came down the stairs and grinned at Dani.

"Hi, Carrie."

"Hi." She said softly. She sidled up to her mother and said something quietly in Dutch.

Ina glanced up at Dani and nodded.

Carrie looked at Dani. "One of our horses just had a foal. Do you want to see it?"

"Sure." Dani glanced at Ina. She just smiled and went about her work, so Dani figured it must be okay.

Carrie took Dani's hand and led her outside. Dani's heart warmed at the feeling of her little hand in her own.

The wonderful, warm smell of hay hit Dani as they

entered the barn. She breathed it in deeply, savoring the comfortable and familiar feeling it conjured up.

She counted six stalls, but most were empty since the horses were out in the pasture. Carrie led the way around the corner to the stall in the far corner.

She gently stepped up onto a bale of straw so she could see better, and Dani peered over the edge into the stall.

Inside, was a tiny, dark brown foal. Its skinny little legs were still slightly shaky, and the foal didn't quite have all its gangly limbs under control yet.

"She's very new," Dani said, smiling.

"Yah, she was born this morning."

"Really?"

Carrie nodded, her eyes on the foal.

"What do you think she'll be named?"

Carrie just shrugged. "I don't know."

They watched the little horse in silence for a few minutes. Dani heard someone approaching and turned to see Willis join them.

He smiled at Dani.

"How's she doing?" he asked, resting his arms on the top of the gate.

"She looks great," Dani said softly. "A Standardbred?" she asked.

"Yep." Willis looked at her. "That's right, you know a little about horses, don't you?"

"A little, but not as much as I should, having grown up with them. They are such beautiful creatures."

Willis looked back to the wobbly foal and smiled at its unsteady movements.

Carrie held out her hand. The foal considered her, and then cautiously made its way toward her. It inspected her hand, and she held very still. Suddenly the foal snorted and jumped skittishly. They all laughed.

"Would you, um," Willis turned to Dani, "have any interest in going to a horse auction?" he asked.

She was startled by the question.

She must have come across as hesitant, because Willis added, "It's a big thing around here."

Dani wasn't sure what to say. If she didn't know any better, she'd think that the look in his eye was a spark of interest in her and this was his way of asking her on a date. She studied his eyes, and he smiled gently, as if not ashamed of what he knew she was reading in his expression.

"Okay," Dani said. "I'm sure I would enjoy it."

"Good." A grin spread over his face. "There's a big one my dad and I like to go to next Thursday in Mount Hope."

His dad would be going—she noticed how Willis smothly slipped that in.

Dani nodded. "Thursday should be fine."

He looked at the foal and leaned back from the gate.

"Well, I'd better get back to work. See you on Thursday," he smiled.

"Ok," Dani smiled tentatively.

Her head was swimming. *What on earth just happened? Was she misreading Willis? Was he really interested in her? What about Mary? What about his being Amish?*

She was surprised at herself that she felt somewhat giddy at the thought of his attention. She had never felt that way before with the several guys over the years that had been interested in her.

Why now, and why with an Amish guy, for crying out loud?

At the same time, Dani felt troubled. *Wasn't he already dating?* While she felt flattered, she was also concerned for Mary. In the little bit she had been around him, Willis hadn't struck her as the flirty type, and unfaithfulness didn't seem to match his character. *What had she just gotten herself into?*

Before long, the little horse laid down for a nap. They watched as she snuggled in and fell asleep.

"Well, she's sleeping," Carrie said quietly, getting down from her perch.

"I think so," Dani whispered back.

As she followed Carrie out of the barn, Dani mulled over what had happened with Willis. Maybe she was wrong and had completely misread him. Maybe the invite was simply a kind gesture to a newcomer. She guessed she would just have to wait to find out in the days to come. She tried to set the thoughts aside.

"Thank you for showing me your foal, Carrie," Dani said as they reached the house. "She is very cute."

Carrie just smiled. "Sure thing."

She skipped off to join the other children.

Rebecca slipped on her shoes and sat down to tie them. "You ready for your lesson?" she asked, smiling up at Dani.

"Yep," Dani grinned.

Rebecca led the way back outside. "First things first," she said. "Catching the horse."

Dani grimaced. She knew what a job that could be.

"Don't worry, we're going to take the old buggy horse. It's not that bad."

And she was right. Rebecca made her way to one of the grazing horses and simply held onto his halter and led him back to Dani.

"This is Charlie."

"Wow," Dani said, stroking his strong neck, "that was sure a lot easier than I expected."

Rebecca smiled. "I hope you keep saying that all night."

She took Charlie to the shop and showed Dani how to hitch up the buggy. It looked slightly complicated at first, but it was actually quite simple. It helped that Dani already knew how halters and reins worked.

"This was actually easier than saddling a horse just for riding," Dani said after they'd finished.

"Yeah?"

She looked at Rebecca. "You've never ridden a horse?"

"As a child, but then it was just our pony, and we didn't have a saddle."

"You mean to tell me you've lived around horses all your life but have never really ridden one?"

Rebecca grinned. "Yah, I guess you could say that."

"Well, you've got to try it! There's nothing like it—the power of the horse under you, flying over the countryside. It's amazing!"

A doubtful expression clouded Rebecca's face. "We're not really supposed to ride our horses," she said finally.

Dani stopped straightening out the reins and looked at her friend.

Oops.

"I'm so sorry, Rebecca, I didn't know," she apologized.

"It's okay. How were you supposed to know?" Rebecca shrugged. "A lot of the girls around here have ridden horseback, but I just never did."

Rebecca finished up and smiled at Dani.

"Now, I'm going to let you drive."

"If you're sure," Dani said, hesitating slightly.

Rebecca nodded.

Dani headed for the left side, automatically assuming that was the driver's side like it was in a car.

"Oh, no," Rebecca called. "The driver sits on the other side."

"Really?" This was going to feel strange.

"Yep."

Rebecca held onto the frame and climbed up into her side. Dani carefully stepped up into the right side.

"Now, there's all different kinds of ways of holding the reins and talking to the horse. I suppose that it's that way with cars, too. Different drivers do different things. I'll show you the way I do it with Charlie, but you might have to do it differently when you drive John and Martha's horse."

Dani quickly found the commands were much like they were for riding—click your tongue to get them going, pull gently on one rein for turns, and pull back on both for backing up.

"You're doing good," Rebecca said several roads later.

"Charlie here is such a good ole boy," Dani said, watching the horse plod steadily down the road. She loved the sound of the rhythmic clip-clop of his hooves on the pavement.

A couple cars had passed them, but Charlie hadn't even so much as twitched.

"What do you do when a horse gets skittish?" Dani asked.

"Mostly just try to get them to come to a stop or slow pace, and then hold them there until they calm down."

"You can turn left here," Rebecca instructed, pointing ahead.

They turned to enter a quiet, country road. It dipped down into woods, the shade from the new leaves on the trees and brush creating a cozy, green canopy around and above them. There were a few bushes loaded with little white flowers, and Dani could smell their sweet fragrance from the buggy.

"What are those white flowers?" she asked, pointing to a nearby bush.

"Oh, those are wild roses," Rebecca answered.

"No wonder they smell so good."

"Yah, they're a sure sign of spring."

The road began climbing a hill, and Dani let Charlie pick his pace.

Driving horse and buggy was actually much easier than driving a car. If you stopped steering a car for one minute, you'd likely drive off the road, but with a horse, especially one this old, they knew exactly where they were supposed to be on the road. You could look at the person next to you for several minutes or out over the fields and neighbors' farms.

Dani settled back to enjoy the scenery and the calm of the evening.

"This is so peaceful," she said, sighing contentedly.

They traveled in silence for a while before Dani dared to broach the subject of Rebecca's phone call earlier that day. She doubted Rebecca had forgotten, but Dani guessed she might be too shy to bring it up herself.

"So," Dani said, looking over at her. "you wanted to share something with me about your phone call this afternoon?"

Rebecca looked down at her hands and then out at the rolling farmland.

"You don't have to tell me if you'd rather not talk about it," Dani quickly added, "but I'm here if you ever need a friend to talk to."

Rebecca smiled, but her smile didn't quite reach her eyes. "Thanks, Dani. I do need a friend."

She looked out again at the trees lining the road, then back at Dani. "You probably are wondering why I don't have many Amish friends I'm close to."

That had definitely crossed Dani's mind.

"Yeah, it did strike me as a bit unusual. Did something happen?"

Rebecca sighed. "Yah."

"It was a guy, wasn't it?"

Rebecca looked at her, surprised. "How did you know?"

Dani shrugged. "I noticed the way you zoned out for a minute when one of the girls at the singing got up to ride home with one of the guys."

Rebecca grinned sheepishly. "You are good, Dani Chadwick!"

Dani smiled.

Rebecca turned her gaze to the road in front of them and sighed. "Yep, that's what happened. I was sweet on a fella, in my heart, of course- I never told anyone about it. Well, my best friend, Susan, must have liked him, too, and she up and started laying on the charm to him. I was never one to flirt with a guy, and I was so disgusted with her behavior. I tried

132

to talk to her about flirting once, but she just got real upset and acted like she was so much better than me because she had a boyfriend and I didn't. That conversation was the end of our friendship."

"Wow," Dani said sadly.

"Yah, we're not miffed at each other anymore, and we'll chat sometimes now, but it's never been the same. I'm just glad she thinks the rift is because of the conversation we had and not because she's being courted by Silas. Truly, it would have broken my heart to have her confide in me about things Silas did or said with her. I'm afraid she would have figured out that I liked him."

"I'm sorry, Rebecca. Disappointed love is a hard thing."

"Yes it is." Rebecca sighed again. "I suppose it just wasn't meant to be."

"God knows best," Dani agreed. "There have been a few guys in the past that I liked, but it didn't work out, and now looking back, I am so grateful God led me away from them. Besides," she grinned, "there are a lot more guys out there. I saw how full the other side of the room was at the singing."

"Yah, but most of them are my cousins," Rebecca said, frustrated. "I am related to nearly the whole church, and the few I'm not as closely related to, that also happen to be my age, I don't care for."

That would be a bummer.

"Which is why," Rebecca plunged ahead, "I made that phone call earlier."

She looked at Dani. "Will you promise not to tell anyone what I tell you?"

Dani looked at her sharply. "Rebecca, what is this about?"

"Please," she pleaded, "will you keep this between you and me?"

Dani looked into Rebecca's eyes, their expression both determined and desperate.

133

"Of course," Dani said softly.

Rebecca relaxed. "Goot."

"The phone call this afternoon was to a second cousin of mine that lives near Mount Hope," she began to explain. "She's been working at a restaurant there, but now she that she is expecting her first child she wants to quit soon. I asked her to see if maybe I could get her job, so she talked to her boss about it. This afternoon I was calling to see what her boss had said."

"And?" Dani asked.

"And I got the job."

Dani could hear the note of excitement and even pride in Rebecca's voice.

"I start next Monday," she told Dani.

"Good for you." Dani thought over what all that entailed for her friend. "So, why is this all a secret? It's not like you're doing anything wrong, right?"

"No, I'm not, but I was afraid my parents might not like the idea. Dani, I need to do this. I need to be able to get out. Who knows, maybe I'll even meet a fella out there."

"Does your cousin know that you're hiding this?"

"No, but she knows how it is. How do you think she got to Mount Hope in the first place?"

Good point.

"How are you getting around leaving for work without your family knowing?"

"I've already talked to a driver who can take me. Mom and Dat think I'm going to be working at Mrs. Miller's Noodles in Fredericksburg."

"You lied to your parents?"

Rebecca looked guilty. "No, not exactly. Dat suggested that I apply at Mrs. Millers, which I did do. I just didn't bother to correct them when I ended up at the restaurant instead." She caught Dani's doubtful look and quickly added, "I don't like that part of it. But if I don't get out, I'm afraid I'll be an old maid and never get married."

"You're still so young—what are you, like twenty?"

"Twenty-one," Rebecca said.

"You've still got lots of time."

Rebecca laughed a single, cold laugh. "Hah! Not in the Amish I don't. Most girls are getting engaged or married at nineteen, or at the very least have a steady man. Me, I haven't even been on a date more than a few times. Before long, I'll end up like my brother Willis, and all the other ones my age will be married already."

Willis? Dani's thoughts sidetracked for just a minute, wondering what that story was. She decided that that wasn't the issue at hand.

Dani could sympathize with Rebecca and the predicament she was facing, but the way Rebecca was deceiving her parents didn't sit well with her.

"Then there's the other reason for me doing this," Rebecca said.

"Another reason?" Dani asked.

"Yah," Rebecca nodded. "Independence."

"Independence?"

"Yah. I have been the good girl my whole life, always following the rules, always doing what I was supposed to, never setting foot outside my life here. I want to see more of the world—to experience what it's like outside my own community."

"Oh, Rebecca," Dani said sadly, "would you leave the Amish?"

"I don't know. I haven't joined church yet, so technically I could still be in my rumspringa time. I'm still allowed to taste the outside world."

Dani didn't know what to say. Her friend had this whole other hidden layer that was completely unexpected. They rolled down the road in silence for a few minutes.

Rebecca looked at Dani. "Are you upset with me?"

"Oh, no!" Dani shook her head. "Just maybe a bit sad. You have no idea what a blessing you have right here in your community. I mean, you have what most Americans would have dream of having—close family, a tight-knit community, a loving church. You are surrounded by people who love God and love you. Why would you want to leave that?"

"I know it seems crazy," Rebecca sighed again. "But I've been inside the box all my life. Even if it is a nice, lovely box, I want to see for myself what it's like outside."

"I can certainly understand that," Dani empathized. "Just please be careful. Say you go out and see what's out there, then what? You know you'll probably want to come back, but it won't be the same. You will have damaged your good reputation and even you will think less of yourself."

"I just have to know what's out there. I want to be able to choose for myself."

Dani looked over at her. "There will always be things you don't know what it's like to experience. I will never know what it's like to go to a bar and get drunk. A godly married woman will never know what it's like to have an affair behind her husband's back. An honest student will never know what it's like to cheat on grades. There are many things in life we won't and should never experience."

Dani could tell Rebecca was thinking about what she had said.

"You may be right... I don't know," she said finally, "but I am still going to work in Mount Hope."

They were silent for a few moments.

"I totally understand you wanting to try something new. I mean, look at me!" Dani held up the reins in her hands and laughed. "But I don't have the consequences you might have to face."

Rebecca was quiet, and Dani was afraid that she had overstepped her bounds as a new friend.

"I really do care about you, Rebecca," Dani added, her

tone more gentle. "I'm sorry if I spoke a little too strong."

"Oh, you're fine," Rebecca brushed Dani's words away. "I wanted you to speak your mind. I've been told that's what a good friend does." She grinned. "You have given me some things to think about."

Dani was relieved to find Rebecca wasn't offended by her words.

They drove on, the conversation turned to other things. They watched as the sun set in the distance. Dani started to wonder about turning on buggy lights as darkness began to fall, but before long Rebecca's home came into view, and Dani directed Charlie down the lane.

They drove up to the shop.

"Thank you so much for the driving lesson!" Dani told Rebecca.

"Oh, thanks for asking me," Rebecca smiled warmly.

Dani walked to the front to Charlie and smoothed his neck. The horse's muscle quivered under her touch, and he turned his head to look at Dani.

"Thank you for a nice ride, Charlie. You're such a good boy," she said, rubbing his nose and between his ears.

Willis stepped out of the shop.

"So, how'd it go?" he asked them as he helped unhitch Charlie.

"It went real well," Rebecca said. "Dani is a natural."

"Well, I had a great teacher and a wonderful horse," Dani said, giving Charlie one last pat.

Willis smiled.

"I think you're good to go as far as buggy driving goes," Rebecca said.

Sure a lot easier than getting a driver's license, Dani thought, but had presence of mind to keep the English comment to herself.

"We can take care of him from here," Willis said as he began to lead Charlie up to the barn. "That way you can go home before it gets darker."

"Oh, ok. Thank you."

Dani turned to Rebecca, who was eyeing her brother curiously.

"Thank you so much." Dani gave her a hug.

They held their hug for a moment.

"Thank *you,* Dani," she said softly.

"I'm here, anytime."

Rebecca nodded and smiled. "Have a good night!"

"You too." Dani waved as she headed down the lane.

She thought of Rebecca the whole walk back to the house. Rebecca had such a lovely, simple life. Why did she want to complicate it? Dani could see wanting to meet other eligible Amish men Rebecca wasn't related to, but the whole "outside the box" idea had her worried. She had heard that some Amish young people left their Amish roots, but she had never expected that with her coming here she would become involved so closely with someone actually considering it.

Dani hoped and prayed that her friend would make the right choice.

CHAPTER ELEVEN

The next day, Dani came upstairs to find Martha tying on an apron.

"Oh, goot," Martha said, "I was chust thinking about calling you. I'm going to make up several batches of Monster cookies here and thought you might want to help."

"Yes, definitely." Dani smiled. She had no idea what Monster cookies were, but if Martha's cooking so far was any indication, they would be delicious.

Martha pulled out three of the biggest mixing bowls Dani had ever seen and began gathering ingredients and setting them on the table.

"I'm planning on making three batches," Martha told her. "Do you know how to follow a recipe card?"

Dani nodded. "Yes, I think so."

"Goot, then you can start by creaming together the sugar and butter." Martha handed her a measuring cup.

Dani started measuring brown sugar carefully into each of the bowls.

Martha pulled out a cordless drill from a kitchen cabinet. Martha must have seen Dani's surprised expression at the sight of the hand tool because she chuckled.

"We will often use these for our mixers," she explained, snapping a drill battery onto the end of it. "Don't worry, this is my kitchen one. John has his own sets for his projects."

Martha handed Dani the drill.

Dani couldn't help smiling to herself. She supposed that when you didn't have electricity, you learned to be creative with other methods.

Carefully, she pulled the trigger and began whirling the butter and sugar together. It actually worked pretty well. Dani had never seen the strange drill bit that Martha had screwed onto the end, but it was obviously designed to mix things.

Martha dumped more ingredients into the bowls, and Dani went one by one mixing them together. She decided that Monster cookies were a unique mixture of oatmeal, peanut butter, chocolate chips, and M&Ms.

When she was done mixing everything together, Martha took the drill bit off.

"You want to lick it off?" she asked, offering it to Dani.

Dani smiled and took the bit. She felt a little silly licking a drill bit, but the cookie batter looked too good to resist.

When the first batch of cookies was done, Martha offered her one of the warm cookies and took one for herself.

"Mmm," Dani murmured. "These are great!"

"I'm glad you like them."

They continued to work on baking cookies for the next two hours. As the cookies cooled, Martha set them in clean, empty ice cream buckets.

140

"These will be put in the freezer for get-togethers or what-not," she explained.

Dani didn't even know you could freeze cookies. She had a feeling there was a lot she would learn living here.

As the days rolled by, Dani began to fit more into her role as an Amish maidly. Martha let her follow her around and help out wherever she could. They began to settle into a rhythm of daily duties as Dani started helping with whatever Martha had on her agenda for the day.

Dani loved feeling more like family now—something she had lost in her life piece by piece. It was fascinating to learn how the Amish did things, and she was trying to pick up Dutch as fast as she could.

As spunky as Martha was, Dani could tell that there were days when Martha was worn out, and Dani was so glad she could help her. Maybe somehow Dani could give back to this couple who was helping her more than they would ever know.

Thursday rolled around, the day of the horse show. Dani realized that she hadn't asked Willis what time to be ready. Fortunately, when she had mentioned it at supper the night before, John had seemed certain that William usually left around eight-thirty.

Dani decided to be ready early just in case. She wore the sage green dress, her hair tucked neatly into her covering. She was getting used to the whole Amish get-up and actually enjoyed the feel of a dress. She did miss doing her hair other ways, but she was content to simplify this area of her life for now.

Dani sat on the front porch around eight to wait for her ride. She wouldn't have minded the walk over to William and Ina's house, but she didn't really want to get herself into an awkward situation if the men weren't ready.

It was a beautiful morning, misty and still. Even the birds were quiet. The sun was just starting to brighten the sky.

Dani looked over the pastures, their gently rolling hills adding depth to the picture before her. A buggy rattled down the road.

Dani breathed in deeply. *What a beautiful life.*

"Thank You, God. Thank You for making this happen for me."

Dani marveled for the hundredth time at how smoothly everything had played out for her. She couldn't have picked a better community or home to stay in. Truly God must have His hand in all this.

A truck pulled into the lane.

Must be our ride, Dani thought.

The truck turned into William's drive and backed up to the barn. Dani watched as Willis led a horse into the trailer.

They must be selling a horse today.

After several minutes, William came out of the house and got in the truck. Willis hopped up next to him, and the truck slowly moved toward Dani.

She got up and walked down the sidewalk to meet them. Willis jumped down from the truck.

"Good morning!" he said with a friendly grin.

"Morning." Dani smiled back.

Willis gestured to the front seat. "You're more than welcome to sit up front," he said, one hand holding the front door, "or you can have the backseat."

Dani glanced at the available seat next to William. She had nothing against the man, but sitting sandwiched between an Amish man and a truck door wasn't overly appealing.

"Oh, the back will be fine," she said.

Willis opened the back door and waited for her to get in. It was quite a step up into the truck, especially in a dress. Willis held out his hand to help her. Dani glanced at him hesitantly, and he smiled gently. She smiled and gladly accepted the help. She stepped up onto the running board and into the truck.

"All set?" Willis asked.

"Yep."

Willis carefully shut the door for her and hopped back into the front.

Dani set her purse on the empty seat next to her and settled back to enjoy the ride. She had a feeling this whole day was going to be interesting.

And not just because of horses.

Dani said hello to William and was introduced to the driver, Andy. He was the same Mennonite boy that had driven her home the other day after dropping off her car.

The men carried on small talk, and a few times she joined in the conversation, but mostly she was content to just watch the countryside sliding past her window. She was delighted to find she could often tell what the men were talking about even though they were using Dutch most of the time. Although she couldn't understand exactly what they were saying, she could recognize enough words she had learned that she could piece together the gist of the conversation.

Willis turned around once to look back at Dani as if making sure she was doing okay, but because he was directly in front of her, it was pretty hard to carry on a conversation between them.

He and his father both wore their Amish hats, but today they were straw ones instead of the black ones worn for the church service. Willis' brown hair flipped up a bit around the edges while his dad's hung very straight. William had on suspenders over a white shirt, but Willis' crisp, blue shirt was simply tucked neatly into his Amish pants.

The closer they got to Mount Hope, the more crowded the county road became. By the time they had reached the town, there were people walking along the streets and buggies and vehicles with trailers congesting the roadways. They pulled into a back way, and Andy rolled down his window to talk to one of the Amish men directing traffic. They were pointed to a barn and got in line with the other trailers dropping off horses.

"We had to be here early if we wanted to sell," William explained. "The actual auction won't start until ten or so."

"Okay." Dani nodded.

The line moved very slowly as one by one the owners filled out the necessary paperwork and unloaded their animals.

"You know," William said, suddenly realizing something, "you could get off here if you want. There's no reason for you to have to wait with us."

Dani looked out at the maze of barns and people milling about.

"Oh, that's okay—I don't mind," she said. "I wouldn't know where to start.

"Here, I'll go with you," Willis offered.

She hesitated, but it did sound more appealing than waiting.

"Okay," she agreed.

They both disembarked, and Dani hung her purse over her shoulder.

"We need to go around to the front to get our tickets," Willis explained as he led her toward the barns.

As Dani scanned the crowd of people, she found that although there were many English people, most of the people there were Amish. It was a strange thought to know that the English people would be looking at her today thinking she was an Amish girl.

She smiled to herself. *Little did they know she could barely even speak Dutch.*

They entered a little shed that served as the ticket booth. Willis was ahead of her, and before she could even dig out her wallet, he had paid for her ticket.

"Oh, no. Here," Dani started fishing through bills.

Willis just waved her on. "Don't worry about it, I've got

it."

They got the top of their right hand stamped and headed out into the auction grounds.

"Willis, you didn't have to do that," Dani said, a little embarrassed he had paid her way.

"Oh, no problem," Willis said, looking down at her as they walked.

"Well, thank you. That was very kind."

"Sure thing."

"Now," he said, pausing, "where would you like to go first?"

"Hmm…I don't know," Dani said, looking around at the various barns.

"You want to start at one end and work our way back?"

"Sure, sounds good."

Willis held the door as they entered the first building. Rows of stalls filled the entire barn. They walked leisurely down the hay-covered aisle, looking at each horse.

"This must be the barn for the standard-breds," Dani said, stopping to pet a horse.

"Yep. That's what sells the most here."

"Isn't that what you use for buggies?"

"A lot of the time." Willis nodded. "Retired race horses come here and work real well for our buggy horses. They are already used to training and they're strong."

"What are you selling today?"

"Oh, she's a two-year-old I broke to ride and pull a buggy safely, and so now she's ready to sell."

Dani was impressed. "Really? You trained her?"

Willis' face flushed as if pleased and shy at the same time at her praise. "Yeah, I have broken a few horses over the years. It's something I really enjoy doing, but I can only do here and there."

"Wow. That's really something," Dani said. She knew how much time and patience went into training horses.

145

She gave the horse a final rub on its nose, and they walked on.

The barns were laid out oddly. Not only were they huge, but they were divided into numerous sections and aisles and areas, with no signs telling you where to go. There were large barn doors on several sections and even though they walked through dozens of them, Willis was careful to always hold them open for Dani. Several times, Willis pulled aside a sliding door to reveal a whole other section of stalls.

"You know your way around here, don't you?" Dani asked as she ducked through yet another doorway.

"A little," he smiled, pulling the door shut after them.

This area was quieter. Looking out over the stalls, Dani couldn't see any horses, but when she glanced into the first one she found out why.

"Foals," she said, delighted.

Willis smiled and rested his crossed arms on one of the stall gates.

The new little horses spooked easily, making them laugh. It was fun to watch them inspect their new surroundings and neighbors and scamper playfully with each other.

After a while, Dani and Willis stepped away and headed out of that section. Willis pulled the door open again, and Dani began to step out.

"Dani!" He yelled and grabbed her arm to stop her. In an instant, she saw a loose horse in the aisle slam into the wall across from her. It glanced her way, and one look from its wild eyes told her she had only seconds to move.

Someone shouted from further down the corridor.

"Shut the door!" Dani cried as the horse started towards them.

With one quick motion, Willis pulled her back and slid the door shut. Dani stood frozen at the sound of the horse thudding against the door.

"Are you okay?" Willis asked. His eyes searched Dani's

in open concern.

"Yeah." She breathed in a deep breath, trying to calm her quivering nerves. "I'm fine. Thanks to you." She looked up to him and smiled weakly.

"One of the horses must have broken free. That's actually why this place has all these doors and aisles—so that they can corral the dangerous animals."

Willis watched her catch her breath for a moment. "Are you sure you're okay? You look pretty shaken up."

"I just got a bit scared. I'm all right now," she said, straightening up.

"Let's go out a different way," Willis suggested, and Dani was all too eager to comply. He pointed towards another door, and she noticed his hand was shaking. The scare they had just encountered affected him almost as much as it had her.

He opened the door on the far side and looked out.

"This one's safe," he said, stepping aside so Dani could walk out.

Willis looked around. "I think we've covered everything in this barn. Do you want to go to the next one?"

"Sure." Dani nodded.

The next barn wasn't quite as big, and as they entered, their eyes had to adjust slightly to the dimmer light.

"This barn here is one of my favorites," Willis said, pleased.

Dani smiled inwardly at his Amish pronunciation of the word "favorite", saying it with an "ite" sound instead of the "it" sound most English people used.

She looked around. In nearly every stall you could see giant horses, their necks and backs easily double the size of a riding horse.

"The draft horses?" she guessed.

"Yep." Willis nodded.

Willis walked up to one of the stalls. Inside was a pair of

the majestic horses.

"They are so huge," Dani exclaimed. "You know, I've never actually been this close to one before."

"They're gentle giants," Willis said. "I would love to train one sometime."

Dani watched as one of the gigantic creatures moved slowly toward its pile of hay. It snorted, making the hay shift and scatter under its breath.

"Their hooves look nearly as big as an elephant's foot," she marveled.

"Yeah, they're impressive creatures," Willis agreed. "That's one of the reasons I like them. In this one animal," he said, pointing to the horse, "there is so much strength and power, yet they are some of the gentlest of horses. And if well-trained, all this power is channeled into wonderful uses. The horse is so many times more powerful that its master, yet because it submits itself to his direction they can get a lot of good done together."

Willis paused, thoughtfully. "I guess that's how it works in our lives too, except that God is much bigger than us, but through submission to Him we can accomplish great good."

Dani glanced at Willis, a bit surprised at his insights and the peek into his spiritual life. She looked back at the horse, pondering what he said.

"Not only does it bring about more good," she said, adding to his thoughts, "but submission ends up also being what is best for the horse. This horse could easily break through this fence and through the barn door if it wanted to, but staying here keeps it dry and fed and safe from cars and other outside dangers."

Willis nodded.

"I suppose that is what a lot of the Amish think about staying Amish?" Dani ventured a bit boldly. "If they submit to the boundaries of the Amish church they will stay safe."

"Yah, I suppose so," Willis said, his words trailing off as

he became lost in thought.

Watching Willis think intrigued Dani. He obviously was a man who pondered the spiritual and deeper things in life.

She looked back at the horses.

After a moment, Willis broke his reverie and smiled at Dani.

"Sorry, I zoned out there for a moment."

"Oh, no; it's fine." She smiled.

"I've had a lot on my mind lately is all."

They continued to make their way through the barn.

"Those black Percheons horses are gorgeous," Dani said, pointing at one of the large horses. The coat and mane of the majestic animal were pure black and shiny as it stood calmly. She held her breath as the horse reached its neck toward her. She held her hand flat as his giant nose sniffed it.

"Sorry I don't have anything for you, Big Boy," Dani said gently.

The horse's warm breath tickled her hand, and she smelled the distinctive grassy smell of horse breath. Dani smiled. She had never minded the smell, and now it joined the other barn smells swirling around her to wrap her in a wonderful whirlpool of familiar and comforting senses.

She looked up to see Willis watching her. She realized she was still smiling and as her eyes met his, she saw a glint of tenderness in his eyes.

Dani stroked the soft nose of the beast in front of her and sighed happily before turning away.

In the last barn, they found a menagerie of horses: several miniature ponies, a few spotted horses and a section of smaller, golden-colored horses.

"Now, this is really bad," Dani said, motioning to the golden horses, "but I can't remember what kind of horses these are."

"They're Halflingers," Willis said. "We use them a lot with pony carts for the children."

"They do look perfect for that," Dani said. The stout little horses were bigger than a miniature pony, but small enough for a child to handle.

"How old do the children have to be to be able to drive a pony cart?" she wondered.

"That depends on the family, but I'd say most Amish children have driven a cart on the road by the time they turn ten."

"Really? Wow."

Dani tried to picture Denise's daughter, Maggie, driving a horse and cart. She could probably do it, but Dani couldn't imagine letting her go out on the road by herself with one. Denise barely let her ride her bike alone in the little street in front of their house, even though they lived in a cul-de-sac and could see her daughter the entire time. It was a wonder that kid could ride a bike at all the way Denise hovered over her girls. Dani suspected that there was a lot that went on when Rob was in charge and Denise was at work that she would never find out about.

Over the loudspeakers, a voice announced that the auction would be starting soon. Willis led the way out of the maze of aisles and toward the auction house.

It was crowded with people when they got inside.

"I'm afraid we're going to have to sit way up," Willis shouted over the din. Dani nodded. She didn't care in the slightest.

They made their way up the wooden platform. It was shaped the same way bleachers were with graduating benches, only these were made of wood.

They picked the first available seats and sat down. Dani looked out over the people below them. It was such a diverse crowd—from the super strict Amish in their dark clothes and vests to a couple fully-decked in Harley leather and bandanas.

The gang's all here, Dani thought dryly.

150

She spied William and Andy at the bottom looking for seats.

"There's your dad," she said, nodding toward the door.

Willis stood up and waved until William spotted him, and they made their way up the bleachers.

"Hi," William said when they reached them.

"Hi," Willis returned. "How'd it go with Mary Jane?"

"Oh, fine, fine," William said. "Unloaded her without a hitch."

Dani realized they must be talking about the horse they brought to sell. The name cast a sudden shadow over her thoughts on an otherwise lovely day. *Willis had even named his horse after his girlfriend?* The more Dani got to know him, the more she liked this Amish guy, but she didn't think it was jealousy that dampened her mood.

She wasn't stupid. She knew from various things throughout the day that Willis was more than just being nice to her. Although he didn't flirt, she saw the spark of interest in his eyes when they talked. She noticed the way he was so attentive to her, and she saw the way he was shaken after the incident with the wild horse.

Sitting there next to him as they watched the horses being sold, commenting about the quality of the horse or the price, Dani also knew there was a great chemistry between them.

The thing that bothered her most was why Willis was letting himself become interested in her while he already had a sweet Amish girl he obviously had cared a great deal for. Dani felt guilty for being flattered by his interest and she felt genuinely sorry for Mary.

Dani enjoyed being friends with Willis. He was a smart, gentle, thoughtful man, and they hit it off well together, but she hated the thought of coming between him and an Amish girl. Mary was the kind of girl he really should be interested in, not some English girl that was only here because she lost her family and needed to sort things out. What was he

151

thinking?

And what should she do?

Dani lost complete sense of time as they watched the horses go through the corral one by one while the auctioneer did his best to drive up the prices.

"Are you getting bored yet?" Willis asked her.

"Oh, no. This is fine," Dani smiled. She really didn't mind except that her stomach was starting to growl. *Was it lunch time already?*

"I'll be right back," Willis suddenly excused himself.

"Okay."

He made his way past the others in their row and down the bleachers. Dani watched as he motioned for an elderly Amish man to go in front of him. Willis followed the older man and disappeared around the corner.

Dani looked around again and realized that she wasn't the only "Amish" girl watching the horses sell. There were actually quite a few. Some were done up to the letter even with their black bonnets as they sat demurely and watched the auction. Other girls leaned casually against the side wall with some Amish boys. One of them was chewing gum and wore her hair parted to the side instead of down the middle like everyone else. Her sleeves were rolled up almost to her shoulders, and she wore ankle-length multi-colored socks instead of the normal, knee-length black socks.

Before long, Willis reappeared on the ground level. He was carrying two bottles of soda pop and a white bag.

Food! Bless you, Willis!

It took him a while to make his way back to their seats.

"Here we are," he said, a bit out of breath as he reached Dani and sat down.

"I hope you like burgers," he said, handing her the bag.

"I love them."

Peering inside the bag, the hot smell of burgers hit her, and her mouth instantly watered. She pulled one out and handed it to Willis.

"There's onion rings, too," he said.

"Wonderful. Thanks, Willis."

"Sure. I had to guess on the pop," he said, holding up the bottles. "Do you like Mountain Dew or Coke?"

"I like them both, so you pick."

"Okay then." He handed her the Coke.

After her own silent prayer, Dani bit into her thick, juicy burger and closed her eyes. Her taste buds thought they had died and gone to heaven. She slowly ate every bite, savoring the goodness.

They were crunching on onion rings when the auctioneer announced that they were starting on the Standard-breds. He switched off with another auctioneer, and in a minute the auction was in full swing again.

Dani quickly realized that the Standardbreds were by far the most popular with the crowd. There were probably twice as many bidders for these as there were for the others that had sold this morning.

A man led another horse into the ring.

"That's my horse," Willis said, nodding toward the dark brown horse.

"Oh yeah?" Dani watched as the auctioneer started the bidding. Hands shot up all over the stadium. She listened as the price quickly climbed. It narrowed down to two Amish men. The auctioneer turned to one then the other, getting the price to rise. Soon, it was as high as either man would pay.

"Sold," the auctioneer shouted. "Number—" he squinted at the white card the winner held up. "three, three, two, one. Number three, three, two, one."

A clerk wrote down the number, and they moved on to the next horse.

"That's not a bad price," Dani said. A lot of horses had sold for much less.

"Yeah, that's better than I was hoping to get," Willis said.

"Good, I'm so glad for you."

Willis looked at her, a smile twinkling in his eyes, but he didn't say anything. He held her gaze for just a second before turning back to the auction. It was in that second and in that look that Dani knew in her heart she had been right all along. Willis did have feelings for her. She could see it in his eyes.

Oh, dear Lord, what am I supposed to do now?

She had never thought in all the experiences she imagined she would have by coming here to Ohio that one might be an Amish man becoming interested in her.

Lord, give me wisdom, she prayed again.

She was going to need it.

She loved watching the draft horses sell. Their massive hooves pounded with each step on the hay-covered ring though they were simply walking calmly. Even though the handlers were grown men, they only barely reached the withers on the giant, magnificent horses.

The draft horses went for much more than the Standard-breds, and she was finding out just how much some people were willing to pay for a horse. She knew they had several expensive horses in their own stables back in Arizona, but watching people scramble to lay down ten thousand dollars or more for a horse was incredible.

William leaned over to Willis and Dani. "You ready to head home?" he asked.

Willis looked at Dani.

"Whenever," she said, shrugging. "I'm not in any hurry."

"Well, it's about two-thirty," William said, looking at his pocket watch. "Maybe we'd better be getting home for chores and supper and all."

Willis nodded. William and Andy stood up, and Dani and Willis followed close behind.

Outside, Andy led the way to the parking lot where he had parked the truck. Because they brought a trailer, he had needed to park in the back.

The group headed toward the truck, but Willis seemed to be looking for something.

"I'll catch up with you," he told Dani and turned to head in another direction.

It was quite a walk to get to the truck. Dani's feet were tired from walking all day, but it had been worth it.

Willis jogged to catch up with them again. He was holding a small plastic bag.

"Here," he said, holding the bag open. "I thought you all might like something cold for the drive home."

Inside were different varieties of ice cream bars.

"Mmm, ice cream," Dani said appreciatively. "Thanks!"

He smiled and offered one to the other guys.

Dani opened the bar once they were on their way home. She loved ice cream and savored every messy bite.

"So, what did you think of the horse auction?" William asked her, turning in his seat to look at her.

"I thoroughly enjoyed it."

"Goot. So, you weren't tempted to buy one of those fancy Percheons?" he joked.

"No!" Dani laughed. "That was amazing how much they went for."

"I saw a horse sell for two hundred thousand once." Andy said.

"That's crazy." Dani shook her head.

"Yeah," Willis agreed, "you could buy a house for that."

"Yah." William folded up the paper from his ice cream bar. "And a house isn't likely to need a vet."

The group chuckled.

They all were in a chattier mood on the way home, and pleasant conversation filled the entire trip.

Andy dropped Dani off first.

Dani hopped down. "Thank you so much for taking me along," she said, "and for the lovely day." Her gaze shifted to Willis.

"Not a problem," William said, and Willis simply smiled.

She shut her door and waved as she turned to head up the walkway.

By now, she came and went in John and Martha's home without knocking.

"Hello!" the parrot squawked, bobbing on his swing. "Hello!"

"Hi, Methuselah," Dani said. She headed to the kitchen.

"Hi, there," Martha greeted her from her spot by the stove, stirring something. No doubt, she was already starting on supper. Dani was quickly learning that an Amish supper often took at least an hour or two to make.

"Hi." Dani set her purse on the floor next to the basement door before returning to the kitchen.

"Did you have a nice time?"

Dani smiled. "Yes, I did."

She washed her hands. "What can I do to help?"

"Well, you can chop this onion here, if you want," Martha said, motioning to a cutting board.

Dani picked a knife out of the silverware drawer. The two women worked together quietly, chatting easily about their day. Tonight they were having pork chops, potatoes, corn, homemade bread, and a pumpkin dessert.

When John came in for supper, he asked about the auction.

"Did Willis sell his horse for a good price?" he wondered, sitting down in his chair at the table.

"Yep," Dani said, setting the last glass of water at its place. "It brought more than he expected."

"Well, it was a good horse," John said. "Any horse Willis trains is a good horse."

"Yah," Martha agreed, carefully setting a hot casserole dish of baked corn on the table. "He's quite a goot trainer."

"That he is." John nodded. "It's a gift from God that boy

has learned to use."

Dani smiled as she slid into her own chair. It did her heart good to hear chatter around her instead of the empty silence of the old ranch house.

They all bowed for the prayer. She had realized, much to her embarrassment, that the Amish prayed silently for their meals. That must have been what John and Martha had smiled about that first day when she was there.

Dani quietly thanked God once again for leading her to this place and giving her such special friends.

CHAPTER TWELVE

Dani was curious to hear how Rebecca's job was going. If she had begun work on Monday like she had told Dani, she would have worked several days by now.

Dani hadn't seen an extra van pull into William's place, but she realized Rebecca probably had to leave quite early each day. She must have simply missed it when it came back in the evenings to drop her off.

Friday afternoon, Dani was walking back from putting a letter in the mail for Martha, when she saw her chance to catch up with Rebecca. The young Amish woman was pulling weeds by herself in a flowerbed on the edge of their yard. Dani put the flag up on the mailbox and headed toward her.

Rebecca looked up.

"Oh, hi Dani!" she said, smiling warmly.

"Hi."

Dani knelt down next to her and helped pick out some of the bothersome weeds growing between the newly blooming lilies.

"I've been thinking a lot about you—wondering how your job's going?" Dani glanced over at her.

"Real goot." Rebecca grinned. "It was a little nerve-wracking at first to make sure I did everything right, but I'm starting to get it. I really like being with all the customers. I'm even starting to make friends with some of the other girls working there."

"Good for you." Dani smiled. "Is today one of your days off?"

"Yah, I'm only on part-time work," Rebecca nodded. "But that's goot with me! Waitressing all day does tire a body out."

Dani thought how most people would take it a little easy on their days off, but not the Amish. Here Rebecca was out busily pulling weeds for her mom. No doubt she had a full day's worth of work planned for the day. Work was something an Amish person expected.

Dani looked around, noticing how well the grass, flowerbeds, and garden were kept up around the large Amish home. Their work ethic was evidenced in their beautiful, orderly homes inside and out.

She turned to her friend. "So, have you told your parents yet?"

Rebecca's face fell ever so slightly. "No."

She looked up at Dani. "I haven't, but I will sometime when it suits."

"Your parents seem very nice," Dani said. "I really think they'll understand."

"I know," Rebecca sighed. "But if they want me to stop, then what am I going to do? It's easier to have them in the dark then to go against their wishes."

"You know, God often works through those around us that love us," Dani said gently.

Rebecca looked out at the fields around them and sighed. "It's not easy, but I do feel like I'm old enough now to be making some of my own decisions."

"Just be sure none of those decisions come back to haunt you. God's plan for us is always the best one."

"Yah, I know."

Dani decided to stop preaching at her friend. Rebecca probably knew the principles in the Bible better she did anyway.

They pulled weeds for a few moments in silence.

"What are you planning on doing this Sunday?" Rebecca asked.

Dani looked confused.

"You know, with it being off-Sunday?" Rebecca added.

"Oh, yeah, there's no church this week, is there?" Dani remembered. "I don't really know. I hadn't thought about it. What are you doing?"

"I think we're going up to our Uncle Eli's place in Applecreek in the morning."

"I really hope I can get some time to think," Dani said. "I feel like I've been so busy since I got here that I haven't really had time to pray and sort out some things."

Rebecca smiled knowingly. "Yah, people think we Amish live a slow life and have all this time." She chuckled. "Our lives are anything but slow. Simple, maybe; but not slow."

Dani smiled. "You are the hardest workers I've ever seen. It's inspiring, really."

"And speaking of working," she said, standing up and stretching. "I'd better get back to Martha before she starts to worry that I'm not coming back to help her finish the housecleaning."

"All right. See ya!" Rebecca waved.

Dani began to walk away.

160

"Oh, Dani!" Rebecca called.

She turned back.

"There's a baseball game in Fredericksburg tomorrow night, if you want to come. A lot of us young people like to go and watch it."

"Sounds like fun!"

"We'll probably take the open buggy, and you're more than welcome to ride along."

Dani smiled. "Sure! That'd be great."

"Okay. We'll head out around seven if you can walk over here by then."

Dani nodded. "Yep. See you then!"

"Yah, see ya."

Dani walked toward the house.

One thing was sure, her social life had expanded faster than Martha's doughnuts in the deep fryer. Here was a girl who went from shopping or going out to eat with the same girlfriend twice a month in a good month, to now doing something several times a week.

She sure wasn't complaining.

Dani walked more quickly to get to the house. She really felt like a good jog, but thought better of it in the dress and all. She envisioned her Amish self running down the lane, skirt flapping, showing the black socks underneath, and kapp strings flying behind her like the tail on a kite. Someone would probably think the house was on fire.

Dani got back to the house and stepped into the mud room. The house smelled like Windex and lemon furniture cleaner with a hint of bleach.

Martha had them scrubbing down every surface imaginable in her house today from the tiny spider webs in the corners of the ceilings, to the upholstered couches, to the hardwood floors. And, of course, all that beautiful wood furniture had to be dusted.

Dani had never minded house cleaning chores, and with

two of them going at it, they could accomplish a lot in one afternoon.

Even with her nose up to it, Dani rarely came across anything that she would have categorized as being truly dirty. She grew up with a dad that didn't clean the house until the spiders were actually wrapping bugs in tiny cocoons in their webs and the mirror was so smudged that if you wanted to see more than a fogged image of your face, you had to wipe a spot clean. Things had changed when she got older and took over the housework, although she still didn't clean anything until it looked like it needed it. But if it made Martha happy, Dani was glad to wipe imaginary dust and smears all day. That was probably the secret to how the Amish women kept their homes so immaculate.

One thing Dani had noticed about the Amish women was how quickly they worked. Even though their movements were graceful and precise, they had learned how to do things twice as fast as any English woman she had seen. It made her feel slow just watching how deftly they did everything.

By the time they were done, it was time to get out the stuff for their quick supper. Dani had learned it meant nothing when Martha labeled a supper "quick". It still meant you were in for some fine cooking. What were "quick" and "easy" suppers in Martha's book were still categorized as "special" and "takes extra time" in Dani's book. She had loved every one of their suppers together so far.

"I think we'll have haystacks for supper," Martha said.

"Okay," Dani nodded even though she didn't have a clue what "haystacks" were. It sounded dry and bland, but she doubted that anything Martha cooked could be either of those.

Martha kept handing her stuff to set on the table- sour cream, cheese, chopped onion, lettuce.

Dani soon realized that haystacks were very similar to what she called a taco salad back in Arizona, but without the

Mexican flavor.

When it was time to eat, she assembled her haystacks toppings on a base of corn chips as Martha had suggested. Dani took a bite.

"This is really good!" she exclaimed, pointing at her plate with her fork.

"I'm glad you like it," Martha said with her typical modesty.

"This might even be my favorite supper so far," Dani said, adding quickly, "but all your suppers have been delicious."

"You're very kind," Martha smiled.

"Didn't I tell you she was the best cook," John asked.

Dani grinned. "That you did."

"Best cook in Holmes County," John winked at his wife.

"Oh, now!" Martha protested.

"Yah," John patted Martha's hand, "I married me the right woman."

"I'm glad you figured that out by now!" Martha teased.

Dani smiled as the two elderly people continued to banter with each other. She suddenly realized that she had missed out on watching her own parents interact with each other. Her smile saddened at the thought of all the memories she never would have.

She wondered if Mom and Dad teased each other around the dinner table. Dad's eyes took on a faraway look like someone remembering a lovely dream whenever he talked about Mom, and Dani could easily imagine the way he must have looked at her across the table.

She couldn't count the many times over the years that she wandered around the house, picking up the frames with photographs of Mom and studying her, trying to know the woman who had loved her baby daughter with all her heart. Dani had no memory of the gentle words her mother must have spoken to her, or the many soft kisses planted on her baby hair, or her mother's hand over her own tiny one as she taught her how to color.

Mom and Dad always looked so happy in the pictures, but as their child, Dani had never been able to witness their love, never being able to see the romance between her own parents or their daily interactions with each other.

And now, with Jeff and Dad both gone, she would never even be able to ask one more question about it. Any thought that popped into her head, any curious questions about Mom, would forever stay unspoken and unanswered.

That night, Dani lay on her back in bed, listening to the sounds of the trees rustling in the gentle breeze and the spring peepers chirping out into the night air. She was glad she had left her window open a crack when she cleaned down here earlier.

Even the night sounded different here than in Arizona. There, the night was silent and still, except for a few horses' whinnies or a lone cricket. Here the night was alive. Above the background noise of the trees and spring peepers, Dani could hear the chattering of an animal—maybe a raccoon— and the occasional faint hoot of an owl. A cow lowed gently as it settled in for the night.

Dani thought back to their supper as she lay there, smiling to herself at John and Martha. She loved the way the older couple's love shown in John's voice when he boasted about his wife or the glint in Martha's eyes when she looked at him. Even though the Amish people were very private about showing romantic affection in public, this elderly couple had allowed her to have a peek into their hearts.

What a wonderful thing to be as old as they were and love each other so obviously after all this time. Dani prayed she might get to experience that kind of lifelong love someday. She knew that kind of love was the real "happily ever after" story.

Dani drifted off to sleep with those pleasant thoughts circling in her mind.

After supper the next day, Dani started to clean up the dishes as usual, but Martha shooed her out of the kitchen.

"Go on now or you'll be late for the ballgame," she said, taking the stack of dishes out of Dani's hands.

A glance at the clock told her Martha was right, and she'd better not argue this time.

"I can help once," John said, standing up and gathering up the cloth napkins.

Martha looked at him in surprise.

"Unless you mind," he said, grinning boyishly at her.

Martha handed him a dishcloth. "Oh, no, you just feel free to help if you want to, Daudy."

John turned to Dani, grinning. "Go on," he said in a low, conspiratorial voice, "Have a nice time."

"Okay." Dani smiled. "I will."

She hurried up the lane to William and Ina's house.

"Hi!" Rebecca waved when Dani reached them.

"Hi!" Dani said, a bit breathless from her brisk walk.

Rebecca was already sitting up in the open wagon parked in the driveway. Willis threw Dani a welcoming smile as he worked on hitching up the horse.

Rebecca and Willis' younger brother, Sam, came running up. "Ready?" he asked. He held onto the back of the wagon and heaved himself up into the cargo section in one smooth motion.

"Isht abot," Willis said, using the Dutch phrase meaning "just about".

"Here, you can sit by me," Rebecca told Dani, scooting over into the middle of the front bench and patting the seat next to her.

"Okay," Dani took hold of the side and hoisted herself up.

"Have you ever ridden in an open surrey yet?" Rebecca asked.

"Nope." Dani shook her head.

One thing that had surprised her about the Amish way

of transportation was how small their buggies and wagons actually were. One would think with their large families that they would have more sitting space, but most of them had only one bench seat. Unlike the buggy she rode at the tourist site, which was more of a buggy limo to the Amish, most buggies on the road had only a stool or single seat in the back where one person could sit sideways. The wagon Dani was sitting in now had the cargo area in the back where Sam and a couple other children could sit, but that was all.

Willis finished and jumped up into the seat on the other side of Rebecca. He gathered up the reins and clicked his tongue. Immediately, the horse started walking. Soon they were rolling down the road.

Dani breathed in a deep breath of fresh air contentedly and let herself relax. She was quickly falling in love with this way of traveling. Other than the fact that it took ten-times as long to get anywhere, traveling by wagon was so much better than by car. It forced you to slow down and kept you from rushing from one thing to the next like all Englishers tended to do.

It was so peaceful watching the farms and cozy homes slide by to the steady backdrop of the clip-clop of the horses hooves.

Sam was chattering in Dutch about the baseball game. Occasionally, Rebecca or Willis commented about what he said or added their own thoughts. As Dani listened, she thought about how beautiful it was, the young people in this family talking together like adults even though their ages varied quite a bit. They had learned to listen to each other and share life together. That was certainly another aspect of life the Amish did better than the English.

They made their way into the outskirts of Fredericksburg. Here, the homes were built close together again and side streets crisscrossed their road. They reached the top of a very steep hill, and Willis slowed the horse. Dani could see that there was a bigger road at the bottom of the hill intersecting with the one they were on. She held onto the side of the bench as they began their descent. This was the closest she had gotten to being nervous on a buggy ride.

Sam continued to talk, clearly unconcerned, and Willis guided the horse carefully until they stopped at the bottom of the hill.

Dani now recognized the larger road as the main street through Fredericksburg. A work truck passed and Willis and Rebecca waved. The driver waved back with a smile.

Willis leaned out to look if it was safe to pull out onto the road. A car was coming, but it was still quite a way off. Willis chose to wait patiently, and Dani wondered about his decision until she remembered how much slower a buggy goes than a car.

The car passed, and Willis turned out onto the road. He turned again at the stoplight—the one and only light in Fredericksburg—and then into the first parking lot on the left.

There were quite a few other buggies parked there, but there were still several spaces available. Willis pulled the buggy into an open spot and Sam jumped out.

"Looks like the ballgame's already started," Sam said, and he turned to high-tail it over to the field.

Dani watched him, amused.

"Sam's in his usual all-fired hurry. He just can't wait to get out there," Rebecca said, shaking her head.

Willis finished tying up the horse, and the little group headed toward the baseball field.

They had to walk past a small car wash on their way, and Dani chuckled as she noticed the sign.

" 'Car and buggy wash,' " she read. "Do you really use the car wash to clean your buggies?"

Rebecca nodded, smiling at her amusement. "Yah, some do. Those vacuums are pretty handy."

Dani could imagine. Still, a buggy-wash was something else she would have never imagined finding in Amish country.

"It looks like the bleachers are full," Willis noted as they got closer. There were clumps of people standing behind the ball fence or sitting in lawn chairs they had brought.

"Let's sit in the grass," Rebecca suggested. "I've been on my feet all day. I'd really like to sit."

"Sure," Willis said. "We should have brought a blanket or something," he said, glancing apologetically at Dani.

"Oh, this will be fine," she said. She was glad she hadn't changed before coming and wasn't wearing one of her favorite dresses.

As they walked toward the grassy area to sit, Willis and Rebecca said "hi" or waved several times as they spotted friends or relatives.

They found a spot where they could comfortably see the game. Sam stayed as close to the game as he could get, holding onto the tall fence near third base with a group of boys.

"Sam really likes baseball, huh?" Dani asked, nodding toward the boy.

"How could you tell?" Willis asked, one side of his mouth turning up into a wry grin.

Dani smiled.

"Yah." Rebecca tucked her skirts under her as she sat down. "I've never seen a boy as crazy about baseball as Sam is. And, let me tell ya, most Amish boys like their baseball."

Dani looked around and noticed that there were a lot of Amish here. In fact, almost all the people watching the game were Amish or plain people of some kind. Even a lot of the players looked Amish, although it was a little hard to tell because some of the boys looked like English boys at first until you noticed their pants. Even with their short English haircuts and polo shirts, their homemade trousers gave them away.

It was different to see a game of baseball without the usual baseball uniforms. Even when she had gone to some of Allie's little league games, each one of the little players had been decked out in their cleats and striped uniforms. It did look like the players here wore cleats, but the two teams simply wore different color polo shirts in lieu of the normal attire.

A couple of the boys looked like they were trying to be cool with their sunglasses and English clothes, even though they were still clearly Amish. Dani found it humorous since they were still far from "cool" to an English teenager, but she kept her thoughts to herself. She supposed maybe they were the cool ones in their Amish world.

The teams switched sides, and Dani focused more attention on the game.

An Amish kid stepped up to the plate and after letting one pitch go, he swung hard as the next flew toward him. His bat connected to the ball with a loud "thwack", and he took off running. The ball soared far into the outfield, and Dani was sure it'd be a homerun. One of the outfielders was running to get under it as it came down, and he jumped up, cleanly catching it.

Every single one of the following batters hit deep outfield balls with barely a foul in the entire inning.

"Wow. They are really good!" Dani said, impressed.

"Yah," Rebecca nodded. "Like I said, Amish boys like their baseball."

"I guess so! Some of these guys look like they could be playing on a professional team."

A player threw the ball from deep in the outfield, and Dani watched, amazed as it easily made it all the way in to the pitcher.

"I'm thirsty," Rebecca said after awhile. "Okay if I go get us some drinks?"

"Sure," Willis said.

Rebecca stood up and dusted the grass off of her skirt.

"I'd like to say 'hi' to Hannah and Verna, too" she said, looking toward the crowd of people. "I saw them sitting on the other side."

"Okay." Willis nodded.

She turned to Dani. "What kind of soda do you like?"

"Oh, a root beer sounds good, but really anything will be fine."

"What about you?" she asked Willis.

"I'll take a Mountain Dew."

Dani pulled her money out of her pocket, but Rebecca spied her and frowned. "Oh, no. I've got it."

Dani insisted, and she was glad when Rebecca gave in.

Rebecca looked out over the field. "Okay, I'll be back in a bit," she said, turning to leave.

Willis and Dani sat, aware of each other, but comfortable as they watched the game, occasionally commenting about a play.

"That boy stepping up to bat is my cousin," Willis said, nodding toward the field.

"Really?" Dani smiled. "How many of the players are you related to?"

Willis chuckled and Dani found she liked the gentle and honest sound of it. "Probably most of them—the Amish ones anyway—if we go back far enough."

He pointed. "The tall guy on second base is my married sister's brother-in-law, and the guy out in far left field is my uncle, my dad's youngest brother.

Dani smiled. "That must be wonderful having family all around you."

Willis looked over at her, "So, what about you? Do you have relatives living close to you in Arizona?"

Dani shook her head and tried to keep the wistful edge out of her tone. "No, the closest family I have is an uncle and aunt who live in Oregon."

Dani looked up at Willis, and the sadness and compassion in his eyes nearly overwhelmed her. She looked away to keep from tearing up.

"I'm so sorry, Dani," he said, simply and sincerely.

"It's okay." She smiled weakly. "That's actually a big reason why I'm here. I needed to get away from all the memories of the ones I've lost."

Willis studied her. "That's pretty brave of you—coming into a new area, trying to fit into such a different culture."

Dani shrugged. "It wasn't so brave. The way the Amish community surrounds a person appealed to that deep sense of loss I felt. Plus, it seemed like the perfect place to get quiet and reconnect with God."

Willis nodded thoughtfully. "Yah, I could see that."

The conversation fell silent and they watched the game. There were two guys on bases with one out. The next player stepped up to the plate. Dani watched as he swung. One strike. The pitcher was winding up for another throw when Willis turned to her.

"Dani, I have something to ask you."

The statement and the way he said it startled Dani. She looked at him. The expression in his dark brown eyes was serious.

"Okay," she said a bit cautiously.

Willis looked out to the ball field for just a moment before looking back into her eyes.

"Dani, would you be willing to spend time with me, to let us get to know each other better?"

Dani froze, completely taken aback. Her mind raced at the realization of what he was asking her. She had known he liked her, but had never expected this, never expected that he would actually ask to date her.

"I…I don't know Willis."

He waited a few moments, allowing her time to process

171

his question and think through her answer.

"What don't you know?" he asked finally.

"There's so many things I don't know. It's so sudden." Dani's eyes followed a ball as it sailed into the outfield. *Dear Lord, what should I say?*

She looked up at him again, and her stomach did a flip as their eyes met and she caught the look of hope mingled with concern in his eyes. *Not now*, she told her heart. Now was when she needed to use her brain, not her emotions.

She knew she needed to explain, to say something, so she decided to be honest.

"Willis, what about Mary?" she began, voicing the one hindrance that was bothering her the most. "How can you spend time with me when you're already dating someone."

Willis startled her for the second time in the last ten minutes by breaking into a huge grin and chuckling.

Dani felt more than a little annoyed. This was no time for laughing.

Willis caught the look on her face and became serious immediately. He stood up. "Come on," he invited. "I'd like you to meet Mary."

Dani hesitated. The last thing she wanted to do was meet some sweet Amish girl that Willis was supposed to be in love with.

"You need to meet her," he encouraged.

"Okay," she agreed, still reluctant.

Willis led her toward the crowd. Dani thought at the very least this short walk would give her a few minutes to gather her thoughts into a more coherent group, but by the time they reached the bleachers, she was no closer to an answer than she had been when he asked the question.

Willis threaded his way through the group to the far end of the bleachers.

"Hi!" he cheerfully greeted someone sitting there. He said something in Dutch, and Dani could pick out "new friend" and "meet you".

She caught up to him.

"Dani, this is Mary," Willis said, motioning to the person.

Dani looked up to see the girl with Down's Syndrome that she had seen helping on Sunday.

Astonished, her eyes darted back to Willis'. He nodded.

"This is Mary," he repeated softly.

Dani was speechless. She looked back at the girl and somehow had enough presence of mind to realize the girl was watching her and waiting for her to say something.

"Hi," Dani said, smiling, but feeling very sheepish.

Mary just looked back at her, her sweet eyes trying to determine what she should do in this situation.

"My name is Dani." Dani paused, but when the girl didn't say anything, she scrambled to make more conversation. She realized that she should probably talk in Dutch. She tried to put together a simple sentence, "Do you like baseball?"

Mary looked at Willis and then back at Dani. Her eyes crinkled ever so slightly with a smile and she nodded.

"I saw you helping on Sunday," Dani told her. "It looked like you were a big help."

Mary's face brightened. "I help Auntie," she said in Dutch, nodding.

Dani had heard people with special needs speak in broken English many times, but Mary's simple, faltering Dutch broke her heart.

"So, Willis is your cousin?" Dani asked.

Mary nodded. She stood up as if she needed to go somewhere.

"Well, we'll be moving on, Mary," Willis said. "I hope you like the rest of the ball game."

"It was nice to meet you," Dani said still in Dutch, hoping she got all the words right.

Mary reverted to her uncertain mode, but Dani was fortunate enough to get her to wave slightly as they left.

173

Dani was still reeling from all the implications of this news as we walked away. So, Mary *wasn't* a girlfriend. In fact, Willis didn't even have a girlfriend. He wasn't being the slightest bit unfaithful when he started liking her.

On top of that, all the attention and rides home and everything that Dani had assumed he was doing for a girlfriend, he was actually doing for a handicapped cousin. She looked at Willis, realizing this man next to her had an incredibly tender and kind heart. Somehow, she had always sensed that, but now she had proof of it.

Once they were away from the people, Willis turned to Dani. "I'm sorry this is such a shock," he said. "I figured you would have known who Mary was by now."

Dani shook her head, still processing the new information.

"Wait! So, the whole time at the horse auction and everything, you thought I was actually dating someone?" Willis suddenly realized.

"Yes, I did."

"Wow." He ran his hand through his hair. "You must have thought pretty little of me."

"Honestly, I didn't know what to think," Dani said. "Going behind another girl's back didn't seem fit your character, but with taking her home and all, I just assumed you had a girl."

Willis was quiet for a moment. They reached their spot on the grass and sat back down.

"Mary is the same age as me so, as cousins, we developed a special bond over the years," he explained. "I think as a child I learned to understand her. Even today, I'm one of the few people she's comfortable with outside her immediate family. So, I help take care of her," he finished simply.

"That's so special and sweet of you," Dani said.

Willis shook his head. "Not really. That girl, even with her challenges and struggles, brings joy to any day. She's as dear to me as one of my own sisters."

Dani smiled and looked back toward where Mary had been.

"Speaking of sisters," she nodded toward the bleachers, "here comes Rebecca."

Willis turned to see Rebecca making her way toward them. He turned back to Dani.

"Please, will you think and pray about what I said, what I asked?" His eyes held such earnestness.

Even with all the questions still buzzing in her head, Dani knew she couldn't say no. Dani held his gaze for just a moment, before nodding. "Yeah," she said gently, "I'll pray about this. I won't give you a careless answer."

Willis nodded, satisfied. "Thank you."

Rebecca was getting close to being within earshot, so they turned back to the game as if they had been watching it all this time.

"Hi!" Rebecca said merrily. "Here are your drinks." She handed each of them a cold can.

"Thank you," Dani smiled up at her and popped her can open. It fizzed and she could smell the root beer. When the foam dissipated, she took a sip.

Rebecca settled back down on the grass.

"So, have I missed anything while I was gone?" she asked, looking out toward the game.

Willis visibly started. He scrambled for words. "Oh! Well, um…"

They had barely noticed there even was a baseball game going on around them while she was gone. The play of the season could have just happened and they wouldn't have had a clue.

Dani quickly jumped in to help him out. "In the last play, that guy on third almost got out, but the outfielder stumbled with the ball," she told Rebecca truthfully.

"Hmm… close one," Rebecca said, seemingly content

with that answer.

Willis and Dani shared a look, and Dani wanted badly to giggle, but settled on a sly smiled instead.

Little do you know how much you missed out on in the short time you were gone, Dani thought. It was amazing how much can transpire in so little time.

Her mind and heart were full as they watched the second half of innings. Although her eyes followed the game, she barely registered what was going on. The sun had sunk low and disappeared behind the trees surrounding the ball field, and the floodlights were turned on. The game slowly wound down to a close.

After the last out signaled the end of the game, Willis turned toward Dani and Rebecca. "Ready to go?"

"Yah." Rebecca stood and dusted off the back of her skirt.

Willis waved to get Sam's attention, and the boy turned to say a farewell to his friends before trotting over to join the rest of his group.

"So, what did you think of your first Amish ball game?" Rebecca asked.

"It was interesting," Dani said truthfully. There were a few other adjectives she could have used—surprising, confusing, startling, puzzling, perplexing, romantic, baffling, unsettling—but Dani didn't think that Rebecca would have understood how any of those could describe a simple baseball game.

They made their way back to the wagon, and Dani waited for Rebecca to climb in. Willis and Sam had been walking behind them, and Dani turned back to see where they were. Sam was talking while Willis listened, his head bent down. For just a moment, Dani studied the man that had just asked to date her. Despite her questions, there was one thing she knew. Underneath the Amish garb and haircut, there was a man with a gentle and tender heart.

Rebecca was settled in and Dani climbed in after her.

Rebecca gave her a curious look. Dani knew Rebecca must have noticed her watching her brother, but she didn't say anything.

Willis untied the horse, and the boys got back in the wagon. Willis carefully backed up the horse, and they were off again.

Dani had never ridden in the dark, and she was thankful only two cars passed them on their trip. It was still a pleasant ride, even if slightly less carefree than their ride earlier. Sam continued to talk up a blue streak about all things baseball. That left Dani to her own thoughts, which suited her mood perfectly. Other than Sam, the night was quiet. Dani looked up at the stars, picking out the few constellations that she knew.

The only interaction she had with Willis the rest of the evening was when they dropped her off at John and Martha's house.

"Thanks for inviting me," Dani said, hopping down. "I enjoyed the ride and the game."

"Sure thing!" Rebecca smiled. "Have a good night."

"Yeah, you too!" Dani waved and caught Willis' eye. He was smiling gently, a thoughtful expression on his face. They held each other's gaze for the briefest of moments before she turned toward the house.

Dani went around the side of the house to the basement sliding door in the back. She really wasn't in the mood for company. Thankfully, the house was quiet when she entered, and she couldn't hear any movement or floorboards creaking on the main floor above her. John and Martha must have gone to bed early.

Dani showered and changed into her pajama pants and a tee shirt. No one had said anything about nightclothes when she became "Amish", and Dani had been glad for that. Some people had comfort foods, but she had comfort clothes. Her soft and loose pajama set was one of them.

177

She knew there was no way she was going to be able to sleep anytime soon with all the thoughts and feelings racing through her mind, so she put some water on the stove to heat up for tea.

A basket of a variety of herbal tea bags had mysteriously appeared on her table one of her first mornings there, just another of Martha's acts of thoughtfulness. Dani hadn't used any yet, but tonight a cup of hot apple and cinnamon tea sounded perfect.

She sighed as she went through the motions of making tea.

Lord, what am I supposed to do with this? she asked for the hundredth time since the ball game.

She still had so many questions. What about his being Amish, for starters? He hadn't seemed as Amish as the other young people for some reason, but he still had the same upbringing and the same rules and church leadership. Surely they wouldn't approve of his dating her. Besides that, she hadn't learned yet what he believed or even really what doctrines the Amish church held.

And why hadn't he already married some nice Amish girl? Was there something about him or something about his past that kept the girls from saying "yes"? There was no doubt he was a handsome guy, and most women would be proud to be the one hanging on his arm.

And what about her? She had come here to get away from the ranch and experience another way of life, yes, but she also knew she had come to find a quiet place to sort out her relationship with God and deal with the grief and pain in her life. The last thing she needed was another complication.

She didn't even know if she was ready to date. She had certainly hoped marriage was in her future someday, but dating someone now, even if she could work out all the difficulties of their different backgrounds, certainly hadn't been on her time schedule.

On the other hand, there was no doubt she was drawn to Willis. Other than him being Amish, he would be just the kind of guy she would want to date. He had a spiritual life and enjoyed thinking about the deeper aspects of life. He was gentle, yet strong; smart, patient, and a man who was able to love deeply as he had showed by the way he cared for Mary. At the same time, he was also quick to laugh and smile and he knew how to enjoy the simple joys in life.

Dani appreciated how purposeful he was in asking her to date. A lot of guys would have just let things continue to play themselves out. Willis had obviously thought about it enough that he was willing to risk his ego and rejection for the sake of being open and upfront about his intentions toward her.

Dani felt respected as a woman in the way he had gone about the whole thing. Several guys had flirted with her over the years to see if she would reciprocate. It made an easy out for them when she didn't. But not Willis. Although it had been easy to read his attraction to her by the look in his eyes and the way he worked things out to be able to be with her, he hadn't once seemed to take it lightly by flirting. Attraction and love were a serious thing to him.

Dani's thoughts seemed to rotate in this same circle with questions and then aspects she appreciated about Willis, but never landing on an answer. At this point, she couldn't see how she could work through all the difficulties with him being Amish, but at the same time, she also had this nagging feeling that she wasn't supposed to tell him "no" either. She didn't feel peace about either way.

In the end, she realized she needed to know more. She needed to have some of her questions answered before she could agree to date Willis.

The warm tea had relaxed her, and the darkness outside had made her sleepy, so she headed for bed.

CHAPTER THIRTEEN

Dani was so grateful the next day was Sunday and that there was no church that day. Ever since she arrived in Ohio, she had been longing to take a walk in the woods, enjoying nature and getting alone with her thoughts and God.

Now, after last night, she had even more to think about.

After a quick breakfast, she poked her head upstairs to let John and Martha know what she was up to.

They were both reading in the living room. John took a sip of his coffee.

"There are several trails through the woods," Martha said.

"Yah," John nodded, folding over the next page in his newspaper, "you can't get lost if you stick to the paths."

Dani smiled. "Okay. I'm going to take along a snack

in case I'm not back in time for lunch, so don't worry about me."

Martha looked knowingly at Dani, wisdom and sympathy shining in her eyes.

Back downstairs, Dani slipped on a pair of black tennis shoes she had picked up at the dollar store and slid open the sliding backdoor. The fresh scent of springtime greeted her, but today the sun was warm and pleasant.

Dani crossed the backyard and entered the woods. She soon came onto a small trail and continued to walk until the houses were nearly out of sight. She let the peacefulness of nature surround and relax her.

She sighed deeply. She had always felt closer to God when she was outside. Not that she couldn't pray to Him in the house, but somehow He seemed closer out among His amazing creation.

For a long time, she let the thoughts of her heart flow out in a silent stream, unorganized and unhindered.

She followed a trail across the side of a ravine to the top. Spotting a boulder, she climbed up on it and leaned against the rough tree trunk it was wedged against. Dani looked out over the trees and plants below her.

Taking a deep breath, she forced herself to think about the one question that had been on the back of her mind for months, the one question that had hindered her relationship with God, the one question she had been trying to avoid for so long.

Why?

So much was wrapped up in that one, tiny, three-letter question.

Here, in this quiet, solitary place, she finally let her tears fall.

Why, God? Why have you taken every member of my family away from me? If You are so mighty, why didn't You let me keep just one of them? Just one? Is that really asking for too much?

She knew all the answers. She had heard them a million times. God is good. God is love. God has reasons we may never understand. God works all things out for good.

In her grief and pain, the answers had seemed weak at best. In the midst of her sorrow they weren't enough. They weren't enough to salve the gaping hole in her heart— weren't enough to make her understand why she had lost so much.

And they weren't enough to take away the anger she felt toward God.

It wasn't so much that she blamed Him for making it happen, but she certainly blamed Him for *letting* it happen. He had known her mom would die of cancer. He had known her dad would have a heart attack when no one was close enough to notice for several minutes, and the ambulance would never have a chance to get there in time. God had known her brother would be on that specific highway at that precise moment and spot to be killed by the driver He knew was being careless. He had known!

He had known all along. Couldn't He have made one of them not happen? It would have been nothing to Him in all His power to heal her mom, or give her dad more warning, or hold that car in its lane to avoid hitting her brother. So, why hadn't He?

It was the hardest battle in her spiritual journey she had ever faced and probably ever would face. She knew she believed. She knew she had a relationship with God. She had felt Him. She had heard Him. She had known He was beside her.

She had also trusted Him, but it seemed like He had let her down.

She had no idea where to go from here. There was no way she could turn her back on Him, no way she could leave the faith that she knew in her soul to be the truth. Yet, somehow her previous view of Him now seemed naïve. She didn't know if she could ever get back to the place she had been before Jeff's death.

She felt stuck. She knew this was an issue she would have to work through. She would not spend the rest of her life as a half-hearted Christian. She had tasted what it was like to be close to God and she desperately longed for that again.

Lord, show me! she cried silently as she looked up through the branches and leaves to the patches of blue sky overhead. *I cannot live without You, and I cannot be angry with You forever.*

In the quiet of the woods, a thought suddenly struck her and she froze.

"I have wept too, child."

The thought was so completely out-of-the-blue that Dani knew it wasn't from her. Her mind went back to story with the shortest verse in the Bible.

"Jesus wept."

She let those words sink in.

Reaching for the bag she had brought along, she pulled out her Bible. She had learned that short verse because it had been part of a Bible trivia game her sixth-grade Sunday school did, but she couldn't remember the surrounding story. Was it in the story of the time Jesus wept over Jerusalem? Or was it when He was on the cross and He told John to take care of His mother? She used the concordance in the back of her Bible and looked up "wept" to find the verse.

Thumbing through the Bible, she found the story. It was the story of Lazarus. Dani flipped back one page to read the entire story.

Lazarus lay on his bed, very sick and getting worse. His two sisters, Mary and Martha, grew worried and sent word to Jesus, their dear Friend, who had often stayed with them.

"Lord, the one you love is sick," their message said.

Jesus replied, "This sickness is not unto death, but for the glory of God, that the Son of God may be glorified."

Dani was surprised as the very next verse read: "Now Jesus loved Martha and her sister and Lazarus." It was as if the writer knew she would be wondering about that. If Jesus really loved them, wouldn't He heal their brother?

But no, He purposely stayed where He was two more days before traveling to Mary and Martha's home. When He finally got there, He was told that Lazarus had already died and had been buried four days ago.

Martha heard that Jesus had come, so she went out to see Him, but Mary, the same woman who had bought expensive perfume and washed Jesus' feet, and the same woman who had sat at her Master's feet while Martha bustled around with hostess duties, stayed in the house.

Dani couldn't help but identify with Mary. Here, Mary had poured out her love for her Lord, yet He hadn't come when she had needed Him most. How well Dani knew the feelings of betrayal and confusion that Mary must have felt in that moment.

Martha met up with Jesus. "Lord, if You had been here," she said honestly, "my brother would not have died."

Jesus and Martha started a discussion about the resurrection. Martha didn't understand what Jesus was about to do, but Jesus got to the heart of the matter.

"I am the resurrection and the life," He told Martha. "He who believes in Me, though he may die, he shall live. And whoever lives and believes in Me shall never die."

Dani could picture Jesus looking deep into Martha's tear-streaked face as He asked tenderly, "Do you believe this?"

"Yes, Lord, I believe," Martha said.

Dani set the Bible down on her lap. Her tears were falling so rapidly she stopped trying to wipe them away. They trailed their way down her cheeks and dripped onto her dress.

"I am the resurrection..." the words echoed in her heart.

"Though he may die, he shall live."

She knew Mom and Dad and Jeff had loved God and they would one day live again. Then, Dani realized the other phrase Jesus had said: "Whoever lives and believes in Me shall never die." Jeff would never die. Dad and Mom would never truly die. They were only taken from this earth and from her for a little while.

Dani felt the question Jesus had asked Martha pointed gently at her this time. "Do you believe this?"

Dani stared up into the sky. *Did she?* Of course, she had believed in heaven and eternal life, but she had never really understood that Jesus *was* the resurrection and that through Him, her precious family had never really died and never would. Through Him they lived and would be raised again someday.

When Jeff had been buried, it had seemed so final. She knew his broken body was in that casket. She knew, as she watched shovelful by shovelful of dirt fall onto the casket, that she was losing the very last remainder she had of him. Even though she truly believed in heaven, she felt like he was taken away from her forever.

But it wasn't forever. And it wasn't final. Compared to the vastness of eternity, it was only for a short time, a little while. He had simply been ushered from one realm into another, more beautiful one.

Did she believe this—really believe this?

Yes, Dani whispered, echoing Martha's words. *Yes, Lord, I believe.*

A great peace settled over her heart.

"I believe," she said again, this time aloud. She looked up to the heavens. "Lord, I believe!"

For the first time since she had started out that morning, she smiled. Tears were still running down her face. She would still desperately miss Jeff, but she would also see him again. He wasn't dead. He would never die.

185

Dani realized that she hadn't yet read the part where Jesus wept, the part that had started this whole train of thoughts in the first place. She turned back to her Bible.

After Martha's discussion with Jesus, she returned to the house and found Mary.

"The Teacher has come and is calling for you," she told her sister.

Mary immediately got up and hurried to Jesus. The Jews who had been with her followed her, thinking she was going to the tomb to weep over Lazarus. They wanted to be with her, to mourn with her.

She reached Jesus and fell at His feet. "Lord, if You had been here, my brother would not have died."

Dani understood Mary's pain. She was asking the same question Dani had been: *"Why, Lord?"*

Jesus didn't answer her. Instead, He saw her weeping and those with her weeping, and His heart ached for her.

"Where is he?" He asked.

As they led Him to Lazarus' tomb, the verse appeared.

"Jesus wept."

Dani stopped and read over the last two verses. She had always assumed that Jesus wept when He got to the tomb because of the death of His friend Lazarus. Dani realized even the people with Him had thought the same as she read the following verse:

"Then the Jews said, 'See how He loved him!' "

But that wasn't the case. Dani reread the previous verses again. They specifically said that it was when Jesus saw Mary's tears and the weeping of those around them that "He groaned in the spirit". Jesus had begun weeping before they even got to the tomb.

Dani sat back, amazed at this revelation. Even though Jesus knew what He was about to do, even though He knew he was going to raise Lazarus back to life and their sorrow was going to be turned into joy in a matter of minutes, still

He so intensely felt Mary's pain that He cried along with her. He loved her so much that He could enter into her sorrow and feel her grief even though He knew it would be taken away in just a few moments.

Dani could not imagine being able to cry with a friend even in the saddest of circumstances if she knew it was all going to be made right in just a moment. Yet, Jesus validated Mary's grief by joining in with her.

Wasn't her story similar? She may have to wait a little longer than Mary to see her brother resurrect, but he would rise again.

Surely, Jesus saw her grief as well and His tender heart felt her pain. Had He also ached for her with each of her family member's deaths, pained that death was a natural part of living in a sinful world, a part that God had never intended when He first breathed this world into existence? Had He been there with her as she wept over the graves of a mother she would never remember, a father she would never be able to lean on again, and a brother she would never be able to say goodbye to?

Dani didn't know how long she sat on that rock overlooking the ravine. She was so overwhelmed by the truths God had spoken into her heart. She cried, finally letting out all the frustrations and pain she had bottled up for so long. In the solitude of nature, with the trees around her like silent witnesses, she took hold of her anger and bitterness toward God and let it go.

Dani cried until she felt like she had spent every last tear she needed to, letting the love and peace of God wash over her. She knew she would always feel the loss of her family, and she knew she would cry again when the memories and loss inevitably washed over her again. But now she knew she had a Friend who also knew her pain—One who knew better than anyone else how to weep alongside someone.

Eventually, she dried her tears as best she could and set

her Bible back in her bag. She took a deep breath and felt her heart settle.

"Thank You, Lord," she said, again looking up in to the sky, but this time with a smile on her face. He had known exactly what she had needed to hear.

He was still with her. He had never left.

After a long time of simply resting, letting the newfound peace and truth seep into every crevice of her heart, she decided to walk some more.

She climbed down from the rock and continued up the trail, this time delighting in the spring blooms of the violets and dogwood trees.

It wasn't long until the trail reached the end of the woods. A field stretched out before her, and she turned to walk alongside it. New corn plants were just starting to show in even rows across the field.

New life was all around her and with her renewed heart, she felt like she had become a part of it, like she was also letting her new leaves unfurl into the warmth of God's sunshine.

Dani walked for a while when she suddenly saw a figure walking toward her. She stopped, nervous to be in such an isolated place with a stranger and then she realized that it was an Amish man. His head was bent in thought as he walked so he hadn't seen her yet. Dani watched the man as her mind raced through her options of what to do. Turn around and start walking? That would be strange and the guy would soon see her anyway. Hide behind a tree and hope he didn't notice? She glanced around. There weren't any large trees close by and the spring foliage was so thin it would be nearly impossible to hide. She looked back at the man. Surprised, she realized it was Willis.

Now she wanted to shrink away more than ever. She was sure her face was a wreck. She always looked swollen and red after she cried, and she had just cried harder than she had in a long time.

He was too close now, and any moment he would look up.

And just then, he did. He seemed just as surprised to see her as she had been to see him, but unlike her, he looked pleased about it.

"Hi Dani!" he called, waving pleasantly.

Dani lifted one hand in a silent greeting and smiled halfheartedly.

Immediately, his happy expression faded and his brown eyes reflected the pain he must have seen in hers.

"Oh," he said, "Dani, I'm sorry. I'll…" He motioned to the path. "I'll just be going."

"It's okay," she stopped him.

His eyes searched hers as if trying to read what she really wanted him to do.

Dani smiled slightly. "It's okay, really. If you don't mind, I'll walk back with you. I was just starting to think about turning around anyway."

"Okay," he said, still a bit unsure.

They turned and started heading back the way she had come. They walked together in silence for several minutes. The sound of old corn stalks and tiny sticks snapping under their feet seemed louder than usual in the quiet.

Dani finally broke the silence. "So, you like to come out into nature to think, too?"

"Yeah." He looked out over the field. "It's always been my favorite way to think."

"Mine too."

Willis glanced over at her and smiled gently.

They walked for several more minutes before Dani spoke again.

"Willis, I have been thinking and praying about your question the other day."

Willis looked at her, and she could see the anticipation in

his eyes.

She continued, "The fact is, I have too many unanswered questions to be able to give you an answer either way."

Willis nodded. "I see," he said, and Dani inwardly smiled at his Amish expression.

She knew her answer wasn't the one he was hoping for, but it was all she could give.

"Well," Willis took a deep breath, "maybe I could help answer your questions? Would you like to talk now?"

"Sure." Dani nodded.

Willis motioned to a dead tree lying along the field. "Do you mind if we sit?"

"No, I'd like that."

They sat down on the large tree trunk with a comfortable distance between each other. After settling in, Willis turned to face her and took another deep breath.

"So, what are you thinking?"

Dani searched his face, trying to decide what she needed to ask. "Some of my questions may seem too personal," she started, then hesitated.

"Dani," Willis said, "please ask me anything you need to know."

She looked at him, but his expression told her he meant what he said. She decided to push ahead.

"Well, one thing I have wondered is why you haven't you married already?" As soon as the word left her mouth, she realized that might have been a just a little too blunt, but there it was. Willis seemed unaffected by it, so she pushed ahead, "Rebecca told me that most Amish young people marry by the time they are barely in their twenties."

Willis looked out over the corn field again, pondering her question. Finally he turned to her.

"I was never the typical Amish young person," he said. "While my friends and family were joining church and hitching up, I found myself suddenly wanting to know why.

Why did we do what we did as an Amish church?"

Dani had sensed before that Willis seemed different than the other Amish she had met, even different than the adults. He had seemed slightly more English or something. Now she understood what it was.

Willis picked up a leaf and absently twirled it as he continued. "I had so many questions those days—questions about God, questions about our traditions, questions about what I really wanted to do with my life. I wouldn't be happy until I knew the answers and I wasn't willing to join a church and blindly follow the course of my Amish friends until I had those answers."

Willis sighed. "Most of my family thought I was crazy, and I'm sure I gave my parents a lot of sleepless nights as the years ticked by. I was so different than all the other Amish young people. I would often come out here in the woods to do my thinking," he said, motioning to the trees around them. "Sometimes, I'd bring a book to read and spend hours out here. When I would get back to the house, Mom would look at me as if hoping I had finally made my decision to join church. It broke my heart to disappoint her time after time."

"So what happened?" Dani asked.

"Well, as time went on I found answers to most of my questions through books I read or talking with my Mennonite boss or my dad. I came to the place where I understood that much of what we do as Amish people is based on traditions from long ago, traditions formed by men who loved God and wanted to keep themselves and their people separate from the world. I began to see that traditions in and of themselves are not a bad thing. We all have traditions, like the fact that we eat our fried chicken hot or like to have pumpkin pie for Thanksgiving. Often, it's just a way of doing things. I just happened to be born into a family that was Amish and held Amish traditions.

191

"Eventually, I came to the place where I felt there was no reason I couldn't live out my faith in God and Jesus in an Amish setting. My mother was having a hard time with my supposed lack of faith. She was so worried about me that she sometimes would lose whole nights of sleep and was even sick for months at a time, probably because of me. I wanted to make my parents happy so when I felt like I had worked through things enough, I joined the church."

"Wow," Dani said, fascinated with his story.

"And, to finally answer your question," Willis smiled, "I never got married because I was going through all of that. I suppose if the right Amish girl had come around in the early days, I probably would have set my questions aside, but none of the girls had struck me as being right for me. Then as time went on, I'm sure a lot of people thought of me as rebellious and a boy that thought too much for his own good. By the time I was ready to join church, most of the Amish girls my age were already married."

"Do you think you would be willing to leave the Amish someday?" Dani wondered.

Willis looked at her. They both knew their relationship hinged on this question.

Willis looked out across the field and was quiet as he formulated his answer. "I have thought a lot about that question." He looked at Dani. "Honestly, I'm not that tied to the Amish church in my heart. If it wasn't for all my family I probably wouldn't be here at all. So, yes, it would be hard, but I could leave the Amish."

"What about you?" He turned the tables. "Could you become Amish?"

"I don't know," Dani answered thoughtfully. "There's a lot about your people and community that I respect and love, but it would be hard for me to pretend to believe in all the traditions. I think I would begin to feel like I was being boxed in by rules I didn't agree with."

"Yah, I can understand that, especially since you're one that wasn't born in that 'box'."

It was quiet for a few moments. Dani broke the silence.

"So, how can you date an outsider when you've already joined the Amish church?"

"Our church does allow it," Willis said. "They wouldn't encourage it, but it's not strictly forbidden."

Dani pondered all the implications of what he was saying.

Willis looked at her, and the corner of his mouth went up into a sly grin.

"You want to make this work," he observed.

Dani smiled back as she realized he was right. "Yeah, I guess I do."

Willis broke into a huge smile and looked down at the leaf in his fingers. It was adorable to see how happy he was at her response.

"So," Willis looked back up, "would you be willing to spend some time with me so we could get to know each other better?"

Dani held his gaze for a moment. "Won't you get in trouble?"

"I'm not sure," Willis said. "It might be best to keep it a secret for a while, if you don't mind."

He caught the doubtful expression on her face, and he continued quickly, "I would like to tell my dad, though. He's very understanding, and he knows what all I've been through and where I'm at now."

"How could we date if we have to keep it all a secret?" Dani asked. "I mean, you can hardly do anything around here without the whole community knowing about it."

"That is true." Willis grimaced. "I'm not sure, but we'll figure something out. We could take walks or picnics out here."

Dani nodded. She could agree to that. Willis wasn't asking to marry her. He was just asking to date. At the very least, she would enjoy getting to know him better and developing a friendship with this intriguing Amish man.

"We won't know unless we try," Willis said gently. "I know there will be some hurdles to cross the deeper our relationship goes, but I also know I really would like to try. Trust me, I've spent a lot of time thinking and praying about this before I asked you last night at the ballgame. If it's God's will for us to be together, He will help us make it happen."

Dani looked into his earnest eyes, struck by the simplicity of his statement. If it was meant to be, it would happen.

She smiled and he smiled back.

"Okay," she said softly.

His smile deepened.

Just then, a mockingbird flitted into a tree overhead. After settling on a branch, he let out a cheerful song.

"I think he approves of our courtship." Willis grinned.

Dani returned the smile. *Our courtship.* The term sounded old-fashioned, but Dani decided she liked the sound of it and she loved hearing the word "our" again. It felt like it had been a long time since someone had used that word with her. It meant she shared something with someone again.

Somehow sharing with Willis seemed perfect.

CHAPTER FIFTEEN

The next week was a blur. Each day was filled with household duties Martha needed done, but Dani was able to slip away most evenings to walk with Willis.

Dani loved their walks. The more she got to know about Willis, the more she liked him.

She felt so renewed after her prayer time in the woods that Sunday afternoon. She finally felt like she was able to come to grips with Jeff's death. She would always miss her brother and there would still be times that she was overwhelmed with sadness, but now it was different. Now, she knew God was holding her hand, whispering promises that one day all would be right. One day, He would wipe away her tears forever. She would see Jeff again.

While her spiritual life soared once again, her relationship with Willis only drew her closer to God. Willis' own love for God and the truth of the Bible inspired her. She loved walking with him and listening to his gentle voice as he explained something he had discovered in the Bible or shared a story from his own spiritual journey.

Sometimes Dani wondered if Martha could sense that something was different about her. There were days she felt so happy, she knew she must be glowing. Dani's cheeks got sore by the end of the day from smiling so much. Her heart felt free and uncluttered.

One afternoon, Martha was more tired than usual and announced she wanted to lie down for an afternoon nap. Dani decided it would be the perfect time to call Denise.

"Hey Dani!" Denise answered. "Great timing. I'm just on my lunch break. I guess it's what, two o'clock your time?"

"Yep."

"I've been dying to hear from you!" Denise chattered on. "So what going on there in Amish country?"

"Well," Dani began, "you wouldn't believe all the new things I've done and had to learn. The lady I'm staying with keeps me pretty busy, which is what I wanted. We're even going to a quilting this Friday.

"Yeah? I still can't picture you in your Amish clothes bent over a quilt and chatting in Dutch with a bunch of Amish women."

"It's a whole different world over here."

"Any cute guys yet?" Denise wondered.

"Actually..." Dani started, grinning.

"Oooh!" Denise squealed. "There *is* someone you have your eye on! Well, it's about time, Girl!"

"It gets better than that." Dani glanced out the window to make sure no one was close enough to the shanty and to overhear her. "We started dating last week."

"What? Really?! Tell me what he's like! Is he Amish?"

"Yes, he is Amish, but mostly for his family's sake. He's very gentle and sweet, but smart and strong in his faith."

"Wow, sounds perfect. What about looks—is he cute? I bet he's got great muscles from working like those Amish people do."

Dani grinned. "Yeah, he has muscles and a cute farmer's tan."

Denise giggled like a teenager.

Dani explained how everything had happened.

"Wow," Denise said. "He sounds exactly like your kind of guy, Dani. I can't believe you're finally dating someone and I'm not even there to see it! I'm really glad for you, though."

"Yeah," Dani sighed wistfully. "I wish you were here so we could go out for coffee or something. I would love having you to bounce things off of. Willis and I have been keeping our relationship hush-hush for now to keep peace with the community, so you're the first one to know."

"Awww, you know I'm always just a phone call away," Denise said.

"Yeah, I know."

It suddenly became quiet in the background so Dani guessed that Denise was in her car again and heading back to work.

"Denise?"

"What?"

"Do you think I'm being crazy?"

"Crazy about what?" she asked.

"About dating an Amish guy."

Denise though for a moment. "Do you have any problems with his beliefs? I mean, his personal beliefs, not what his church tells him?"

"No," Dani answered honestly. "He's more grounded in the Bible than I am."

"Do you think God is leading in this or are your emotions and his farmer's tan the only reason you agreed to date?" Denise half-teased.

"No." Dani chuckled. "You know me better than that, Denise."

"That's true. Looks were never a top priority for you."

"It's the weirdest thing, Denise. I feel such a peace about the whole thing, even though I can't figure out how it will all end up working out. I feel such a connection with Willis, like he's an old friend and yet so much more than a friend. I've never felt that way with any other guy. It's like we're just meant to be together or something."

Denise chuckled. "It's called falling in love, Dani."

"But to an Amish guy? I would never have seen that one coming. Why did God let a great guy cross my path here? And now?"

"Maybe that was part of His plan all along," Denise said. "Dani, I wouldn't worry about his being Amish. If God is in this, He will make the way clear. Besides, you said yourself that you love the Amish."

"Yeah, but you know I could never be one of them permanently. I can play the act for awhile, but I couldn't live it for the rest of my life."

"Yeah," Denise agreed. "Rob and I will be praying a lot for you."

"Thanks, Denise. You have no idea how much that means to me."

"We love you, Dani. We want to see you happy."

Dani smiled. "I know."

"Well, hey, I'm sorry, but my break is over, and I'd better run," Denise said.

In the background, Dani could hear Denise's high heels clicking across the pavement. "Oh sure. It was great talking with you."

"Anytime, Dani! You know I love hearing from you."

"Yeah. I'll call you again soon."

"You do that."

They hung up and Dani sat for a moment, processing Denise's words and missing her. The dial tone on the phone reminded her to hang it up. She looked down at it as if seeing it for the first time and stood to hang it up.

Later that evening, Dani walked down the path in the woods to meet Willis. It was a perfect night for a walk.

Willis was waiting for her when she reached their usual meeting spot. He smiled tenderly and held up a beautiful red tulip he had been hiding behind his back.

"Oh!" Dani said, surprised and pleased. She took the flower. Its petals were so perfect and thick that they almost looked fake.

"One of the last of the season," Willis said.

"How in the world did you sneak that out here?"

Willis grinned. "Very carefully."

Dani smiled.

"You want to walk?" Willis asked, motioning toward the path.

"Sure." Dani nodded. "It's such a lovely evening."

They walked in silence for a few minutes.

"I talked to my dad today," Willis said.

"Oh yeah?" Dani turned to him, curious.

"Yeah. He said that he already saw it coming."

"Really?" Dani asked, surprised. "How could he have?"

Willis smiled. "A beautiful, sweet English girl coming into our community with a desire to enter a new world and a willingness to learn? Yeah, it wasn't hard. Especially when he noticed me watching you at church."

Dani blushed at his compliments. It was strange. She had never been one to blush before, and guys had given her many compliments over the years. She guessed she now knew the guy truly meant the words, and now she also really cared about what the guy thought of her.

"You were watching me back then?" she asked, pleased, but still a bit embarrassed.

"Oh yeah. I was watching you from the first day you got here. I saw the way you were helping Martha on your very first evening at their place. I saw how you were with Carrie after church meeting and how you smiled at Mary. You can

199

learn a lot about a person by watching them when they don't know you're looking."

Willis looked over at her. His eyes were soft and full of meaning. Looking into them, Dani had the feeling there was a lot more Willis wanted to say, but he simply smiled gently.

They continued up the trail until they reached the log they had sat on that first walk. It had become "their" log and was usually the destination point of their walk. Often, they would sit awhile before turning back and heading home before it got dark.

"Willis," Dani began after they had sat down on the tree, "I think I should tell John and Martha about us. It's starting to get awkward and weird with me going on a walk nearly every evening. Even if they don't always know I'm gone, I'm sure they've seen me several times."

Willis was thoughtful. "Yeah, I've been thinking about it a lot, too, and I think you're right. I don't know what will happen, but I think it's time to let others know about us."

Dani nodded.

Willis continued, "I still feel the Lord's blessing on our relationship."

Dani agreed. "Yes. I haven't had a doubt his whole time."

Willis smiled. "It's so strange that even though we were raised worlds apart, we fit together so well."

"I know, I have thought of that, too. I would have never thought I would date an Amish guy."

"We're not all that bad now, are we?" he teased.

Dani laughed at his boyishness. "No. Well, at least you're not."

Willis looked at the sky. "We'd better head back."

Dani sighed. "Yeah, I think so."

"Just think, tomorrow we won't have to sneak out here."

"Yeah, that will be nice. So," Dani said, "what's going to happen when the community knows we're dating."

Willis shrugged. "It's hard to tell. I'm sure I'll have a few talking-tos, but it probably won't get worse than that."

Dani searched his face. "Are you going to be okay if the community thinks less of you because you're dating an outsider?"

"Honestly, I'm sure it will be a bit uncomfortable at times, but I'm a little used to it. I've always been the odd one. No," he shook his head and a big smile spread across his face, "I can't wait for people to know."

He looked over at her. "I feel so blessed to get to be your boyfriend. It's like I won the lottery or something. I'm ready for the whole world—English and Amish—to know that I am the one dating Dani Chadwick."

His words warmed her heart and made Dani feel special. But then, Willis always made her feel special, as if their relationship was the most precious thing in his life. She knew she was the lucky one.

Willis suddenly had an idea. "We should do something special tomorrow, with it being our first date out in the open. We could get a driver to take us somewhere."

"Okay," Dani agreed. It would be weird to be driven on a date, but she would have to live with it.

"I know just the place. Can you come over around five, you think?"

"Yeah, that should be fine. Martha and I are going to a quilting, but I imagine we'll easily be back by then."

"Good. I can finally take my girl on a proper date."

"You know I've never minded the walks," Dani said. "It's a perfect way to talk."

"I know, but I'd like to do better than that for you."

They reached the spot where they usually parted ways.

"See you tomorrow, Willis." Dani smiled gently.

"I can't wait." He grinned

They waved as they headed off in their separate directions.

Dani was back at the house just as the sun said goodbye

to the world with its finale of orange and pink streamers across the sky. She leaned against the outside wall next to her basement door and watched.

She felt so blessed and happy.

"Lord, thank You," she breathed.

She didn't have to tell Him what she was thanking Him for. He already knew. That one, short prayer was the one thing on her heart as she thought about her time here in Amish country. She had experienced so many rich blessings here—her journey to peace with Jeff's death, all the special people she had met and little lessons she had learned, and her relationship with Willis.

Every single good thing she could hoped for in coming on her trip into the Amish world had happened and then some.

Her heart was overflowing with gratitude as she finally turned in and entered the house.

She could hear John and Martha still milling about upstairs, so she decided to go ahead and tell them the news.

She came up through the basement stairs. Martha was sweeping the floor, but she looked up and smiled at her.

"Have a nice walk?" she asked.

"Yes, it was lovely."

Dani cleared her throat. "There's something I've been wanting to tell you both," she said, looking over at John who was working on something in the living room.

He looked up, and Martha glanced at her curiously.

"You see," Dani began, "I haven't been taking all of these evening walks by myself."

"You haven't?" Martha asked, surprise and confusion written across her face.

"No," Dani shook her head. She had their full attention now. "I've been walking with Willis."

John and Martha froze, shocked by her news.

Dani smiled uncertainly. "We've decided that it's time to

let everyone in the community know that we're dating."

"Dating?" Martha repeated incredulously.

John leaned back in his chair, pondering the situation.

They didn't smile. They didn't congratulate her. Instead, they looked troubled. Dani held her peace and waited for them to say something.

Finally, John spoke.

"You know we really like you, Dani," he said, "but you aren't one of us. You're not *really* Amish."

Dani listened respectfully.

"It's really not goot for an Amish member to be dating an Englisher," he continued, trying to couch his words kindly.

"Willis told me that it would be something not strictly forbidden by the church," Dani said as gently as she could.

John nodded and smoothed his long, white beard.

"That's so, but just because something may be allowed doesn't mean it's best."

Dani wasn't sure what to say. She couldn't break up with Willis simply because John and Martha wanted her to, but she certainly didn't want to come across as rebellious, either.

An awkward silence filled the living room. What else was there to say?

"Well, I guess I'd better head for bed," Dani finally said and turned to go.

"Dani," Martha laid her hand on Dani's shoulder, "please, we're not upset at you. We're just looking out for the good of the community."

Dani managed a smile and nodded. "I know. And I understand. Thank you, Martha."

As she headed down the stairs to her apartment, her heart that had moments before been as light as a puff of dandelion dancing on the morning breeze, was now heavy. She hadn't expected John and Martha to respond like this. She supposed she hadn't realized Willis wouldn't be the only one facing some unpleasant reactions. She just hoped what happened this evening was the extent of it.

"Lord," she prayed, "if this is really Your will, help me to respond rightly. Give us wisdom in the coming days."

CHAPTER SIXTEEN

Martha and Dani headed out early the next morning for the quilting. Well, early for Dani anyway. She was quickly learning that getting up each morning at six or even five was barely early for the Amish.

Their lives may be more simple, but they definitely kept busy. Dani had a whole new understanding of what it meant to work hard. Except for Sundays, not a day had gone by since she had got here that Martha wasn't bustling around working on something.

John, who had to be well-past retirement age, continued to work full-time and after dinner, he often went back outside to work on something around the house.

Martha led the way to the garage and stepped up into the

205

buggy. Dani was proud of herself to have been able to hitch it up for her this morning. Dani handed Martha the sewing basket she had carried for her and climbed up in beside her. Martha pulled out a couple of wool blankets from the back.

"It's a bit nippy this morning, not?" she asked, handing one to Dani.

Dani smiled at the Amish expression.

"Yeah!" She rubbed her hands together. The cold air seemed to go right through her dress. She noticed leggings of some kind peeking out underneath Martha's skirt. *Smart.*

They tucked blankets over their legs, and Martha picked up the reins. The buggy lurched into motion, and soon they were clip-clopping their way down the road.

Dani wondered if Martha would mention her relationship with Willis on the ride, but she was relieved to find Martha seemed at least a little friendly this morning.

She took in the peaceful morning. The dew still clung to the tall pasture grasses, outlining hundreds of spider webs scattered over the fields, and a light fog clouded the low dips and valleys.

Dani turned to Martha.

"So, where is this quilting being held today?" Dani asked conversationally.

"It's at Reuben Nisley's," Martha answered. "His wife, Sarah, is my sister."

"Oh, yeah?"

Martha nodded. "We're going to be working on making a quilt for an up-coming wedding for another sister's youngest daughter."

"Wow, what a nice wedding present!"

Martha smiled gently as if amused that Dani would think something so commonplace was so special.

"Do you usually make quilts for wedding gifts?" Dani asked.

"Oh, sometimes. Often someone wants to do that for them

and organizes it all. We've actually gotten away from it more than I'd like to admit. It's so easy to pick up a comforter at the store anymore. I'm afraid we're slowly losing some of our independence from the world."

"Well, today you're gaining one new quilter," Dani said.

Martha smiled at her. "Yah, that is true, isn't it?"

She turned the buggy down a lane to another beautiful Amish home. She pulled up to the shop.

A boy, maybe nine or ten-years-old, ran up to the buggy.

"Mornin'!" he said. He held onto the horse's bridle while Martha slowly got up out of her seat.

"Oh, the old bones ain't what they used to be," she said, grimacing.

"Does this colder weather bother you more?" Dani asked, concerned.

"Yah, I probably better pick up some arthritis tonic next time we go out again."

Dani stepped down and reached in to retrieve the basket before following Martha up the walk. Instead of going up to the front door, though, Martha took the sidewalk leading around to the walk-out basement.

They entered to a scene that Dani imagined many photographers and painters would have begged to capture. In the middle of the room was a long quilting frame. Around it sat a dozen or so Amish women in a spectrum of ages from a stooped, white-haired elderly woman to a teenager with a sweet baby face, her blond hair already loosening from the confines of her covering in tiny wisps. Each of the women was sitting up to the beautiful quilt, a needle in hand.

Two babies played on a blanket nearby, toys scattered around them. Dani had decided that there was nothing in the world as cute as an Amish baby with their tiny shoes and little Amish clothes. She couldn't help smiling at their rosy-cheeked, chubby faces.

The quilting group looked up at them as Dani shut the

door behind her.

"Come on in," said one of the women. Dani assumed she must be Sarah.

Dani was delighted to spy Rebecca the moment she came in. Rebecca motioned for Dani to sit in the corner next to her. Dani smiled and pulled up a chair.

"Mornin'!" Rebecca smiled brightly.

"Hi!" Dani sat down. She looked around the table. "Just you here today?"she asked, not seeing Ina.

"Yah, Mom wasn't up to coming today."

Dani thought that sounded strange, but Rebecca quickly changed the subject before she could ask more.

"Have you ever quilted before?" Rebecca asked, handing Dani a needle already threaded and connected to the quilt.

"No. I really have no idea what I'm supposed to do."

"Oh, don't worry, you'll do fine," Rebecca assured her. She gestured to her own needle. "What you want to do is poke through all the layers of the quilt—the top, of course, down through the batting and the back. Then, come back up close to the same place you went down. Here," she handed Dani a thimble, "you're going to want one of these."

Dani put it on her right thumb as she had seen Rebecca do with hers.

Rebecca continued, "It helps to have one hand underneath the quilt so you can feel if you go all the way through the layers to the back."

"Won't I poke myself?" Dani asked, looking at the sharp needle in her hand.

Rebecca grimaced. "Yah, you might a few times, but you'll learn how not to."

Dani certainly hadn't thought a simple, peaceful quilting would be adding to the calluses and scrapes her hands had already collected over the few months of being Amish. These hard-working women must have hands as tough as leather after living like this all the time. That, or they were a lot more careful than she was.

Dani watched carefully as Rebecca wiggled her needle in and out with her middle finger and thumb a few times before pulling it through, making several neat, tiny stitches at once.

Dani bit her lip in concentration and began her first stitch. She decided she better not try to be as fancy as Rebecca, so she aimed for just one simple stitch.

She carefully felt the needle go through and pulled it out with the hand under the table. She poked it back up next to where she thought it had gone in. It ended up nearly an inch away from her first stitch, so Dani took it out and tried again. It took three tries to get it close enough to make a small first stitch.

Dani sighed.

"That's fine," Rebecca said encouragingly.

"But twice as big as your stitches," Dani groaned.

"Don't worry about it," Rebecca smiled. "That is the beauty of a homemade quilt. It doesn't matter if your stitches aren't perfect."

"If you say so." Dani's eyebrows arched, skeptically. She tried again. This time it went a little better.

A woman passed them on the way back from taking care of one of the babies.

"How's your job going, Rebecca?" she asked pleasantly.

A look of panic crossed Rebecca's face, but she quickly pasted on a smile. "Oh, fine."

"You know, my sister used to work at Mrs. Miller's, too."

"Yah," Rebecca nodded, "I remember that."

"Well, I'm glad it's going well for you."

Rebecca smiled again, and the woman moved back to her spot down the line of women.

Dani looked at Rebecca.

"You haven't told them yet?" she whispered.

Rebecca looked down the quilt to make sure no one was listening to their conversation. The other women were all chatting and laughing softly about something. The closest lady was an elderly lady, and Dani guessed she couldn't hear very well. Still, the two kept their voices low.

"No, I haven't." Rebecca said.

"But why?"

"Because," she glanced nervously at the other women again, "I've been sort-of seeing someone and I can't mess it up yet."

"Seeing someone?" Dani asked, her curiosity piqued.

"One of the other waitresses has a brother who has been coming to the restaurant quite often for a piece of pie and coffee. She told me the other day that he has his eye on me."

"Is he Amish?"

Rebecca nodded. "From what little I've seen and what his sister says, he seems real nice. She invited me to come over some evening for a singing or supper so I'll probably get to meet him better."

"Wow." Dani took in the news. "Rebecca you really should tell your parents."

A brief look of frustration came over Rebecca. "What? And have mam upset at me, too, like she is with..."

She stopped and quickly glanced up. Dani could tell from her face that she had said more than she had wanted to.

"I'm sorry, Dani," she said sincerely. "The whole thing has me so mixed up."

Dani suddenly understood. "Your mom was upset with Willis? Is that why she isn't here today?"

Rebecca nodded sadly. "Willis told us last night that he was dating you. Dat already knew, and I knew that Willis was interested in you, but Mam was totally surprised. I'm sure Willis will tell you, but it didn't go well."

Dani's heart sank. "She felt that badly about it that she wouldn't come to a quilting?"

Rebecca nodded. "She always told us that it was her goal in life to keep all of her children in the Amish church."

Dani was speechless and saddened for Willis. Why did caring for her have to make things so difficult for him?

"But why would she be upset with you?" Dani wondered, returning to the original subject. "You said the guy is Amish."

"I don't know," Rebecca sighed. "Maybe she wouldn't be all that upset. Even though he's a part of a newer order church, at least I'd still be Amish. I just don't want to upset the apple cart just yet."

"But you're lying to them, Rebecca."

A look of guilt passed over Rebecca's face. "I know, and I really don't like it anymore than you do. I'll fix it as soon as I can."

"Willis said he's taking you out tonight?" Rebecca asked, clearly done talking about her dilemma.

Dani couldn't help but brighten. "Yes, but he didn't tell me where."

"He'll think of a real goot place, I'm sure."

Dani smiled. "I'm sure anything he picks will be fine."

She looked up at Rebecca. "What do you think about our relationship—of Willis dating me even though I'm not Amish?"

Rebecca pondered the question for a moment before answering. "That first day Willis walked you home after singing, he surprised me. He's not usually that bold, especially not with girls. Then, as I thought about it, I realized how he was simply able to see past your Englishness to the lovely, sweet woman you are. I had been drawn to you from our first meeting. It was no wonder my brother was, too." She looked up and smiled sweetly.

Dani's eyes grew moist as she listened to her kind, honest words.

"So," Rebecca took in a deep breath and threaded her needle through the quilt once again, "I won't stand in your way. Besides, who am I to talk?" She looked up and smiled a lopsided grin.

Dani smiled back. "Thank you, Rebecca."

A woman sat down closer to them and struck up a conversation with the elderly woman. Rebecca and Dani exchanged glances, knowing their private conversation was over for the time being.

Dani mulled over Rebecca's words as she painstakingly made another stitch.

She was troubled for Willis. She didn't worry so much that he might break their relationship off. She knew he had already weighed the consequences long before he made his announcement to his family and even before that, when he decided to ask to date her in the first place. She only wished he didn't have to go through his mother's disappointment.

God, make a way, she prayed silently in her heart. *Give Willis wisdom. Help him to know what to do.*

It wasn't the first time she had prayed for Willis. It felt so right and wonderful to lift him up before their Father. She loved praying for him throughout the day, thinking about what he might be doing that very moment, knowing he was likely thinking about her and maybe even praying for her at the same time. It was such a beautiful thought, two young people in love simultaneously lifting each other up in prayer. How could a relationship like that go wrong?

Dani contentedly listened to the women around the tables chatting in Dutch. Even with their near-constant talk and occasional laughter, it was a much quieter group than a group of English women this size would be. Dani was glad she could understand a lot of what they were saying even though much of it was news about people she didn't know.

Dani had figured out by now that the Amish identified people by their dad's name as well as their own. She guessed that was because there were so many of them with the same first and last names. So, for example, she would be Bill's Dani and Rebecca would be William's Rebecca. A few of them had funny nicknames they were called by instead, like Hogger Danny, a guy that raised hogs for his living, or Stumpy John, a man that had a huge stump in his yard. Dani loved the thought that people in a community knew each other so well that even if you called them by their nickname, everyone would know exactly who you meant.

The quilters took a long break for lunch, and a few of the women chatted with Dani. For the most part, she had found the Amish women to be a very warm and caring group. Many of them were gentle, quiet, and shy. When Dani first came to Fredericksburg she had thought maybe they didn't like her. As time went on and they got used to her, they warmed up, and Dani was on friendly terms with all but the very shyest ones who still seemed to avoid her.

And probably Ina now, too.

Dani grimaced, remembering what Willis must have had to deal with last night. She wondered how upset an Amish woman got. They certainly seemed so demure and kind.

One by one, the women made their way back to the quilt. The ones with children left to put their babies down for naps.

Dani sat back down at her spot at the quilt. She was determined to get the hang of this quilting thing. She wasn't too bad at the one-stitch-at-a-time method, but that made her progress excruciatingly slow. In all the morning's work, she had done maybe a ten-inch row. She watched Rebecca again, her fingers deftly moving the fabric onto her needle, down and up, then pulled it through. Dani decided to try.

Slowly, she poked her needle in and, feeling with her other hand to be sure just the tip went all the way through, she directed the needle back up through the fabric. She had three stitches on her needle before she pulled it through.

It worked. It was nowhere near as tiny as Rebecca's stitches, but there they were—three little even stitches. Dani was proud of herself and tried it again.

After two more hours, her back was tired of hunching

over the quilt and her fingers were sore from working the needle. She was grateful when Martha spoke up.

"Well, I think I best be going and getting on supper if you're ready to go, Dani" she said, tying off her needle and carefully poking it into a pin cushion.

Dani nodded in agreement. She looked over at Rebecca. "Thank you so much for teaching me how to quilt." She helplessly looked down at her needle, not sure what to do with it.

Rebecca followed her gaze. "Oh, don't worry about that," she said. "I'll knot it for you."

"Thanks."

Martha came over and looked at Dani's work.

"Well, it looks nice," she said, smoothing the quilt with her worn and weathered hand. "You did real well for your first time."

"Oh, thanks," Dani said, pleased at her approval.

Martha looked over at Rebecca and her tone turned serious, "Tell your mother I said hello, Rebecca."

She looked up. "I will," Rebecca said and shot a glance at Dani.

They said their goodbyes to the group.

When they settled in their buggy and were on the road again, Martha turned to Dani. "So, what did you think of your first quilting?"

"I enjoyed it," Dani said. "My fingers are sore now, but I had a lovely afternoon."

"Goot," Martha smiled. "I thought it looked like you were havin' a nice time."

The ride home was a bit quiet, and Dani could tell Martha was tired.

"How about you rest when we get home and I'll get working on supper," she offered. It would only be about three o'clock when they got back, plenty of time for her to get the most of supper prepared before getting ready for her

214

date with Willis.

Dani could tell Martha was tempted to take her up on it.

"Willis and I are going out tonight," Dani said.

Martha looked at her, surprised. "Oh, you are?"

"Yes," Dani nodded, "but I could easily get everything cut up for haystacks so all you'd have to do is put them on the table."

"That would be nice, Dani, if you're sure you don't mind." Martha sighed heavily. "You'd think after sitting all day a body would be rested, but I'm just all done in."

"I'm glad to do it."

Back at the house, Dani insisted on putting away the horse and buggy. That done, she headed into the house and found Martha in the kitchen.

"Here's most of the food items," Martha said, adding a head of lettuce to an array of other items on the counter. "You know where to find it if I forgot something."

Dani was already washing her hands, but she looked up to smile at Martha. "That I do. Now, you go enjoy your nap. I'll wake you before I leave around five."

Martha looked at the clock. "Oh, I'll probably be up by then, but please wake me if I'm not. This old body just needs a bit of recharging."

She headed to her bedroom, and Dani got out a knife and cutting board. It was quiet, working by herself in the big kitchen, but she relished the peacefulness as she sliced and diced. The beautiful grandfather clock in the living room kept her company with its rhythmic and gentle tick, tick, tick.

It gonged out four o'clock by the time she had everything chopped, the meat cooked, and the table set. She set the last bowl back in the gas refrigerator and surveyed her work. She turned the stovetop off, but left the meat on the hot burner and headed downstairs to change.

It was such an odd feeling, getting ready for a nice date,

but not being able to do much different than she did every day. There was no make-up, no special dresses, no jewelry to decide on, or curls to set.

Dani picked out the burgundy dress, one of her favorites from Rebecca. The color brought out the natural rose tint in her cheeks and lips and the reddish highlights in her light hair. Looking at herself in the mirror, she touched up where her hair had loosened, tucking stray wisps back up under her covering where they belonged. After tidying her hair, she carefully placed her covering back on, letting it sit back just a bit further than usual.

She studied her reflection in the mirror. *What else could she do?* Suddenly a thought hit her. Maybe she had brought some kind of perfume. She rummaged through her suitcase with her old English clothes.

When she had packed and headed for this trip, Dani wouldn't have been thinking she needed any perfume, and she definitely wouldn't have imagined that she might need it for a date with an Amish man. She smiled to herself. So much had happened to her in so little time. How quickly life can spin in a direction you never would have dreamed of.

Dani spied a bottle of something in the corner of one of her suitcases. *Aha!* Dani pulled it out to find it was a bottle of body spray.

Dani read the label. *Lily Path.*

She popped off the cap and smelled it. It was a bit sweet, but the warm undertones gave it enough of a perfume scent. She decided this would do, especially seeing as it was the only thing she had available.

Dani looked around, making sure she hadn't forgotten anything before she headed back upstairs.

Martha must have gotten up because she was working on something in the kitchen.

"Did you have a nice nap?" Dani asked.

"Oh yes," Martha looked up and smiled. "Thank you for

doing all the fixings for supper."

"Sure, no problem."

Dani walked over to the living room to watch for the van that would be taking them on their date. She didn't have to wait long. A minivan pulled into Willis' drive, and she saw him walk out to meet the driver. Her stomach did a little flip at the sight of him and excitement for their evening together.

Dani popped her head into the kitchen. "The driver's here."

"Okay," Martha said.

No "have a nice time" or "enjoy your evening". It felt odd, but Dani understood why Martha didn't seem pleased that Dani was going out tonight. Dani decided to just be thankful that she didn't make this strained situation any more unpleasant than it had to be.

Dani headed out to the end of the sidewalk and waited for the approaching van. It pulled up to the walk, and Willis slid open the side door for her.

The driver turned around in his seat to greet her, and Dani saw it was a gray-haired older gentleman. He smiled at her.

"Hi. I'm Roger, and you must be Dani."

"Yes," Dani nodded and smiled.

"All set?" he asked, glancing at Willis.

"Yep."

Roger turned back to the front and began pulling around to head out of the driveway. Country music was playing on the radio, eliminating the need for any conversation with Roger and helping to ease what might have been an awkward setting for Dani.

She looked up at Willis. He was watching her, with a mix of tenderness and admiration.

She blushed and smiled, and he returned her smile.

Dani wasn't the only one who had thought of perfume. The instant she had gotten in the van she had smelled the wonderful, rich scent of men's cologne. Willis had good taste.

The ride up was fairly quiet. They asked each other about their days, and Willis laughed at her tale of her first quilting. Roger hummed along contentedly to the songs on the radio, allowing for them to talk without feeling the need to include him.

After about a half hour drive, they pulled into a parking lot. The surrounding area was farms and countryside with no other stores in sight. The large building in front of them was designed to look like a chalet, and the sign above it read, "Alpine Alpa."

This must be the restaurant. Dani had no idea what kind of food to expect from an "Alpine Alpa," or from a chalet, for that matter, but she was ready to enjoy whatever Willis had picked for them.

As she unbuckled and picked up her purse, Willis jumped out and hurried to her side to open the door for her. Roger was already heading into the restaurant, kindly giving them space.

"Thank you," Dani smiled at Willis as she stepped out of the van.

"My pleasure," he winked.

"Are you hungry?" he asked as they headed to the front doors.

"A little," she admitted.

Suddenly, high above them on the front of the building, two shutter doors flew open, and a full-sized puppet popped out.

Dani started and grabbed Willis' arm.

"Welcome to Alpine Alpa. My name is Hilda," the Swiss woman mannequin began.

Dani held a hand to her chest and caught her breath. She looked over at Willis and then back at the talking Hilda. She burst out laughing.

His eyes shone with amusement. "Are you all right?" he

asked, his voice wavering with his own laughter.

Dani nodded, still laughing. She took a breath. "Yes, I'm fine."

She realized her hand was still on his arm, and suddenly she was very aware of how strong his muscles felt. Dani dropped her hand instantly, and Willis pretended he hadn't noticed, although the grin he was trying to hide told her that he had been fully aware of her hand on his arm.

So far in their relationship, Willis hadn't so much as tried to hold her hand, and Dani had decided it was better to let him be the one leading their relationship, so she was careful not to overstep the boundaries he hadn't crossed yet. She never would have thought in her English life that she could fall in love with a man so deeply without having even kissed him.

"Whew!" she said, wiping her eyes. "I have never been startled before by an oversized Swiss woman jumping out of a wall."

Willis chuckled. As they neared the restaurant entrance, Willis reached to pull the door open for her.

Inside, Dani found that the place was much more than just a restaurant. Tiny stores on either side of the main hallway gave it the feeling of a little mini-mall.

"This place is huge," she said. "A lot bigger than it looks from the outside."

"Do you want to shop some, or would you rather eat first?" Willis asked.

"I think I'd rather eat, if that's okay with you."

"Sounds good to me."

They casually made their way through the building. One section had a floor-to-ceiling mural made from a photograph of a city street from some European town. Dani stopped and studied it. There were wrought-iron benches placed in front of the wall to give you the illusion you were a part of the old city.

219

"Could you imagine living there?" Willis asked.

Dani's gaze wandered to the towering Alps in the background of the quaint town. She shook her head in amazement. "It's so beautiful."

Behind her, music suddenly started playing. Willis and Dani turned around. A group of puppet Swiss musicians on a stage began blowing horns and beating on drums in time to the music.

A young couple stood nearby with a little boy, and Dani assumed that they had been the ones to put in the quarters to pay for the little show.

The musicians played and danced rhythmically with the music. The boy giggled and laughed, delighted with the puppets. Dani looked up at Willis, and he grinned. All of the adults chuckled as the boy squealed out another burst of laughter when the puppets twirled.

The puppets wound down their song and bowed before returning to their original frozen positions. Willis and Dani smiled at the couple and continued their leisurely walk.

Eventually, the hall led them to the restaurant part of the building. As they turned the corner to enter, Dani was awestruck by the place. The ceiling above the dining area was two or three stories up and painted to look like the sky with twinkling stars in it. Starting on a ledge above the far booths, was an alpine scene painted across the entire wall that met up to the painted sky. A motorized train made its way through bridges and tracks incorporated into the scenery.

In one corner, there hung a ceramic mountain boy climbing up a rope, and on the awning above the kitchen area was a life-sized set of Alpine men, each with a horn so long it was played with one end resting on the ground, its front end curling up just above the grass and edelweiss.

In the middle of the dining area a real waterfall cascaded down, the water seeming to come from the painted hillside into bronze tubs, one pouring into the other until they reached the small pool at the bottom.

Next to her along the wall, was a miniature scenery with tiny chalets set on ledges carved out of a mountain and goat herders watching over their flocks. A herd of cows in a neat row traveled on a small conveyer belt on their way to the barn to be milked.

Willis was watching her, when she finally turned to him.

"This is amazing," she said. "I've never seen anything like this since Disneyland."

He smiled at her pleasure. "I thought you'd like it."

The hostess in a Swiss red and white outfit smiled and motioned for them to follow her. Dani couldn't help looking around, taking it all in as they followed her. It was the most enchanting restaurant she had ever set foot in.

They sat in a booth set under the waterfall.

Dani sighed happily.

"So," Willis looked at her, "this was a good choice?"

"This was a perfect choice."

"You haven't even tried the food yet," Willis teased.

"With this backdrop, I'd be content with a bowl of oatmeal."

Willis opened his menu. "Well, it doesn't look like you'll have to do that."

Dani looked through her menu.

"I've heard that they have really good fish," Willis commented.

"Mmm." Dani could already taste a hot, flaky cod.

In a few minutes, the waitress came by and took their order.

"I'll have your salmon dinner with a side salad," Dani said, pointing to the number.

The waitress finished taking her order and turned to Willis.

"Just make that two of those," he told the waitress.

221

"Blue cheese dressing on your salad as well?"

"I'll take French if you have it."

"Yes, we do." The waitress nodded as she jotted down the change. She took the menus from them.

"It'll be out in a few minutes," she said before hurrying off to hand in their order.

Dani looked around at the restaurant.

"Looks like Roger's enjoying himself," she said, nodding toward the buffet line where the older man was scooping food onto his plate.

Willis smiled.

They were silent for a few minutes, taking in the beauty of their surroundings and simply relaxing in each other's company.

Dani turned back to Willis.

"So," she said gently, "I heard you had a difficult evening yesterday."

A shadow crossed over Willis' face, but it left just as quickly as it had come.

"Yeah, it wasn't one of my better ones," he said ruefully.

"Your mom was pretty upset, huh?"

Willis sighed. "You could say that."

Dani studied him, concerned. She felt like somehow she should offer him a way out of his painful situation, but her heart ached at even the thought of losing him.

He must have read her train of thoughts because he reached across the table and took both of her hands in his, a gesture he had never done before.

"Dani," he said earnestly, "I knew she would react that way. I knew exactly what I was getting myself into when I asked you to date me. I weighed the consequences long and hard before I ever asked you."

Willis looked deep into her eyes. "I decided getting to know you was worth whatever it took."

Dani held his gaze for a moment, and his deep brown

eyes never wavered. The intensity of his response shouldn't have surprised her. That was just like him, to think through a matter so thoroughly that by the time he made his decision, he knew he could stand by it, confident that it was the right one.

"It just makes me feel bad that I am the one causing you so much trouble."

"Trouble, Dani?" Willis smiled. "My life has felt richer, more complete now that you're a part of it. I wake up every morning smiling to myself. I go throughout my day feeling so blessed by God that He brought you into my life. You're not trouble to me, Dani. You are..." he searched for words, "a pure treasure," he finished.

Dani could feel the tears welling up in her eyes as Willis spoke, and when she blinked, two tears fell onto her cheeks.

"Okay," she whispered. She pulled one hand from his and wiped the wetness off her cheeks. She smiled at Willis.

He held her hand a moment longer, then squeezed gently before letting go.

The waitress soon appeared and set their steaming plates in front of them.

"This looks delicious," Dani said.

"Can I get you anything else?" the waitress asked.

Dani looked around at the table and shook her head.

"Not right now, I guess," Willis answered.

"Ok then, enjoy your meal." The waitress smiled and left.

Willis looked across the table at Dani. He held such a loving, tender look in his eyes.

She couldn't help but smile at him. *What had she done to get such a great guy?*

"Ready to pray?" Willis asked.

Dani nodded.

Willis led in a simple, but heartfelt prayer. He thanked God for their relationship and asked for continued wisdom. He prayed for his mom that she would forgive him and one day understand why he had chosen the path he had.

After the "amen", there was a brief pause as they both picked up their forks and took bites.

"Hmm," Willis pointed at the fish with his fork. "This is really good. You made a good choice."

Dani nodded, her mouth still full.

"Everything looks delicious," she said finally, looking around at the home-style rolls, buttery potatoes, and crisp salads.

"You know, I was never used to praying out-loud before," Willis commented.

"Really?" Dani had never thought of it before. Being Amish, most prayers were silent–just between yourself and God.

Willis nodded. "I had prayed somewhat verbally in my own walks in the woods with God, but other than over a few meals, I had never prayed with another person before you."

Dani let what he said sink in. So, she was the first person Willis had trusted with his prayers. Soon into their dating relationship, he had been the one to suggest that they pray together. It had been such a wonderful experience, bringing perspective to their relationship and drawing them closer as they understood better the other's walk with God.

"So, how was that, praying out loud for the first time?" she wondered.

"It was a bit awkward at first," Willis admitted.

"I wouldn't have known."

"Maybe not." Willis looked thoughtful. "Prayer is really a vulnerable thing, you know. At least it can be if you're truly honest in your prayers."

Dani nodded.

Willis continued, "It's like you're letting another person have a peek into your soul."

She considered him. "You miss that in the Amish church, don't you?"

"That depends on the people. Some are content to just follow the rules, and others want to understand more and are willing to share their struggles. It's like it is anywhere else, I suppose. You have some people that are more open and others that go through life without really wanting to think about spiritual things."

"I'm guessing your dad is one of those more open type?"

"Where do you think I got it?" Willis grinned boyishly. "Yeah, ever since I was a teenager, he began letting me into some of his world, tossing around questions about what he should do in certain situations, and being honest enough to tell me if he didn't really know the answer to my questions.

"My mom is actually the more 'spiritual' one, from an Amish viewpoint. She's the one that wants to do everything exactly by the rules of the church. While my dad wants us to be the best people we can be, Mom's goal is to make us children into the best Amish we can be."

Dani thought about that for a moment.

"You wouldn't know it," Willis said, buttering a roll, "but a lot of times it's really the women that are the ones running the Amish. It's not always the case, but more often than not, if you really think about it, they tend to be the ones keeping everyone in line. Sure, the men believe in following the rules and staying Amish, but the women are often more passionate about it."

"So, your dad is still okay with you dating me?" Dani asked.

"He's not happy about it," Willis said, "but I doubt he'll say or do much."

"What about the rest of your family—your siblings at home and your married sisters?"

"I don't know. The ones at home only care because of the way it affects our mom. The married siblings and a few of my uncles will probably give me a talking-to at some point."

"That's a lot of pressure from your family."

225

"Yes it is," Willis agreed. "But I've been through it before."

Dani didn't remind him that in that situation "before", he had eventually given in to his family's wishes and joined the Amish church.

She had to trust God in this. She wouldn't spend her time trying to ensure Willis would never break off their relationship. There was little she could do anyway, and worrying about it wouldn't help anyone. Again and again, she had to mentally set Willis back into God's hands. As much as it would hurt to lose him, she had to trust that God's will was best.

For both of them.

"Rebecca is pleased with our relationship, though," Willis told Dani.

"Is she?"

"She has a pretty high opinion of you."

"That, or she just doesn't want to see her older brother stay a bachelor for the rest of his life," Dani teased.

Willis chuckled. "Well, there is that too."

They had finished eating and were lazily drinking their raspberry iced tea—another thing Dani had been introduced to in Amish country.

"Hey," Willis pulled a watch out of his pocket and looked at it, "do you want to see the cuckoo clock?"

"What?" Dani laughed.

"It's the world's biggest cuckoo clock. They let it play on the hour."

"Let me guess—that's here too?" she asked. *How many surprises could one tucked-away restaurant have?*

"Yeah. It's outside though. Do you want to see it?"

"You have to ask?" She smiled. "What time is it?"

"We have fifteen minutes or so, so if you want dessert or anything…"

"Oh, no. I had more than enough already."

Willis paid the check and led Dani toward signs pointing the way to the cuckoo clock.

To get in, they had to wind their way up ramps that led them to a well-lit patio near the roof of the building. When they reached the landing, they saw they were the only ones up there, so they had their pick of the seats in the viewing area.

"Oh, wow," Dani said, stopping to look at the clock.

If you could call it that. The cuckoo clock was huge, probably at least twenty-feet tall. It looked like an elaborate, chalet-style playhouse with its little doors and painted grass in front.

"Look at all the trim work and the curtains and doors," Dani pointed out. "That must have been such tedious work to paint."

"You love details," Willis noted, sounding pleased.

She paused. "Yes, I guess I do."

"I'll have to remember that."

Willis and Dani sat in the middle aisle a couple rows back to wait for the clock to start.

"I have something I've been wanting to ask you, Dani."

She turned her attention to him. "Okay," she said, a bit hesitantly. The last time he told her that had been the night of the baseball game when he had asked her to date him.

"This may seem like a strange thing to ask," Willis began, "but would you mind if I hold your hand?"

Dani smiled and relaxed. "No. I wouldn't mind."

Gently, almost shyly, Willis picked up her hand that had been resting on the bench next to him. Holding it in one hand, he studied it and traced the outline with his finger. He turned her hand palm-up.

"You weren't kidding about your hands. Your poor fingers have been taking a beating lately," he said, noticing the scrapes and new calluses.

"I don't know how the Amish women keep their hands

227

from getting rough like mine with all the work they do every day." Dani sighed.

"No, you have beautiful hands," Willis contradicted. "Smooth hands aren't as pretty as the ones that have seen some work because you know the woman that owns them sure isn't gawly."

"Gawly?" Dani scrunched up her face at the word. "I don't think I've learned that one yet."

"Sorry. It means 'lazy'. You know the word for 'horse', right?"

"Isn't it 'Fawl'?" Dani asked.

Willis nodded. "If someone has a lazy horse, sometimes we'll call it a 'Gawly Fawly.'"

Dani smiled. She had found the Amish enjoyed putting together words that rhymed.

"My grossdaudy used to tell me that you were a man once you had calluses," Willis said, gently rubbing his thumb over the rough spots on her hand. "He used to get me and my boy cousins comparing palms to see which one of us was the manliest." Willis chuckled at the memory.

Dani smiled, watching him reminisce. "That must be so wonderful to grow up with all your family around you."

Willis must have caught the tone of wistfulness in her voice, because he looked at her for a moment, understanding and compassion in his eyes.

"Yes, it is," he said softly. "Family is a precious gift."

They sat in silence for a few moments, each lost in their own thoughts.

"You're still dealing with the pain of losing him, aren't you," Willis said softly.

"Yes, I am," Dani sighed. "And I probably always will."

Willis squeezed her hand.

The strength and warmth of his bigger hand around hers felt wonderfully safe and protective.

Suddenly, the cuckoo clock came to life.

A bird popped out of a window in the upstairs.

"Cuckoo, cuckoo," it sang before slipping back behind the door.

On the second-story roof, a little Swiss man came to the front and rotated to face the large bell that sat in the middle of the fake yard. He lifted his painted sledge hammer over his shoulder and swung it at the bell to chime out the hour.

At his final stroke, alpine music began to play and more Swiss puppets began to move. Each of them played a different instrument. A circular conveyer belt brought the various puppets, through one door, around to the front of the stage and back into another door.

In a side yard, a Swiss boy and girl danced together to the music.

The show lasted about ten minutes before everything slid back behind to its original position and the music stopped.

"So what did you think?" Willis asked.

"That was great." Dani smiled. "At least this time, I didn't let the Swiss people scare me."

"I don't know, I kind of liked it when you did," Willis said, grinning boyishly at her.

Dani couldn't help smiling, even as she tried to make a face at him.

Willis laughed. "If that was supposed to be a scowl, I can see I have nothing to worry about in the future."

"I will have you know I can make a very good scowl if I need to," she protested.

"Can you?" Willis asked, unconvinced. "And you know this how? You've practiced in front of the mirror or something?"

Dani shook her head, laughing.

They made their way back down the ramps.

"So, does this place have any more secrets I should know about?" she asked.

"Not that I know of. Just the shops, yet."

They made their way back downstairs and followed the hallway back toward the shops. In one of the tiny shops, Dani picked up a couple of postcards of the place to send to Denise. Another store was filled with hundreds of cuckoo clocks.

"Oh," Dani breathed, entering the shop.

They took their time, slowly walking along the walls and pointing out unique ones. Almost all of the clocks were turned on, the host of pendulums ticking creating a gentle backdrop. They must have been set to various times, because every once in a while one would come to life and chime out the hour. Willis and Dani would pause in their walk to watch it before turning back to the wall in front of them.

"Oh, look!" she pointed out. "There's one that looks just like the big one here."

Willis nodded. It was the perfect replica of the giant one upstairs, down to the colors of the paint and even each tiny musician. Dani stopped in front of it, wishing she could justify the six-hundred dollar price tag.

"The work is so beautiful on all of them," she said, looking around at the many varieties. There were huge clocks with meticulously carved pine cones and branches down to tiny cuckoo clocks painted in bright colors.

"I think the work is done in Switzerland." Willis noted.

"Really?"

That might explain some of the prices she had seen.

Eventually, they made it all the way around the shop, and Dani reluctantly moved to the next store.

The last store they went into was a bulk food store. Dani picked up some items for her breakfasts and some things she thought John and Martha might enjoy.

Willis insisted on carrying most of her bags.

"I only have three, and they're not heavy at all," Dani said, chuckling.

"All the better–I can just carry them all, then."

Dani handed the bags over. "You're going to make me into a gawly lady yet."

Willis shook his head. "I can't picture you ever being lazy."

They walked out of the building.

The motion sensor picked up their movement, and Hilda popped out again and began her speech.

"Goodnight, Hilda," Dani said ruefully.

Robert was already in the van, reading a newspaper. He saw them and started folding the paper back up.

"Did you get enough to eat?" Willis asked him as they climbed in.

Robert patted his stomach. "Oh, yeah."

The ride home was relaxing. Willis held Dani's hand the entire trip. She loved the feel of hers in his larger, but gentle one.

Robert was singing off-key to a country song. It ended, and another one started. Dani smiled as she recognized the song as one of her favorites. She hummed along with it and tapped her foot to the beat.

"You know country music?" Willis asked, surprised.

Dani laughed. "I may not look like it now, but I *was* born and raised on a ranch, remember? Everyone plays and loves country music on our ranch."

Willis looked pleased.

Dani nodded toward the radio. "This is one of my all-time favorites."

The corner of Willis' mouth turned up in a grin. "So, not only are you familiar with country music, but you actually like it?"

Dani smiled. "Depends on the song, but yeah, I like a lot of the songs. I think I'll always be a country girl at heart."

"I should have known." Willis smiled.

"So, what about you?" She turned to him. "I mean, I know you only sing accapela and can't have CD players or anything, but you must have been exposed to other music at least a little bit."

Willis nodded. "We might not have it in our homes, but most of us have listened to anything from rock to hip hop to classical."

"Rock?" It was Dani's turn to be surprised.

"Oh, yeah. You'll hear them every once in awhile–a young guy with a boom-box in the back of his buggy. You can hear the thump of the beats as his buggy rolls by."

Dani giggled at the picture. "That is hilarious."

"I know, but to answer your question–my Mennonite boss plays the Christian radio in his shop, but that plays preaching more than music. I like quite a few of the songs they do play, though."

Christian radio, huh? That must have been another way Willis was influenced spiritually. Dani knew from her own experience that it was hard to listen to a good Christian radio station on a regular basis and not grow in your spiritual journey and understanding of the Bible.

Willis continued, "As a whole, most of us Amish like our country music, and I'd have to say that's what I'd be most likely to pick that for background music if I had to choose."

Yet one more thing they had in common. It was amazing how different people could be in the way they grew up, and yet how similar they could be the things they liked and the beliefs they held. Willis and she came from entirely different worlds, and yet Dani had never met an English guy who shared so many of the same opinions that she had.

From what she had seen and what Willis had told her, Dani doubted that there were very many Amish young men like him and even fewer young women. She had been plunked down in the one community and in a house just down the driveway from one very unusual Amish man.

As she pondered this, she was reminded again at how good God was; how mysterious were His ways.

CHAPTER SEVENTEEN

The morning breeze was chilly. It would get warm later, but now it was a perfect temperature for working outside in the flowerbeds.

Martha was working on her hands and knees a few yards down from Dani. Pulling the tiny little weeds from among all her flowers and bushes and covering them with fresh mulch would take several hours, but Dani enjoyed the work. It was peaceful and quiet work, the kind she could do absently while lost in her own thoughts.

For some reason, her emotions had been running the full gamut today. This morning, she woke up with a song on her heart. She had a sweet time reading her Bible, and as she tidied up her little kitchen, her thoughts naturally went to Willis.

She had finally come to admit to herself that her feelings toward him had deepened beyond that of attraction or even affection.

She loved that boy. She felt it as deeply and as surely as she had loved Jeff or Dad or Denise.

Dani had never known what it felt like to be in love. It seemed like nothing in the world could touch her and her happiness. As long as she had Willis, that was all she needed.

She wished she could see Denise to have a face-to-face conversation with her. She wanted to share her over-flowing joy with someone.

Her thoughts suddenly turned to Jeff. What she wouldn't give to be able to talk with her brother right then about Willis and about everything that had happened since his death. He would have been so happy for her.

Unexpectedly, a rush of sadness came over her, and she couldn't help the sudden tears that spilled over her cheeks. She leaned against the door frame and looked out at the morning sky.

Jeff would have liked Willis. Dani could easily imagine the two of them talking over horses or ribbing each other or having a deep conversation about marriage and life. Jeff would have embraced and loved Willis as a brother.

But they would never have that. The two men in her life that she had loved the most would never get to meet one another this side of heaven. If the day came and she walked down the aisle to become Willis' wife, Dani knew she would instinctively look, but would find Jeff's spot empty. She wouldn't be able to find her brother's smiling face among all the faces in the filled pews.

Dani watched as the last pink wisps in the sky faded. She let her tears fall as they willed, washing over her soul, soothing the pain in her heart.

The thought struck her that if Jeff hadn't been killed, she would never have come to Ohio, and she never would have met Willis.

She thought about that for a moment. She couldn't accept

the idea that her joy now justified Jeff's death, but she knew God could bring a good thing out of a bad situation. It didn't mean that the bad went away, and it didn't mean that God caused the bad to be able to bring the good. It simply meant that no matter how terrible a situation, God always had a way to bring something good out of it.

And for her, out of her grief and pain, God had brought her more good than she could have imagined. She had come to Ohio praying for healing, and God had given her so much more.

Jeff would have liked that. He would have liked to know that she met Willis because of his death, that he was inadvertently the cause of some of her sweetest moments.

Her heart calmed and her tears faded. In the bathroom, she washed her face with cold water to try to help take away some of the redness before she headed upstairs to see what she could help Martha with today.

Upstairs, the house was quiet as she looked for Martha. Through one of the windows, she spied the Amish woman's blue dress outside. She apparently was already busy at work in the flowerbed. Dani slipped on her shoes to join her.

Martha smiled when she saw her. "Goot morning."

"Morning." Dani smiled.

Martha and John had been just a bit colder toward her than when she first got here, but Dani could tell they were trying to hide it. She could understand why, even if she was disappointed by their reaction.

Dani doubted it helped her case that Ina was Martha's sister. Surely, she would have shared her frustrations with Martha at some point.

To her credit, Martha had said very little about it over all the time they had spent working together. John commented on it a few times when it came up, but he seemed to avoid the subject whenever possible.

It was quiet as Martha and Dani worked carefully around

each plant.

Dani thought if she could only pick one word to best describe Amish life, that would be it—quiet. She had been used to living alone and she would have thought her life was fairly quiet compared to most, but living here in Amish country had taught her a whole new dimension of the word.

Here there were no phones to ring, no television to make noise in the background, no radios or CD players to play even the softest of music. The loudest thing in the house was Methuselah's squawks or the clatter of dishes when they were being washed. Even the hum of a dishwasher or dryer was missing.

The Amish people even talked quietly. Many times Dani had to strain to hear what one of the women was telling her.

She admired their quiet spirit. They were slow to express their opinions, careful in their decisions, and content to let others go ahead of themselves.

Other than wishing for a little music here and there and the evening news, Dani loved the lifestyle. It created such a peaceful environment, the perfect place for her to reconnect with God.

Martha was straining to push a wheelbarrow full of mulch up the small rise to where they were working. Dani jumped up.

"Martha! Here, let me do that."

She took the handles from Martha and pushed it up the hill.

Martha wiped her forehead with the back of her hand. "I guess I am not as young as I once was." She chuckled ruefully.

Dani set the wheelbarrow down in front of the flowerbed.

Standing this close to Martha, Dani could tell she was studying her.

"Oh," Martha said softly, "you've been crying, Dani."

"I was hoping you didn't notice," Dani smiled shakily.

"But why? There is no shame in it. Even the Lord Himself cried."

There was that verse again, the one that had been the beginning of the turning point in her grief.

Martha went on, "You know, we are meant to bear one another's burdens."

She took a few steps to the picnic table sitting close by and sat down. "Aw," she sighed. "It does feel good to sit."

Dani knew Martha was hoping that she would sit next to her, but she wasn't really ready to share her heart with the Amish woman. She would rather have gone back to work, but she decided to humor Martha. She took the seat next to her on the bench.

Martha was very quiet as she looked out over the yard and garden.

She finally spoke, "I lost a child once."

Dani looked up at her, surprised by her words.

"She was three-years-old, the spitting image of John with all the spirit and joy of a three-year-old."

"I'm so sorry, Martha," Dani said sincerely.

Martha nodded, acknowledging her words.

"It had been a busy day like all my days were back then with five children under eight-years-old. I thought the oldest was watching Susie, but by the time I realized she wasn't... it was too late. We combed all the fields and barns looking desperately for her. Finally, hours later and after nearly the entire community was out looking for her, someone spied her little dress stuck on some brush in the pond."

"Oh, Martha!" Dani ached for her friend.

Martha wiped a tear off her cheek. "See, thirty-two years later and it still makes me cry. I see three-year-old little girls and remember how my little Susie was at that age. I see our children gathered around at family get-togethers and I often wonder how many more people and grandchildren we have missed getting to love because she never got to live a full

237

life."

Dani's tears were falling now. Martha's pain was all too familiar to her.

They sat for awhile, both too full of emotion to speak.

"Does it ever go away?" Dani finally whispered.

Martha shook her head. "It never does. Because you can never stop loving the one you lost. The pain fades, time dulls the sharp edges, but you will always miss that precious part of your life."

They sat for a long time in silence, grieving together, sharing in the pain of someone lost.

Those moments with Martha at the picnic table became a turning point in their relationship and helped heal the small rift that had come between them. Dani knew Martha couldn't be happy that she was dating Willis, but now Dani felt closer to the woman than she ever had. She knew Martha hadn't liked the distance between them anymore than she had. It touched her that Martha had been the one to open her heart first.

Willis and Dani took walks together nearly every evening and an occasional buggy ride up to the ice cream shop. The store had a soft-serve machine that made over thirty flavors.

"How is the black raspberry?" Dani asked as they waited their turn to order.

"I've never had it," Willis said. "Actually, I haven't tried many of the flavors. I usually just get chocolate or twist."

"Let's try a different flavor every time we come here," Dani suggested on a whim. "Maybe we can try them all."

"Serious?" Willis asked, smiling.

"Sure."

"Okay, but I'm going to save the pina colada for last."

Dani chuckled. Willis hated coconut.

"And I'll save the peanut butter for last," she decided.

"I thought you liked peanut butter?"

"I do, but it sounds like a strange flavor for soft serve ice cream." Dani wrinkled up her nose.

It was their turn to order and Dani picked the strawberry cheesecake flavor while Willis chose caramel. They took their cones out to the picnic tables in the front of the shop and lazily ate their ice cream.

Dani loved how Willis was content to do the simplest of things together. He didn't need their relationship to center around exciting outings like some of her other dates in the past had. Instead, he was happy just to be with her, sharing their hearts, sharing life.

One evening, they were heading back home from a walk. The sun was just going down, turning the horizon a gentle orange hue. The bellies of the few fluffy clouds floating in the sky reflected in a brilliant pink.

"What do you see yourself doing ten years from now?" Dani asked Willis as they watched the sunset and walked.

He looked at her, a glint of humor in his eye. He knew she was hinting at more with such a loaded question. Willis hadn't brought up the topic of engagement yet, even though they had often talked about marriage and issues surrounding it. They both knew their relationship was heading toward that.

"Well," he looked out to the fading sun, "I would hope to be settled down by then with a wonderful, beautiful wife and maybe three or four happy kids."

"Three or four, huh?" Dani asked, not bothering to hide the laughter in her voice.

"Yeah," he nodded, smiling. "I would enjoy branching out into some other kind of work—maybe open my own shop or something. I wouldn't need a big place, but I'd like enough land for the kids to run and to be able to own some animals."

It sounded perfect.

"What about you?" he looked down at Dani.

She pondered his question for a moment. She laughed. "I

239

honestly can't think of much I would change about your picture. Except I would add a dog."

"Would you?" Willis smiled.

"I'd like some big ol' sweet dog to run around with the kids and make footprints on the deck. I want my future to be filled with as much life as possible."

Her own words surprised her. She had never phrased her dreams for her future that way before, but it was exactly what she wanted—life. She didn't care about muddy prints on the porch, or toys strewn around the yard, or piles of laundry. Right now, as crazy as it sounded, those nuisances sounded like bliss. They were evidence of life—full, alive, and happy.

Willis squeezed her hand. "I hope with all my heart yours is, Dani."

As they rounded the bend around the barn, they could see a group of people at Willis' house.

"What's going on?" Dani asked.

"I don't know. It looks like something's wrong."

The adults stood around talking and even the kids stood by quietly. That was the first indication of trouble. Usually the children would be off together, running and playing.

Willis and Dani picked up their pace. As they reached the sober group, their concerned eyes turned to Willis and Dani.

"What's going on?" Willis asked John, the first person they came to.

"Rebecca never came home," John said. "She should have been back at five and it's now nearly eight o' clock."

Ina ran up from the phone shanty. "I finally got through again at Mrs. Miller's and spoke with a manager. She's not there. William," Ina looked anxiously at her husband, "she never has been there."

"Not been there?" her husband asked confused.

"That's what they said. They said that she never was even hired there. The manager said just now that they do have a

'Rebecca Steiner' but no records of a 'Rebecca Hostetler'."

"Our daughter's been hiding something behind our backs?" William seemed more hurt than angry.

"I think it might be."

Dani inwardly groaned. *Oh, Rebecca, what have you gotten yourself into?*

William ran his fingers through his hair. "What can we do next? We don't even know where she was supposed to be?"

"I can help," Dani said simply.

All eyes turned to her.

"Rebecca never worked at Mrs. Miller's, but she was working. She has been a waitress in Mount Hope at Mrs. Yoder's Restaurant."

Ina was speechless, but William jumped into action.

"Ok, now we're getting somewhere. I'm going to call them. Hopefully there's still someone there to answer the phone yet."

He hurried back down the drive to the shanty and Dani glanced over at Ina. She hadn't taken her eyes off Dani and now they narrowed.

"Why did you not tell us this?" She barely could keep the anger from her voice. "Our own daughter and you knew, for how long?"

"I've known about it for a couple months now," Dani answered frankly. She could have told her how she nearly begged her daughter to tell Ina about the deception, but Dani knew Rebecca was in enough trouble already. There was no need for her to add to it.

Ina wrung her hands and turned away, trying to keep her anger under control. Dani had never had someone so angry at her, but she knew most of Ina's frustrations were really with her daughter instead of with her.

Willis pulled Dani off to the side.

"You knew?" he asked quietly. Even he seemed a little taken aback by her revelation.

241

She nodded. "Will, I asked her many times to talk to your parents, and she said she would in her own time. What was I supposed to do?"

Willis nodded, understanding, "Ok." He looked at the group behind her. "We need to find her now."

William came back from the phone shanty. "She did work there today, but she's not there now," he said, breathless from his jog back. "Her supervisor said she had asked to clock out early—around four, but he doesn't know where she went from there."

"So, what do we do, William?" Ina was growing frantic. "Where could she have gone?"

"Should we call the police?" John asked.

William pondered the question. Normally, the Amish were hesitant to involve outside, English authorities, but in emergency situations they were grateful for their services.

"I know where she went." Dani stepped forward again.

"You?" Ina scoffed. "How is it that you, an English woman, knows more about the whereabouts of my daughter than even I do?"

Dani didn't bother to answer. Not now. She turned to William.

"Rebecca told me that she might go home for dinner some evening with another Amish waitress."

"Do you know the waitress' name?" William asked.

Dani shook her head. "She didn't tell me, but I do know that she has a brother named Marcus, and that he comes to the restaurant fairly frequently. Someone at the restaurant should know which waitress that is."

"And I suppose this 'boy'," Ina spat out the word, "is the reason Rebecca is going to their house for supper in the first place?"

"So," William said, his voice low and calculated, keeping his frustration under control, "I find out that not only has my daughter been lying to us about where she was working, but she has also been seeing a boy behind our backs, planned on going to his house, told you about it, and to top it all off, is now missing."

There was nothing Dani could say.

William turned. "I need to call the restaurant back," he said, trying to hide his emotions.

At that moment, a car pulled into the lane. It pulled up to the drive and they all watched in surprise and relief as Rebecca stepped out.

The group was quiet as Rebecca shamefacedly walked up.

"Where have you been, Daughter?" William asked, anger and disappointment etching his words.

"Never mind," he held up his hand as she started to stammer out an answer. "Now is not a good time. Please. Just go inside. We'll talk about this later."

Rebecca glanced at Dani as she turned away.

When the door shut behind her, Ina turned back to Dani.

"You!" Ina pointed a finger in Dani's face.

The Amish woman tried to lower her voice. Her jaw clenched as she fought to keep composure.

She spoke in quiet, clipped words. "You have been nothing but trouble to this community. First, you pull my son away from his Amish faith and now this...this—encouraging our daughter to go behind our backs and see a fella?"

Dani kept her tone even, "Ina, I didn't encourage Rebecca to hide this from you. I thought she should tell you both."

William spoke up, "But the fact still remains that you were the one she felt she could talk to. You were the one she thought her secret was safe with. Why do you think that is?"

Dani had nothing to say.

Ina was on the verge of tears. "Why have you come here to this community? Why do you have to be here? Do you want to cause heartache? Do you want to tear families apart?"

Dani looked around at the group. Each one was silent,

243

their faces mirroring the same concern and accusation on William and Ina's faces. A pain shot through her heart as the realization dawned on her.

They didn't want her here.

She looked up into Willis' face. His eyes were troubled, but not condemning like the others. He, too, was silent. What could he possibly say in her defense? Their accusations were true. She was tearing apart a family and a part of their community.

The thoughts swirling in her head stilled as she looked from one quiet Amish face to another.

She knew what she had to do.

A tear slid down her face, not only because of the pain she had caused them, but also because of the pain she would now be inflicting on herself.

"I'm so sorry," she whispered to Ina and William. "I'm sorry," she repeated, looking to John and Martha and the others. She avoided Willis' eyes.

Dani turned and headed down the driveway to John and Martha's home.

Willis hurried to catch up to her.

"I have to go," she said, her voice choked with emotion.

"Dani, they'll get over it. It'll be okay."

Dani shook her head and took the shortcut through the grass instead of taking the sidewalk down to her apartment.

"Dani, please!" Willis grabbed her arm turn her face him.

He searched her eyes, and she couldn't bear looking into them, the ones she had learned to love so much. But she had to answer him. He deserved that much.

Dani took a deep breath to try to calm her emotions enough to speak. It was impossible to stop the flow of tears, and she didn't even attempt to wipe them away.

"Will, your mom is right." She looked away to keep her composure. "I have to go. I can't let you do this to yourself."

"Go?" Willis' stunned voice was a low, tortured whisper.

"Dani, please."

"I lost my family, Will. I know what it feels like. I won't let you lose yours on account of me."

"But, Dani," His eyes filled with tears as they searched hers, trying desperately to convey the depth of his feelings, "I love you."

"I love you, too," she whispered, "more than I imagined I could." Dani was barely able to get the words out through her tears. "That is why I have to let you go."

"No, Dani, please! We'll find a way to work this out."

"You have a beautiful life here," she tried to smile through her tears, but failed miserably. "You have something most people only dream of having."

"Please, Dani. You mean more to me than all of that."

"But what about years down the road? I know what it's like to lose your family. On top of that, you would be losing everything you know if you left the Amish and this community. I can't let you make a decision you will later regret. I can't bear to be the cause of that kind of pain."

Willis was quiet. He knew that he couldn't promise he wouldn't miss his family or his community.

Dani squeezed his hands, then let them fall from hers. She had to go before her heart ripped in two.

"Goodbye, Willis," she whispered.

Tears slid down his face, and he was too choked up to say anything. His eyes pleaded with hers, and the raw sorrow on his face nearly crumbled her resolve.

She turned and went into the house.

She didn't look back.

She couldn't.

CHAPTER EIGHTEEN

In her room, Dani dug frantically for her cell phone. Finally finding it, she held down the power button to turn it back on. The light turned on, and she watched it begin booting up. Good, there was enough battery power for her to call out.

She called the airline and booked a flight out in the morning. It was expensive since it was last minute, but she didn't care. She could not stay here a day longer.

Dani needed to get a rental car, which meant she would have to find someone to drive her out in the morning. She grimaced, realizing she didn't have a number for a driver. She would have to try to get one from the phone shanty.

She began packing up her things, waiting for thicker darkness before she walked out to the shanty. She didn't want Willis to see her or try to talk her out of what she knew in her heart she had to do for him.

Dani couldn't keep the tears from falling, and at times they were so thick it made it hard for her to see what she was doing.

She packed up everything that was hers from the kitchen. She certainly hadn't expected to leave anytime soon, so her things were scattered throughout the apartment. She walked through the rooms, gathering the items: a book on the table, a sweater on the couch.

About an hour later, it was fully dark and Dani decided to chance the trip out. She had heard John and Martha come in a while ago, and she hoped everyone else at Williams' had already left.

She slipped outside and headed to the shanty. Everything was quiet. She reached the shanty and found, to her relief, that there was quite a few names on the list of drivers.

She hurriedly copied them onto a scrap of paper and returned to the house. She stood outside while she called the drivers. It was late to be calling, but she would need to leave around seven-thirty to be able to get to airport in time.

George, the guy that had driven Willis and her on their date, was the first one she called.

He picked up on the third ring, and she could tell from his voice he had been sleeping.

"Hello?" he said, a bit groggily.

"Hi, is this George?"

"Yes."

"Hi, George, this is Dani—Willis Hostetler's girlfriend." Even as the words slipped out of her mouth, she realized they weren't true anymore. "Willis' friend," she corrected, her throat tightening with tears again.

"Oh, yeah." George recognized who she was.

She cleared her throat. "I'm so sorry for calling you this late, but I have an unexpected flight I need to take in the morning, and I need a way to get to the rental car place in Wooster."

George thought for a moment. "I don't have anything in the morning until eleven. I can take you to Wooster if you want."

"That would be great."

They finished the arrangement. George would pick her up around seven.

Dani was relieved to have that detail taken care of.

She packed up her things in the bathroom and began working on the bedroom. She found her suitcase of English clothes and set it on the bed. Opening it, she looked down at her piles of shirts and jeans. She looked at her own reflection in the upright mirror.

She wasn't ready to return to her English self. She walked slowly towards the mirror. Standing in front of it, she began pulling out the pins that held her covering on. One by one, she slid them out and poked them into the pin cushion Martha had given her. When they all were out, she reached up with both hands and carefully took her covering off.

She continued to watch her reflection as she took off the hair net and began pulling out the hairpins that held her bun in place. She set them and the folded hairnet on the dresser and watched as her hair untwisted and fell around her shoulders.

Dani stared at herself, letting the realization of what was happening fully sink in.

It was time to leave her fantasy land and return to who she really was.

She took each of the Amish dresses off their hangers in the closet and carefully folded them into a neat pile on the dresser. Martha would know someone who could use them. Maybe Rebecca would even take them back. Dani did keep the burgundy one—the one she had worn on her date with Willis. It would always remind her of him and her happy times in Amish country.

She hugged it to herself and took a deep breath.

Lord, help me.

She knew what she was doing was the right thing, but

why was it that the "right thing" was often the single hardest thing to do?

She wished she could spare Willis and herself the pain they were now going through. Why hadn't she been able to see down the road far enough to see what their relationship would eventually cost Willis? She had somehow been under the illusion that they could date and even marry with little more than a frown from his family and community. She was sure they wouldn't like it, but she'd had no idea how much it would sever Willis from them.

Dani knew looking into the pained eyes of William and Ina, that if she married their son, she would be breaking apart their family forever. Sure, they would still get to see him, but it would never be the same. Willis would become an outsider and looked down on as the black sheep of the family. His parents would warn the younger siblings about the way their oldest brother fell. Willis would never be able to have a relationship with them or others he loved, like Mary, if he walked out of the Amish church.

How had she missed that? After spending months with the Amish now, how had that escaped her?

Willis had fully known these things, and he had still chosen to be with her. Dani smiled through her tears at how loved she had been. It was a beautiful, precious gift—one she would cherish until the day she died.

It was also one she had to give back.

Dani finished packing, more slowly now. The urgency she had felt had turned into sadness over saying goodbye to a place and a people she had come to love.

After she had found and packed everything, she stacked her three suitcases by the door.

By now she felt exhausted from all the emotional strain. Dani fell asleep under the hand-stitched quilt, her hair falling over the side of the embroidered pillowcase for the last time.

Her alarm woke her up at six o' clock. She got ready

quickly. It felt so strange to be wearing jeans again, and she felt exposed and immodest with her hair falling down around her face.

Dani knew from all her mornings here and from the creaking of the floorboards above that John and Martha were already up, so she walked up the stairs.

She opened the door and stepped onto the main floor. John and Martha were sitting at the table and looked up as she entered. Dani caught the look of sadness in their eyes when they saw that she was back in her English clothes. The fact that they didn't look surprised told her that they somehow knew she was leaving.

They were quiet, waiting for her to talk.

"I guess you know I'm heading out," she started sadly.

John nodded. "We wish you wouldn't have to."

"I do too," Dani said sorrowfully, "but it's for the best."

John sighed, "Yah, maybe it is."

She could see from the solemn look on their faces that they really did wish she wasn't leaving. They couldn't in good conscience encourage her to stay, but they wished there was a way she could.

"Do you have time to eat?" Martha motioned to an empty chair.

Dani's throat thickened as she sat down. She would miss these meals with the Amish couple, miss all the banter and conversation.

John passed her a bowl of scrambled eggs, and she dished out a tiny helping. As good as Martha's cooking was, Dani doubted she would be able to swallow very much this morning.

They ate mostly in silence, but it was a sad silence more than an awkward one. They eventually got up from the table.

"I don't know how to thank you for all you've given me," Dani began.

John waved it off. "You've been the one that's blessed us

with all the help you gave Martha."

Dani knew when Martha cleaned her room later she would find the check Dani had slipped under her pillow. She could never repay them for all the experiences and joy she had living with them here in Amish country, but she hoped the check would help express it.

The grandfather clock chimed out six forty-five.

"Well, George should be here soon," Dani said.

She wanted to give John a hug, but settled for a handshake, knowing he'd be more comfortable with that.

"Take care," he said, his voice husky.

"You too." Dani smiled sadly. "Thanks for everything."

She turned to Martha. She looked about to cry. Dani hugged her. "Thank you for all you taught me."

"Ah, I will miss you, Dani. You're a special young lady," Martha said.

"I'll miss you, too," Dani said quietly.

They held their hug for a moment. When they finally let go, Martha's eyes were red.

"Write us sometime," she said, smiling bravely.

"I will."

Dani looked around. "Goodbye, Methuselah."

The bird bobbed and turned upside down on its branch, but for once he was quiet.

"Well, I'd better get my bags."

"Do you need help with anything?" John asked.

Dani shook her head. "No, I can get it. Thanks."

"It looks like George is pulling into the lane," Martha commented, looking out the living room window.

They said goodbyes once more before Dani headed back down to the basement for her things.

She carried her suitcases through the basement door to the waiting van.

She was setting the last bag in when she heard a voice behind her.

251

"Dani?"

Her heart stilled. She knew that voice all too well.

She turned to see Willis standing there. Their eyes met, and they couldn't say anything for a moment. His eyes were a bit swollen, no doubt from tears and a lack of sleep, but they held such a look of love and longing that it broke her heart all over again. Dani knew exactly what he was feeling.

"Please stay, Dani," he whispered.

The tears couldn't be held back any longer. "You know I can't," she said. "I have to do this."

"I'll do anything to keep you." His eyes pleaded with hers.

"I..." Dani held his gaze as the tears fell onto her cheek, "can't."

They stood there for just a moment, their eyes speaking the sorrow and love they couldn't put into words.

Willis seemed to remember something, and he held out a package.

"What is it?" Dani asked, peeking into the bag.

She pulled out the object.

"Oh, Willis!" she held her forefinger to her upper lip to keep from sobbing. It was a cuckoo clock, the one that was a miniature of the huge one at Alpine Alpa.

"It was going to be an engagement gift," Willis said, "but I want you to have it."

Dani looked up at him. *An engagement gift? They had been that close to being engaged?*

She couldn't hold it back any longer. She set the clock on the van seat and threw her arms around Willis.

"Thank you, Willis," she said through her tears. "Thank you for everything, for bringing so much happiness to my life here."

Willis couldn't speak. Dani could feel his shoulders shaking as he silently wept.

They just held each other for a moment.

When they broke, she whispered, "I have to go."

Willis wiped his eyes.

She stepped into the van.

"Fill your future with lots of life, Dani," he said gently, his voice cracking.

Her throat choked up and she nodded. Before she could say anything, Willis managed a tender smile and slid the door shut for her.

She wanted to say something, but there wasn't anything to say that could sum up what she was feeling.

Willis stood in the drive watching them leave, and she turned to see him. That picture of him, the Amish man she had learned to love so deeply, standing there alone in the driveway, would always be etched in her memory.

The van turned out of the lane, and the barn took Willis from her sight.

She turned back to face forwards, trying to block out the painful thoughts whirling in her head. She would never see that face again. She would never look up into his smiling eyes or see his tall figure coming down the lane to meet her.

She had lost every one of her family members, and now she was losing one more precious part of her. Only this time was different. She had chosen it.

She ran her fingers along the smooth wood on the clock next to her. She would treasure it as long as she lived.

The ride to the car rental was quiet. George understood her lack of conversation, and he hummed along quietly to his music, giving her privacy.

Dani thanked him and paid him generously before getting into her own car at the rental.

When she was alone and on the road, she took a deep breath. She had cried so much in the last ten hours.

She was so tired of weeping.

Lord, help me.

From the moment she had realized that she needed to leave, she had felt such a sense of peace over her decision. She had to rest on that and the fact that she had done the right thing, the truly loving thing for Willis.

Somehow, in the days to come, she would get back to normal. Her heart would eventually stop bleeding, even though there would always be a deep scar.

It would be strange to get back to her English life. Her eyes had been opened to such a different way of living. She was coming home with a new outlook on life, one she had learned from the quiet people of Holmes County.

She knew she would need to begin work again. If she learned one thing from Martha and the Amish people, it was the blessing of hard work. It left you feeling satisfied and productive.

She would also go back to church. She needed people. She would never be able to be a permanent part of an Amish community, but in her own way she could draw strength from her own community of sorts—people of faith that God had put in her life around her.

She knew she would miss the Amish. As she drove through the farmland, she tried not to think of all she was driving away from, all she had loved and would never see or experience again.

God had clearly led her to this place, and He had used it to teach her so many lessons. She would always be thankful to God for taking her on this expedition through Amish country.

The Amish people would forever have a special place in her heart.

CHAPTER NINETEEN

EPILOGUE

Dani walked through the stables. In the early morning, the horses were still sleepy and quiet. She had come to love this morning stroll.

One of the horses stuck its velvety-soft nose through the bars of the stall, hoping for attention. She stopped to pet him.

It had been nearly three months since she got back to her Arizona ranch. She was slowly learning to enjoy her own life again. It wasn't an Amish one, but it was the one God had given her.

The first couple of weeks had been most difficult.

She had asked Denise to pick her up from the airport. Denise had been surprised by Dani's sudden return, but understood when Dani told her she didn't want to talk about it right then.

As soon as Denise found her at the airport, she wrapped her friend in a tight hug. Dani couldn't hold back the tears any longer.

"Oh, Dani," Denise said sympathetically.

After a long hug and Dani felt like she could move again, Denise led her to the car.

On the way home, Dani filled Denise in on all that had happened, and Denise had cried right along with her.

"Do you want me to come in?" she asked when she pulled

up to Dani's house.

"No, it's okay."

"You sure?" Denise looked concerned.

Dani nodded. "Yeah, I need some time to process."

"Okay, call me if you need anything, please."

"You know I will." Dani shut the car door. She waved as Denise pulled away.

She carried the suitcases to the door and unlocked the door.

The familiar smell of the house hit her. She was home.

She shut the door behind her and leaned against it. The house seemed desperately still and quiet.

She couldn't help the sudden rush of emotions that she had been bottling up all day. Dani slid to the floor and finally let herself fully weep, right there in front of her door.

Her heart ached at the loss of Willis. He had completed her in such a way that she had never thought possible. She had loved him deeper and more intensely than she had thought she was capable of.

Father, help me. Help me see beyond the fog. Help me get through one more sorrow.

"I am with you, Child, even to the end of the age," Dani heard the gentle of words of Scripture.

The tears subsided eventually, and she simply sat and breathed in deeply, letting her heart settle.

God knew the pain she was in. She would be helped. He would give her strength to move through one day at a time.

When she felt calmed and ready, she carried the suitcases to her room upstairs and began unpacking. She spied the cuckoo clock, still in the brown paper bag Willis had put it in. Dani smiled sadly and pulled it out.

It was beautiful. She carried it downstairs and found a spot for it in the entryway, a place where she would see it several times a day.

She set the clock to the current time and hung it gently on

257

the wall. She worked the weights and watched as the clock began ticking.

Thank you, Willis, she whispered, grateful for much more than just the clock.

Even with all the pain she was experiencing now, she would not undo one day of their courtship. She was thankful for every happy moment she had spent with him.

The days moved by slowly, but began to pick up speed as she started getting back into the swing of things around the ranch. On her first Sunday back in Arizona, she visited Denise's church and met several lovely people. Of course, Denise was thrilled that she was there.

Denise and Dani spent several long afternoons together. Denise was so fascinated with all Dani had learned and experienced in Amish country, and Dani loved reliving it.

Mercifully, Denise hadn't tried in all the last three months to match Dani up with anyone, which had to be far and away a record for her. Dani knew her friend must have understood just how true and deep her relationship with Willis had been. Denise knew if Dani was ever going to love someone again like that, it was going to take a lot of time.

Dani still thought about Willis every day. She missed him terribly. Just to talk with him and hear his voice again would have been such joy.

She had thought maybe he would try to call her, but he hadn't. She had been disappointed, but she knew it was for the best. He must have known as clearly as she had that she had made the right choice.

She prayed often for Willis throughout the day, asking God to bless his life. Once, she even asked God to bring him a wonderful, young Amish woman into his life. She choked up in the prayer and couldn't help the sobs that overtook her.

The ache that she felt over a love that strong, yet a love she had to keep to herself, physically hurt.

Dani was learning that she had to rest on God's strength

many times, and her trust in His love for her carried her and kept her when she would have crumbled on her own.

She reached between the bars and rubbed the horse's head between its ears.

God had been faithful. Every day, she learned more and more of His grace and all the blessings she was surrounded with. He was teaching her to focus on those beautiful things in her life instead of the losses.

On the far side of the barn, she heard one of the workers come in. She glanced at her watch. It was about that time.

She sighed and patted the horse one more time, reluctant to go. There was something so peaceful about being in the huge barn in the morning quiet before starting on the tasks for the day.

"I was told that I might find you here," a voice broke the stillness.

Dani froze at the sound of the voice- a voice she knew so well. Surely her heart was playing tricks on her.

She turned.

There in front of her, standing in her barn in Arizona, was Willis.

She was utterly unable to speak or move.

Willis smiled the same gentle smile that she had so desperately missed these last few months.

"Hi, Dani."

She held her fingertips to her lips to keep from crying.

She flung her arms around him and couldn't let go for several minutes.

"You're here," she whispered, finally able to talk. Tears of joy spilled over her cheeks.

She pulled back from him and realized he looked different.

"You're not Amish!" she exclaimed. His hair was cut short like an English man's, and he wore a striped polo shirt tucked into jeans. He looked even more handsome than he had when he was Amish.

Willis shook his head. "I left the church soon after you came back here."

Dani's thoughts struggled to keep up with all that was happening. "Then why...why didn't you..." Dani's voice trailed off, the implications of it all sinking in.

"I didn't contact you right away, Dani, because I had to know that I was doing the right thing and not making my decisions based only on my emotions. I felt so overwhelmed with feelings for you, and I had to be certain that they were leading me in the right direction."

That was like Willis, so careful and sure.

Dani searched his eyes. "But what about your family, Willis?"

"I love my family, and I always will. But," Willis brushed aside a loose strand of her hair, "I can't live without you. As loving as it was of you to leave, that wasn't your decision to make, Dani. You know, and I know that I was never really Amish at heart."

"Besides," he added, his tone turning lighthearted, "I figured you could use another horse trainer down here."

Dani smiled. Her heart was full and overflowing with joy. God had brought her Willis back to her. He had given her back the dream she had placed in His loving hands.

"So, what does all this mean?" she said softly.

Willis looked into her eyes, all the love in his heart making his eyes sparkle.

Those eyes. This man she loved so much.

"It means," Willis said tenderly, as he picked up her hands in his. His eyes were shining with happy tears. He knelt down on the stable floor.

"Dani, will you marry me?"

260

The Author

Amber Willems grew up in a plain church. She learned the history and culture of Anabaptist ways first-hand as she went to church, quilted, gardened, canned, and was taught the simple ways of life.

She lives with her husband and children in the rural and rolling hills of Holmes County, Ohio, the largest settlement of Amish in the world. Her husband has lived in the area his entire life and works as an office manager and one of the few "English" employees of an Amish company. They are blessed to count his co-workers and bosses as dear friends.

Amber draws upon her own experiences, facts, and love for the Anabaptist lifestyle in the stories and articles she writes.

Thank you for reading this book! If you enjoyed it, please consider leaving a review on Amazon. It would mean so much to us and really help promote this book!

Thanks in advance!

Amber shares about Anabaptist lifestyle, living in Holmes County, and connects with her fans and those interested in the plain ways on her Facebook author page:

Living Among the Amish/Amber Willems

https://www.facebook.com/livingamongtheamish

Scan this code to take you directly her page:

Through the Glass

Made in the USA
Las Vegas, NV
11 November 2021

34243762R00156